Her Many Faces

A Novel

NICCI CLOKE

WILLIAM MORROW
An Imprint of HarperCollins*Publishers*

HER MANY FACES. Copyright © 2025 by Nicci Cloke. All rights reserved. Printed in the United States of America. No part of this book may be used or reproduced in any manner whatsoever without written permission except in the case of brief quotations embodied in critical articles and reviews. For information, address HarperCollins Publishers, 195 Broadway, New York, NY 10007. In Europe, HarperCollins Publishers, Macken House, 39/40 Mayor Street Upper, Dublin 1, D01 C9W8, Ireland.

HarperCollins books may be purchased for educational, business, or sales promotional use. For information, please email the Special Markets Department at SPsales@harpercollins.com.

hc.com

FIRST EDITION

Designed by Bonni Leon-Berman

Library of Congress Cataloging-in-Publication Data has been applied for.

ISBN 978-0-06-339504-6

25 26 27 28 29 LBC 5 4 3 2 1

HER MANY FACES

For Chris, for everything

1

Katie

COCKTAIL HOUR. MARCH HOUSE COMES alive with the slosh of martini, the stench of aftershave; business is over for the day.

I weave through them all, take the elevator down to the calm and quiet of the lobby. Step into the corridor, where the only eyes on me are oil-painted and safely trapped in their frames.

I take a breath. Tray steady, the palm of my hand perfectly flat. Cocktails balanced precisely. Door opened with my other hand, quick swoop of the tray through the gap, and I'm into the private dining room again, listening to the four of them laugh.

"So I told her, 'Listen, sweetheart, I could buy this plane, your entire fleet of them, right now,'" one of them says. I dig my nails into my palm.

Lucian catches my eye. Fatherly smile. Grandfatherly, I guess. Anyway: he's not a lech. I get a lot of *those* smiles, slimy and hard-eyed, a snake's tongue flickering over my skin. But Lucian looks only at my face, wants to know how I am, are they working me too hard, have I brought any of my sketches to show him?

Smile. Set the drinks down and murmur politely back. Short and sweet. I'm supposed to be invisible tonight.

"You should have told her, 'Sweetheart, I could buy *you.*'"

Hyenas laughing. They don't care I'm here. The things I've heard in this room, in all of the rooms in March House. Sharp, the feeling of it, like walking over broken glass. Each prick a shock.

I retreat. Wondering how to get through the night.

It's simple, really.

Step back outside into the quiet of the corridor. Leave them to it;

listen to the tick of the clock, the night slipping slowly by. The wine with it. Their faces flushing, their voices getting louder.

Wait on their every need; appear before they even know they want me. Decant and pour, serve and clear.

My moment will come.

Wait.

2

Tarun

"Katherine"

YOU WERE A CHALLENGE. I should be honest about that.

I'd just sat down at my desk in chambers when my phone rang. When I looked down and saw Ursula's name on the screen, my first instinct was to ignore it. I answered only out of a sense of duty to someone who had been a good friend to me when I really needed it, and I regretted it almost as soon as I heard her brisk voice.

"Welcome back," she said, and then she told me about you.

You were twenty-two, a waitress at March House—a private members' club in the heart of Mayfair whose patrons were some of the wealthiest and most powerful people in London. You were accused of murdering four of them.

I imagined the scene. The private dining room with its antique oak table; at the head, Lucian Wrightman, the owner of the club, with the poisoned bottle of brandy in front of him. Two of his guests, the property magnate Harris Lowe and the Chief Secretary to the Treasury, Dominic Ainsworth MP, had died in their seats, while the third, oil baron Aleksandr Popov, had been found on the floor several feet away. An attempt to raise the alarm that he had been unable to complete before being overcome.

A lethal dose of hydrogen cyanide prevents the body's cells from using oxygen, resulting in confusion, dizziness, seizures, and rapid cardiovascular collapse before a victim's inevitable loss of consciousness and death.

It was a cruel way to kill someone. I had, unfortunately, seen worse.

You'd abandoned your post and been captured on CCTV leaving the club shortly after midnight, and had subsequently been arrested attempting to flee London via an early-morning train at Paddington. You told the arresting officers, "They deserved it."

So yes, you were a challenge.

You refused to speak during your interviews in custody. Ignored the duty solicitor and were equally unwilling to communicate, at least initially, when your father hired Ursula as her replacement. And while she seemed confident in your case now, it was clear to me that you would need a highly competent barrister to represent you in court if you were to have any chance of walking free.

I should have been flattered, then, that Ursula had chosen to instruct me. Instead, as I read through her notes again, I felt only dread.

3

John

"Kit-Kat"

YOU WERE A GIFT. UNEXPECTED but not unwanted, a daughter making her late entrance after two sons. Your mum turned thirty-eight three days before you were born; no age at all, really, but we'd thought, after Bobby, that she couldn't carry another baby. We'd been lucky enough to have the boys and had made our peace with it, been content with our little family.

And then there you were. The sweetest girl, seven pound nothing and happy to be held by anyone who'd have you. Born smiling, we used to say, though Bobby, who was having trouble adjusting, would always tell anyone else in earshot, "It's just wind!" He had a habit of eavesdropping on adult conversation, snatching up phrases like a magpie. You may remember a time when you were small and he liked to tell people you were an "axe-dent."

It was Stephen, eleven years your elder, who took his role as your protector seriously, right from the start. When you were a toddler, he used to hold your hand to cross even the quietest street, and as you grew, he was always there to swoop in when you—adventurous, mischievous, ever the explorer—decided to climb a tree or a fence, or to try and ride your little blue trike backward or to crawl into the chimney looking for Father Christmas. You loved the stories he invented for you, a bear called Howard and a brave girl named—at your insistence—Pancake, adventuring through faraway lands and magical worlds with the dubious guidance of the WotsitPotsit Bird. Nothing made you laugh more than that badly behaved bird, and whenever we were out in the garden or on the beach, I'd catch you craning your face to the sky, hoping to catch a glimpse of him.

Your mother and I worried about you as you got older, more so than we did the boys. Perhaps that's normal. It's frightening, sending a daughter out into the world. And you were so headstrong, so fearless, that I would lie awake some nights, wondering what the world would make of you. Wondering what you would make of it. It seemed to baffle you, sometimes—at four, five, six, you were a ball of questions: *Why is that man sleeping on the pavement? Why is that lady sad? Why do I have to go to school? Why do we live in a house and not on the beach? Can I learn to fly a plane? Can I have cake for breakfast? When is it Christmas again?*

So often I felt I was disappointing you with my answers, realized the inadequacy of saying *Well, sometimes people are sad* or *That's just the way we have to do things.*

You were angry one weekend, aged six, when I wouldn't let you camp alone in the field behind our house. Your mother had been trying to get you into the stories she'd loved and so you'd been listening to audiobooks of the Secret Seven and Nancy Drew and had fallen in love. You wanted to look out for robbers and smugglers, making notes in one of your schoolbooks by torchlight. I told you it wasn't safe. "But why, Dad?" you asked, so impatient with me. And I found I couldn't tell you that smugglers are not one of the things people fear, out in the dark of night. Stephen, humoring you, offered to camp in the garden with you, and Bobby, always afraid of missing out, suddenly became enthusiastic too.

Stephen and I set up the tent together, you bouncing in before we'd even finished pegging the guy ropes to the ground.

"Perfect," you said, flopping onto your front, a notebook already open in front of you, an old pair of binoculars your uncle had bought the boys looped around your neck. "Get in, get in!"

I left you to it, and later, I watched through our bedroom window as night fell, the glow of your torches flickering through the canvas of the tent. It was colder than forecast and when I came out to check on you, I half expected you to want to come back inside.

But you were already tucked in a sleeping bag fast asleep, your brothers reading their books peacefully on either side of you. Stephen, aged seventeen and probably wishing he was out with his friends, smiled at me and took the extra blankets I'd brought. Bobby, ten and usually far too cool to be seen with any of us, pointed at the notebook. "No smugglers or robbers," he said, "but we heard one owl and one car alarm."

You came in the next morning, not long after dawn, your hair a scarecrow's nest and your pajamas damp with dew from the grass. You had your toy cat, Pudding, under one arm and your notebook under the other, and you were the happiest I'd ever seen you.

4

Max

"Killer Kate"

YOU WERE THE STORY I'D been waiting for.

Everyone had heard about March House. A place where you needed more money than sense and an invitation to join. Where rock stars snorted coke in the toilets with world leaders, and Hollywood heart-throbs hobnobbed with royals, and where some of the biggest business mergers and policy decisions of the past century were said to have been made.

A murder there would always have been a peach of a headline, but the identity of the victims made it particularly fucking juicy. The owner, Lucian Wrightman, wasn't exactly a household name, but he was richer than God and tipped for an OBE in the coming honors list. Dominic Ainsworth, a political cartoonist's wet dream with his neat little side parting and eager pink face, had had a disastrous outing on breakfast telly two years earlier as a junior minister, and had somehow since been promoted to a role at the Exchequer, despite giving the impression he'd struggle to manage a weekly shopping budget, let alone the country's finances.

Then you had Popov, a billionaire tycoon with fingers in lots of pies, not least as the new owner of a Championship football club—spawning a slew of Mumsnet threads about how hot he was. Harris Lowe looked practically pedestrian in comparison; he was heir to the Lowe's Diamonds fortunes and head of Lowe Estates, which happened to own half the property in Mayfair—including the very building you murdered him in.

They had a clutch of marriages and affairs and a shocking—sickening—amount of personal wealth between them. Very naughty boys. We were all just waiting to hear exactly what they'd done to become targets.

Then came news of your arrest: a waitress at the club, aged twenty-two, barely five feet two and a mousy little face, looking like you wouldn't say boo to a goose.

The whole thing went from nought to feeding frenzy in record time, headline after headline for days, click rates to die for on every article we posted. And once you were charged, I set about finding out everything there was to know about you.

5

John

"Kit-Kat"

YOU BROUGHT ME FLOWERS ONE Father's Day. You'd been for a walk with Stephen while the rest of us were out, had broken off stems from people's front gardens while he wasn't looking. You presented them to me with your hands still streaked with soil, a gap in your smile where you'd lost a bottom tooth and a smear of green pen still staining your cheek where you'd drawn yourself "a tattoo" days earlier.

"Sorry," Stephen said. "I did tell her not to."

"Boys don't like flowers, stupid," Bobby told you, and you looked genuinely puzzled.

"Everyone likes flowers," you said, and you turned to me for confirmation.

"I love flowers," I told you.

"So did the people who planted them," your mum said. "Bobby, get your things. Kit, are you ready?"

You looked at me and shook your head. "I want to stay here today," you said.

You'd always loved going to the gym when Bobby was training. As a toddler, you'd treated the place like a giant soft play, often needing to be fished from the landing pits beside the parallel beams and the vault table, where you liked to bury yourself beneath the foam blocks. Now that you were older, Julia, who adored you, would sometimes take time out to help you practice your handstands or to plait your hair in various complicated ways, while Peter ran through Bobby's routines with him.

"You can't," your mum said. "Come on, get a move on."

"Please," you said, turning to me.

"I have to drive Stephen back," I said. "You don't want to be stuck in the car the whole day."

"Yes I do," you said, case closed, and you ran to get your shoes and your Nintendo DS.

Your mum shrugged and smiled at me. "At least you won't get lonely on the way home."

"Can't you come and watch me?" Bobby asked, his small frame dwarfed by the kit bag slung across his body.

I tried to make it to as many of his practices and meets as possible. We had hired a new vet at the surgery, making my workload a little more manageable, and your mother and I divided things equally between us where we could—drop-offs and pickups and birthday parties and your swimming lessons and playdates. But Peter was your mum's friend, now Julia too, and so gradually it became her thing, the other commitments mine.

"Next weekend, I promise," I told him. I kissed them both and herded you and Stephen into the car.

I hadn't wanted Stephen to go to Sandhurst. It hadn't really occurred to me, when marrying your mum, that the military line in her family might be expected to continue with any children of our own. When the three of you were younger, I'd tuned out your uncle's and your granddad's comments, had thought that Stephen—endlessly patient and kind to a fault—would be a good teacher or a nurse, perhaps a writer. You still talked about Howard and Pancake and the Wotsit-Potsit Bird.

But Stephen had been set on it, and even I could see it had been the making of him. Glancing at him in the passenger seat, confident and calm, his hair shorn, I almost did a double take, unable to reconcile him with the skinny, sweet little boy I remembered.

As we joined the motorway, we passed the time talking about some of Stephen's fellow officer cadets and his instructors and the exercises he would be taking part in during his final term. You played your game, ignoring us. At first, you'd shown some interest in the survival skills he'd learned, were particularly excited about building your own camouflaged shelter behind your mum's rose beds, but you'd been up-set when, in his second year, Stephen had been on an exchange to West Point in the States and you hadn't seen him for three months, and since then you ignored all talk of his training as if that might make it go away.

"Will you be home in time to go to the farm?" you asked when we'd fallen quiet.

"Not this year." Stephen turned in his seat to talk to you. "But when I get back, I'll take you to London, okay? Top deck of the bus, all the sights. Like I promised."

"Fine," you said, rolling your eyes and turning the volume up on your game.

But when we dropped him off, you, suddenly solemn, hugged him so tightly he let out a surprised puff of air. I met his eye, and he smiled at me.

"Be good, okay?" he said to you, ruffling your hair, and you pulled back and told him that you would.

Aged seven, you liked to draw, working your way painstakingly through a book you'd found at the library, though it was too advanced for you, your tongue poking out of the corner of your mouth as you tried again and again to follow the steps to draw a dog. You loved to learn about the world, liked copying pictures of things you thought Stephen might like—Angkor Wat and the Great Wall of China, the "Great 8" animals of the Great Barrier Reef, and a cockscomb plant whose flowers looked like brains that you found in an old gardening manual of your mum's.

You were helpful, always appearing at my side in the kitchen or garden, asking if I had a job for you. "Your little shadow," your mum said once, though you were just as likely to curl up next to her on the sofa while she was marking homework. You liked company, liked to talk. You always had something to say, always a question to ask.

The four of us traveled up for Stephen's passing-out parade, you and Bobby dressed smartly with your hair combed neat. I felt so incredibly proud of you all as I moaned at you to pose nicely for the photos. And as we walked back to the car afterward, you and your mum were ahead, you tugging at the waistband of the tights that were too big for you, a grass stain on the hem of your dress. Your mum put her arm round you and squeezed you, and you looked up at her and beamed.

I think of that moment often, perfectly framed in my mind, a post-card from another time. I want to step inside it, race to catch up with you both, to fold you into my arms and never let go.

You turned eight the following summer. Your birthday was on a Mon-day, an injustice you were deeply unhappy about, only compounding your upset that Stephen was still two months away from returning from his first deployment to Helmand Province. But you'd been cheered up by your presents—the beautiful set of encyclopedias that your mum had found for you, the games and clothes and hair braiding set you'd chosen for yourself—and had gone off to school happily enough.

That morning we went shopping for the birthday dinner you'd re-quested: burgers, hot dogs, and your mum's macaroni cheese. We drew the line at the champagne you'd asked for.

"Where has she even heard the word *canapé*?" your mum asked, frowning at the list you'd carefully written out for us.

I pushed the trolley on, adding mince for the burgers. "I blame *Ratatouille*."

"Maybe *we* have the champagne," she said, consulting the list again. "That seems fair, don't you think?"

It was unusual for us both to have a day off together—your mum's school was closed for emergency water pipe repairs, and I'd taken one of my many accrued annual leave days after repeated badgering from the practice manager. Back at the house, I made us sandwiches, and we took them into the garden, the day warm and bright. We sat and listened to the birds singing in the oak tree above us.

"She was such a lovely baby," your mum said. "Remember the cheeks?"

"The wrist rolls."

Your mother pressed a hand to her chest. "Perfection."

There was a single, sharp ring of the doorbell. "It's probably the cake," your mum said as I got up. "The woman said between one and two."

But when I opened the front door, there was a man of about my own age, sweating in his suit. Everything about him precise, calm. Only the slightest tremble in his voice gave him away as he came into the living room, sat us both down, and delivered the news.

Stephen, killed by a car bomb on a patrol base in Nad Ali.

Your mum, sitting beside me on the sofa, let out a single, indecipherable sound and curled over onto her knees, her hands covering her face.

You liked our casualty visiting officer, a young man from the same regiment as Stephen who had sisters of his own and often took the time to sit and talk with you. I heard you once, on the afternoon he'd come to assist us with funeral plans, telling him about the letters Stephen had sent you, proudly showing him the little blue sheets of paper with their jokes and doodles, Stephen's descriptions of the camp and the things he missed most from home. I noticed the way you spoke in the present tense about him—*he says it's really hot and the food's okay and that Cheryl Cole is visiting soon for Pride of Britain and he'll say hello from me*—and the gentle way the CVO used the past tense in response: *It sounds like he was a lovely brother. I bet he missed you a lot.*

When your mum found the letters on the kitchen table, she gathered them up and hid them on a high shelf in a cupboard. "It's upsetting her," she said, though I worry, now, that the opposite was true.

Stephen was buried in a military cemetery in West London, and your uncle Neil traveled down from Scotland to be a pallbearer. He'd served in the Gulf War before returning to run your mum's family's farm when your grandfather had become too ill to do so, and when I came down that morning, feeling sick to my stomach, he was dressed in uniform in the kitchen, making breakfast while you and Bobby sat quietly at the table. For a second, I thought it was Stephen standing there, and it was only in that moment, as Neil turned round and I saw it was him, that it truly hit me that I wouldn't see Stephen again.

Afterward, you kept a photo of Stephen in his uniform—one of the ones I had taken at his passing-out parade, you grinning beside him—on your bedside table. I noticed, over the months that followed, how it moved position every few days. Sometimes facing your pillow, at other times looking out at the room, once or twice on your windowsill or dresser.

And I felt *glad* that you were touching it, holding it, while I was walking round the house with my eyes fixed on the floor, too scared to look at any of the family photos we'd hung so carelessly, so obliviously, as if they were from a never-ending supply. You were remembering Stephen. As if you were the only one brave enough to do so.

6

Tarun

"Katherine"

I STAYED LATE AT CHAMBERS that night, rereading Ursula's email. I was grateful that she had contacted me directly rather than my clerk. I'd felt that the time was right for my return to work, but now, looking at the details of your case, I was no longer sure.

I focused on the specific points of law a jury would need to be convinced of to convict you of the murders. In doing so, I set about applying pressure to each piece of the prosecution's case in turn. Searching for the gaps, the weak spots. The things that said *there is doubt here.*

There was no doubt you were in an undesirable position. You had served the group all night, in a dining room on a floor separate from the rest of the club and its patrons, and the only fingerprints found on the poisoned bottle of brandy belonged to you and Lucian Wrightman himself. You had fled your shift early without telling anyone you were doing so and, when apprehended by police, had declared that the victims deserved it.

But that didn't mean I couldn't see those weak spots in the case against you. I could begin, reading those notes, to imagine myself standing up in court, the lines of cross-examination I might pursue against the witnesses who would be called by the prosecution. I stepped unexpectedly back into a self I had once known so well, and it felt good.

Just as quickly, a familiar feeling crept over me: the sensation of walking along a cliff edge, not knowing when the ground might crumble beneath me. I read what Ursula had written about you again, and then, knowing it was a terrible idea, I read some of the news coverage of your arrest.

There is a principle in my profession known as the cab rank rule: a barrister may not discriminate between clients and must take on any case, provided that it is within their competence and that they are available and will be appropriately remunerated. Justice must be freely accessible to all, meaning that one cannot turn down a client simply because a case may be contentious, unpopular, or difficult to defend. I had never strayed from this code of conduct. Had always represented every client to the very best of my ability.

But I was not the same person anymore. And I was no longer sure that this case—or any—was within my competence.

I called Ursula as I walked home.

"I'm not sure," I said, when she answered. "I'm not the right person for this."

"Of course you are," she said.

"I'm not ready—"

"You are ready," she cut in, in a tone that brooked no argument. "And you can help her."

I was silent, the entrance to the Underground station looming ahead of me.

"She isn't Marla, Tarun," Ursula said.

I hesitated for a second, winded.

"Come on," she said. "I need you. And you need this."

7

John

"Kit-Kat"

IN THE MONTHS AFTER STEPHEN'S funeral, when the house felt too quiet, too still, you were always there with your questions, your stories about your day, your funny little ways. You insisted on coming with me to walk the dog each night, waiting by the door in your pajamas with your coat zipped over the top. You and me and Wilbur, who endured your hugs and teasing and your games of hide-and-seek, walking the same loop across the meadow and the dunes and down to the beach. You told me it was the best bit of your day, but once, a couple of months in, I overheard you telling your mum that you didn't want me to be lonely.

As time went on and we settled into a new kind of normal, you were always trying to make us laugh. You could make your mum and me cry with your impressions of celebrities and neighbors and my customers at the surgery; I still remember how uncanny your old Mrs. Pollock was, the way you'd stand with one hand on your hip, berating the imaginary receptionist: *I've told you a thousand times, this waiting room is too cold for Bitsy!*

Though you weren't particularly academic, you liked school. You loved art and anything creative, especially when your teacher brought in a sewing machine for you to try. You came home so excited about it that your mum went up to the loft and brought hers down, and the two of you spent the rest of that summer going to charity shops, buying baggy old T-shirts and dresses that you cut with painstaking concentration, trying out stitches and techniques from another library book.

She wore a top you made when she went out for dinner with Julia one evening, and I thought you might actually burst with pride.

All the while, the collection of medals and trophies displayed proudly in Bobby's room grew larger, his confidence with it. I stood watching him on the parallel bars one afternoon in early 2010, not long after he'd turned fourteen, and was completely blindsided by how strong he looked, how elegantly he moved.

"I think he might be one of the most naturally talented gymnasts we've ever worked with," Peter said, coming up beside me. "You must be very proud."

"I am."

"Big things," he said, clapping me on the back. "The boy's going to do big things."

The after-school and weekend training sessions and meets intensified after that. I tried to be around as much as I could, so that you could stay at home instead of waiting for hours on end on the balcony of the gym, reading or drawing in your notebook. You told me repeatedly that you hated it, that everyone was annoying, that gymnastics was the stupidest sport.

But your mum said that you often asked if you could have a turn, could sometimes be found in whichever corner of the gym was quietest, trying out the balance beam or the horse in your school uniform and socks. You came home upset one evening because Peter had told you off for climbing on some old equipment you'd found in a storeroom.

"It was dangerous," your mum said. "Don't sulk about it."

"It wasn't dangerous," you told me later. "Peter was horrible to me. He said I had to stop sneaking around and trying to be the center of attention all the time." Your eyes filled with tears again as you said, "I don't even know what that *means!*"

Bobby was invited to a selection event for an official Team GB development program. It meant staying in London for three days, time off school. Peter would attend as his coach, and I managed to book leave so I could go with them.

"I want to come," you said, a week or so before. "I want to see Diagon Alley."

"It's not real, idiot," Bobby said, at the same time as your mum told you, "You've got school."

"It's not fair," you said, your voice growing plaintive. "Bobby gets to go everywhere."

"You'll get plenty of trips when I'm in the Olympics," Bobby said, grinning, and you rolled your eyes.

"*Not* going to happen," you said, but Bobby, on cloud nine, took no notice of you.

Your night terrors began around that time. Waking soaked in sweat, or sleepwalking into our room, babbling about bad men, death, fire. It had been two years since Stephen died and your mum banned you from taking out scary books from the library, grounded Bobby for showing you horror movie trailers on YouTube. When I suggested, six months on, that we actually needed to find some kind of counseling for you, she dismissed the idea. "She'll grow out of it," she said. "I was the same, at her age."

"This is different," I said. "She's gone through something traumatic, we all have. She needs to talk about it."

"You're making connections that don't exist." She was irritated now. "It's just a normal thing, and she'll grow out of it."

"But why *should* she, when we can get her some help?" I was tired by then of the belief, handed down to her by your granddad and his father before him, that things should be borne or suffered silently through, that airing our problems only gave them oxygen to burn brighter.

"I'm not having this conversation again," she said, going into the en suite and closing the door on me, and I walked over to the bed and screamed into a pillow.

But to you, we always presented a united front, and when you had a run of good nights, sleeping soundly through, I let the idea of counseling drop.

One afternoon, Bobby came storming into the kitchen, complaining that he couldn't find his grips.

"Those are new. Please tell me you haven't lost them," your mum said.

"I *haven't*," Bobby said hotly. "They were in my room, and now they're gone." He thundered back up the stairs and went into your room.

"Hey!" I heard you shout. "You have to knock—"

There was a crash, and your mum and I both hurried up to see what was going on. Bobby had pushed your books and pens and pencils from your desk, and now began ransacking the drawers.

"*Bobby*," your mum said, shocked, as you leapt from your bed, the wool you'd been attempting to knit with tumbling to the floor.

"Stop touching my things," you shouted, your mum just catching you before you could get to him.

"Enough." I pulled Bobby away by the shoulder. But as he removed his hand from the back of the bottom drawer, he brought out the brand-new grips. We all stared at them.

"I was just borrowing them," you said in a small voice.

There were several similar incidents over the following weeks. A tracksuit top went missing, never to be found again, and Bobby's kit bag was left unzipped on the front step in the rain. A leotard had a tear down the back when I came to remove it from the washing machine.

Your mum sat you down after your bath one night, you wrapped in your dressing gown with your hair still wet.

"It's normal to feel jealous," she said, combing your hair. You winced. "But I want this behavior to stop," she continued. "You should be happy for your brother. You should be supporting him."

You opened your mouth, ready to argue, but then you closed it again. "Okay," you said.

That weekend, I took you and Wilbur up the coast for a walk through the forest, a place you'd loved to come to when you were little and liked to help Stephen and Bobby make dens between the trees. I could picture you in your tiny wellies, arms loaded with twigs and sticks and your face scratched and beaming, so pleased with yourself. Now you were quiet, walking along with your hands stuffed into your pockets, your shoulders slumped. You barely looked up as we followed the trail, ignored the ball Wilbur kept dropping at your feet.

"Let's go and get cake," I suggested. "Maybe a hot chocolate?"

You smiled and nodded, but you still seemed a million miles away.

When we were sitting in the café, our drinks steaming in front of us, I asked you if everything was all right.

You bit your lip. "I need to tell you something."

"Okay." I folded my hands in my lap.

"I don't think you're going to like it," you said.

"You can tell me anything."

You swallowed. "When I was at the gym with Mum the other day, I saw Peter taking pictures," you said.

Your cheeks were burning; that's the thing I remember most. You were never shy, rarely blushed, and yet now you could hardly meet my eye.

"What do you mean? Pictures of the session?"

"No." You shook your head. "Pictures afterward. In the changing room. In the . . ." You blinked at me. "In the showers," you said, your voice almost a whisper now. "He was standing at the door and nobody had seen him and he was taking pictures."

8

Max

"Killer Kate"

MY WIFE, ANYA, HAD HER own opinions of you. "She looks so sweet," she said, scrolling through her phone at breakfast. "It's sad, really, isn't it?"

"Sad for the men who were murdered, sure."

She got up from the table, started clearing the mess of crumbs and juice our hurricane of a six-year-old had left in his wake. "Imagine how her parents must be feeling. What do you think happened?"

I shook my head. "I'd like to find out."

I found the picture of you she'd seen on the BBC, an old one ripped from social media: you in a park, smiling like sunshine personified with an ice cream in your hand. She was right: you did look sweet. I imagined that same conversation happening over coffee and cereal in kitchens across the country. What had happened in that club? Why had you done it?

Good questions. I wanted to be the one to answer them.

That day, I started trying to track down people who knew and would be willing to talk about you. Your parents had been easy enough to find—your mum's picture all over the school's website, and the one for the veterinary surgery where your dad worked listing a phone number and email address for me to try. I'm guessing I wasn't the first or last journalist to contact them, and I didn't hold out much hope of my calls being returned.

Your brother was on Instagram. Not much personal information given away, just artsy-fartsy shots of London—blurry buildings through rainy bus windows and nighttime streets streaked with headlights—and pretentious flat lays of books he was reading: a classic Agatha Christie with a coffee and croissant, a P. D. James beside a boiled egg and soldiers and a chintzy teapot. None of his own face and none of yours. But in his bio, the place to find him: *Owner of @wilburscoffee.*

Wilbur's was already busy, the tables out on the pavement full and a queue for the counter inside that never really seemed to subside. I joined the end of it, pretending to admire the display of cakes. The place was full of yummy mummies and hipsters with their matcha lattes and cold brews, buggies and expensive bikes parked between tables. It was a prime spot, right off Newington Green, and I bet the rent was astronomical.

There were two girls behind the counter, no sign of Bobby. Maybe keeping a low profile while your mug shot was still fresh in people's minds. I toyed with the idea of using a cover story to ask for him, possibly pretending to be a concerned friend, which had worked for me in making reluctant sources materialize in the past. But no need—just as I reached the front of the queue, he appeared, a phone wedged between his shoulder and ear. I ordered a black coffee from one of the girls, watching him as he stood at the other end of the counter, searching through a stack of documents. In person, there was some family resemblance, same mousy hair and freckled skin, but he was more striking than you, strong jaw and bright blue eyes, and looked like he took better care of himself.

He found whatever he was looking for just as the girl handed me my coffee. I tapped my card on the reader without really paying attention, instead noticing the way your brother kept his head down as he weaved his way out through the tables and onto the pavement. He looked bruised somehow, scared, like he was afraid of being noticed or spoken to. I took my coffee and hurried after him.

He was walking fast, already a little way down the street when I called his name. He turned, and when he saw me, a stranger, his face hardened. But he stopped walking.

"Max Todd," I said, jogging to catch up with him. The paper cup was thin, and I hadn't taken a sleeve for it, the heat of the coffee already burning my hand. "I work for the *Herald*. I'd really love to talk to you about your sister."

He flinched, already turning away. "No comment."

"It must be a terrible shock, all of this," I said, because a little kindness right off the bat usually goes a long way. You'd be surprised how far a bit of empathy gets you with some people.

To my surprise, he laughed. A bitter, hurt kind of laugh that told me he'd talk. Eventually.

"Nothing Kit does shocks me anymore," he said. "Please, leave us alone."

But he took my card when I offered it. I watched him walk away, turning that line over in my head. *Nothing Kit does shocks me anymore.*

Now I really was interested.

9

John

"Kit-Kat"

THE DAYS THAT FOLLOWED WERE rough; I find it difficult to remember them now. That night your mum asked you, over and over, *Are you sure?* while you sat at the kitchen table and cried. Bobby flew at you when he heard what you'd said, his face scarlet as he spat, *Liar.* I grabbed him, his wiry frame now knotted with hard muscle, my heart pounding against his back as I locked my arms round him and held him.

Your mum tried to stop me at the door when I said I had to report it. Over her shoulder I saw you standing there, looking small and scared. I pushed past her and found my phone.

When a member of staff rang to let us know the gym was closing temporarily, Bobby punched a wall so hard that his knuckles split open with the plaster. I cleaned and bandaged his hand, and when I was done, I kept hold of it. "I know this is awful," I said. "But I'm here for you."

"She's lying," he said. "And you believe her and not me." He pulled his hand away.

You refused to leave your room all week. That night I came up to see you with two plates of food on a tray. You were curled at the end of your bed, reading a book, and I noticed you were wearing an old sweatshirt of Stephen's.

"Hi," you said.

"Hi." I put the tray down on the bed beside you and then took a seat. You watched me, cross-legged on your kitten-print duvet, trying to eat lasagna, and then picked up your own knife and fork and started eating too.

"Everyone's going to hate me," you said. "They're all talking about it at school."

"It's a small town," I said. "Everyone talks about everything and then they forget."

"Okay," you said, though you didn't sound sure.

"You did the right thing," I told you, and I saw your shoulders drop, just a little, as if a weight had been lifted from you.

We ate in companionable silence after that. I took the plates down to the quiet kitchen and washed them while Bobby and your mum watched a film in the living room.

10

Tarun

"Katherine"

MY FIRST MEETING WITH YOU made me nervous; I won't pretend otherwise.

I'd told Ursula I wished to see you alone, and if she thought that unusual—or the fact I had asked to do so at this early juncture—she said nothing. Perhaps she thought I was still finding my feet again, overcautious about ensuring I had everything I needed to proceed with the brief.

The truth, however, was that I wondered if you were guilty, and hoped I might be a better judge than she was.

You were sullen, staring at me as I took my seat opposite you in the private room the prison had assigned for us. You were sitting on your hands, the sweatshirt you were wearing swamping you, and your hair was unwashed and uncombed.

"Hello, Katherine," I said. "My name is Tarun Rao, and I'm the barrister that Ursula has instructed on your behalf."

You eyed me warily and then looked away. "She says you're the best," you said.

My last murder client had said something similar to me, and this did not reassure me.

"There is significant evidence in the case against you," I said. "I'd like to hear your version of events."

You began picking at a loose thread on the cuff of your sweatshirt. "She didn't tell you?"

"I'd like to hear it from you."

You chewed your lip. Nerves, perhaps, or the pause of someone trying to ensure they had their story straight.

"I went to work as normal," you said. You still didn't meet my eye. "It was a private dinner, one of Lucian's, and I did what I always did. I served the food, served the wine, served the brandy. I didn't kill them."

"The Crown Prosecution Service are proposing that you brought the poisoned bottle of brandy into the club."

"I didn't. It was already in the room when I arrived."

You looked at me as you said it, your clear green eyes locked on mine, and I understood for the first time why Ursula believed you.

"You ran away before your shift was over," I prodded.

"I hated it there. I'd had enough."

"So you just walked out, there and then, without telling anyone?"

You nodded, your expression hardening. You didn't like being questioned, which did not bode well.

"You told the police the men deserved it."

Again, you hesitated. "I didn't mean that. I didn't know what I was saying."

I sat back in my chair and let a silence unfold between us.

"What's going to happen to me?" you asked.

"If you're found guilty, this offense meets the criteria for a whole life order, meaning a life sentence with no possibility for parole."

You looked as though I had slapped you. "*Will* I be found guilty?"

I knew that I should respond reassuringly, pragmatically. But instead the only answer that came to mind was *Should you be?*

John

"Kit-Kat"

IN THE SUMMER OF 2014, we headed for Scotland. It had been three years since Peter and Julia had moved away, two and half since we'd heard the investigation had been dropped. You'd cried when I told you the news.

Peter had been popular locally, and I can't pretend I didn't notice the way people avoided me after he left, the slight frostiness with which a lot of my patients spoke to me.

But you'd turned eleven, then twelve, then thirteen, seemed to be doing well at senior school. You still spent hours carefully sketching or sewing, sometimes doing your maths homework at the dining table so one of us could help you. When I look back now, it seems obvious how little you talked about friends. How few names you mentioned when recounting your days at school. We were too distracted to notice.

Bobby had failed his exams and refused to retake them, had begun smoking cannabis so regularly that I'd stopped noticing the smell on his clothes, stopped being shocked by his red eyes, his long disappearing acts to friends' houses. He sat in the backseat of the car now with his headphones in, ignoring all of us. As we drove up the rutted track to the farmhouse, I looked in the rearview mirror and saw he'd fallen asleep, his head bouncing gently against the window.

As children, you'd all loved Neil, who had taken over the family farm when your granddad retired. We'd always spent our summer holidays there, Neil telling you ghost stories out in the dark barn or letting you sit too close to the firepit he'd built so you could toast marshmallows.

But when we arrived this time, he wasn't going to play the fun uncle.

"You've grown, kitten," he told you, barely glancing at you before switching his attention to Bobby. "And what's the problem with you, then, eh?"

"Good to see you too," Bobby said, but the sarcasm fell flat, and I could tell he was nervous.

"Go and put some trainers on," Neil said. "We're going for a run in ten minutes."

"Can I come?" you asked, and Neil shook his head. "Me and Bobby have got some talking to do."

That night I walked in to find Bobby at the kitchen table with a laptop, applying for jobs, and realized that your mum had been right. Neil had known how to get through to him.

I went to our bedroom to tell her and found her at the window, watching you in the garden with Wilbur. You were getting him to chase you, one of his favorite games, your hair flying behind you and your cheeks flushed. You looked the happiest I'd seen you in a long time.

"I'm glad we came," I said, and your mum startled, lost in thought.

"She's so like my mother," she said, still watching you. "I hadn't noticed."

I hesitated. She rarely spoke about your grandma, who'd died when you were still a toddler, but when she did, it often sent her mood spiraling to a dark place.

I put my arm round her. "I think she's just our Kit," I said.

12

Max

"Killer Kate"

AFTER I MET YOUR BROTHER, I realized this was going to be a big deal for me. I mean, obviously you were clickworthy. You were young, reasonably attractive; the four victims were high-profile enough that there was plenty of mileage to be had in that alone. That was my job: finding the headlines that people couldn't resist opening, making sure we were always first in line with those stories. It was never going to win me a Pulitzer but I think old József P. himself would've understood: the sensational stuff was what got the traffic, and that paid the bills. I was good at it.

But there was more to this. There was more to you.

And that was the *point* of it all. The reason I went down this path in the first place, the way I'd felt when I read *In Cold Blood* for the first time, aged fifteen. Writers like me were supposed to shed light on the darkest parts of our society, to truly show the reality of the world we live in. To explain why people do bad things, to find closure—justice—for everyone involved.

Your story? It felt like a chance to really do that.

Especially when I realized Hasan was working your case. That, I guess, was my first real stroke of luck.

We'd met five years earlier, when I'd been working on my first book, a deep dive into the cocaine trade in the UK, formed entirely of conversations with five anonymized real people connected to it: a dealer, a middle-class dinner-party user, the mother of an addict, a kid caught up in county lines, and a detective from one of the Met's crackdown operations.

The Met officer was Hasan, and we'd been friends ever since. The book, meanwhile, had generated a brief flurry of moderate excitement from the industry and then been conspicuously absent from the shelves or the review pages, and nowadays it was something that Hasan and I didn't speak about. C'est la vie. Genius hits a target that no one else can see, as Schopenhauer said.

We met at a pub just off Broadway Market, and I bought the drinks as usual. Fair enough; I remembered what it was like to be young and hemorrhaging most of my salary on rent, working too many hours to actually spend any time in the shoebox flat it was all going toward. Hasan's girlfriend was drifting along like a typical Gen Z, but he reminded me of myself: a workaholic, hungry for it. That day, his hair was still wet from the shower, the bags and circles under his eyes telling a tale of naps grabbed between night shifts, his stomach growling as he glanced at the menu.

"Sounds like this March House thing's going to keep you busy," I said.

"Understatement." He rolled and then unrolled his sleeves, his foot tapping against the tiled floor. He was a ball of energy and caffeine, just like I'd been at his age, and that was usually when it was easiest to catch him off guard.

"I've been doing some digging into Kate Cole. It's hard to see how she ended up doing something like this."

He raised an eyebrow at me, a kind of *you don't know the half of it.*

"I shouldn't be telling you this," he said, taking a sip of his beer, enjoying it, "but check out a site called the Rabbit Hole."

13

Gabriel

"K. C."

YOU WERE THE PRETTIEST GIRL I'd ever seen.

I was fifteen and had wet dreams about Jennifer Lawrence, my maths teacher, and you. Back then, I blushed pretty much as soon as you walked past me, but that didn't matter. I was invisible to everyone then, even you, and that suited me just fine.

Before everything, I grew up sick. That's how it feels, when I think of being a kid. Chicken pox, a thousand puking bugs, one long Christmas spent picking impetigo scabs. Chest infections, allergic reactions, every cold and flu that came to town. And then, when I was fourteen, a virus that hit me hard, for no reason anyone could ever figure out, and left me stuck in bed while they tried to decide what the hell was wrong with me.

When I told you that once, those exact words, you laughed. "Any day now," you said.

The summer of the sickness was also the summer my mum finally saw sense and broke up with her boyfriend, Dave of the bad breath and polo necks, and decided it would be best for both of us if we moved somewhere new, ideally somewhere with fresh sea air, like I was a Victorian kid with rickets.

She settled on Devon and then on Combe Little—close enough to see the sea but from a flat we could just about afford the rent on—and we packed up our stuff into a grand total of twenty-three boxes and loaded up a hire van with my auntie Shelley in the driving seat. Shelley bought us a pizza while we unpacked, and the three of us sat out in the flat's little courtyard, listening to the seagulls and the silence while Shelley drank three Cinzanos—the box of booze being the only one she'd helped unpack—and Mum hummed happily to herself.

A week later I started school, painfully and obviously the weird new kid, and I did my best to shrink into the shadows at every opportunity, scuttling around like a wood louse running from rock to rock and wondering how long I could get away with nobody noticing me. Choosing the quietest corner of the canteen to eat my sandwiches, trying not to make eye contact with anyone or in any way draw attention to myself.

You sat at the table in front of mine about ten minutes before the end of lunch with a half-eaten slice of pizza and a can of cream soda. You had your back to me, and I watched you carving your initials into the bench as you ate. *K. C.* I liked the sound of them in my head, the way they made a name of their own.

Mum got a job at a guesthouse near the beach, cleaning the rooms and washing the sheets, which meant she got up at five each morning, and I got myself breakfast and went off to school without saying a word to another human until my form teacher called my name in registration. In the evenings, Mum worked in an old people's home on the outskirts of town, helping with the dinner trolley and washing more sheets and playing cribbage with an old man who thought she was his daughter, and I got myself dinner and made sure there was always enough for her and that the flat was tidy and warm when she got home. She was happy, and that made me happy.

I finally worked up the courage to join Warhammer Club, which was a great decision because I made a friend, Bart, who was kind and funny and, most important, could help me navigate my way round the school. Once we were walking to biology and you were hurrying in the opposite direction, your head down. "Who's that?" I asked, feeling uncharacteristically brave.

He looked at you and then raised an eyebrow at me. Bart's eyebrows did a lot of the talking for him a lot of the time, sometimes disappearing up under his fringe or crawling right down into one long line when he was really thinking about something. "Katie Cole?" he asked. "Why?"

I shrugged, already embarrassed. "Just wondering."

"She's trouble," he said. "Everyone will tell you that."

But I didn't have everyone to ask, just him, and it didn't stop me looking for you each time my mind started wandering at school.

My mum turned forty that winter, and I decided I was going to make her a cake. I'm not usually ambitious, but I'd watched a lot of *Bake Off* that year, and I guess might have developed unrealistic ideas about what was achievable with a bit of time and a positive attitude, so I chose a Black Forest treble-tier number with chocolate-dipped cherries on top. I waited till her first night shift at the old people's home that week and headed straight off on my bike to buy all the stuff for it, riding down the hill toward town and picking up speed.

I didn't see the car reversing off the drive in front of me. Probably I was miles away, imagining myself winning *Bake Off* or running through the *Call of Duty* mission I was meant to be playing that night with Bart, with no bandwidth left available to see the souped-up Vauxhall crossing the pavement in front of me. I smashed into the side of it, and the next thing I knew, I was on the ground as the bike hit the pavement in front of me, its back wheel spinning.

The wind must've got knocked out of me or something, because I remember just lying there and hearing a car door open, the clump of boots on the pavement.

The next thing, I'm being lifted up by my T-shirt or my neck, and my ears are still ringing, and there's this red-faced guy launching spit all over my face while he's telling me I'm a fucking moron and a little shit and that he's going to rip my fucking head off.

"Hey," you said, from the pavement on the other side of the car. "Want to say that again so I can be sure I got it?"

We both turned to look at you, and you waved and pointed at your phone held up in front of you.

"I didn't quite catch you reversing into my friend," you said, with the sweetest smile. "But I definitely have you threatening to kill him, which really seems like a strange way to apologize for a situation that was one hundred percent your fault."

I'd never, ever, in my whole life been happier to see someone.

The guy let go of me. Or at least my feet touched the ground again.

"He's dented my car," he said.

"Then you should look where you're going," you said, the phone still held up, you still giving him that sweet smile.

The guy looked at you and then at me.

"Fuck this," he said, or something like it, and before I could even draw a full breath, he was storming back round to the driver's side, the car reversing the rest of the way into the road with a squeal.

When he was gone, there was just you and me and a valley of pavement between us, and I finally got round to feeling the full force of the humiliation of the whole thing.

"Thank you," I said.

"Are you okay?"

I looked down at myself. "I . . . think so?"

"Are you sure?"

I was worried my legs were shaking so much I'd have to sit down on the curb before I fell over. Or that I might cry, which in front of you might actually have been even worse than getting beaten up.

"I'm fine," I said. "Honestly."

You smiled at me, like you were waiting to see what I'd say next, and I realized I was gawping at you like some bug-eyed fish, like you were some mythical being who'd swooped down on a lightning bolt or Pegasus or something.

"Thanks," I said again, like a total idiot. I swear, with every second that passed, a little bit more of me curled up and died inside.

You stepped forward and lifted my bike up from the ground. "Look where you're going this time, okay?"

I took the handlebars from you and watched as you walked away in the orange glow of the streetlights.

"Hey," you said, turning back round. "What's your name, anyway?"

14

John

"Kit-Kat"

YOU GREW QUIETER AS YOU turned fifteen and started studying for your GCSEs. You frustrated easily—emptying the wastepaper bin in your room, I often found scratched-out notes and crumpled attempts at essays or art assignments. You still made clothes, your room filled with stacks of fashion magazines and scraps of fabric, the sewing machine often juddering through the floorboards late into the night. You also liked to listen to music while you were alone, sometimes lying on your bed with your eyes closed, your speaker turned up as loud as it would go.

Your mum was not shy about strolling in and turning it off. But I liked some of the artists you liked, had taken you to see Joanna Newsom and Sufjan Stevens before. You tried to teach me about the others when you were in a chatty mood, playing me Wolf Alice and Kendrick Lamar, Alabama Shakes, Jenny Hval and Beach Slang.

I came into your room one afternoon with a stack of books and magazines you'd left scattered around the house, and found you at your desk, frowning at your laptop. I told you that dinner was almost ready, and you nodded, distracted.

"Can I show you something?" you asked.

You played me a video of the footage from 9/11: the planes colliding with the twin towers, one after the other, the footage slowed right down as someone in the corner of the screen speculated about inconsistencies in the way the buildings had collapsed.

"Isn't this crazy?" you asked. "Can you believe we haven't heard about this before?"

I put down the books on the edge of your desk. "We haven't heard about it because that person doesn't know what they're talking about. Where did you even find this?"

You ignored me. "But what if it *was* staged, Dad? And the war was all because of a lie?"

You said it so earnestly that I felt unnerved. "It wasn't, Kit-Kat. This is just a made-up conspiracy theory. There's a million of them out there, about all sorts of things."

"I don't think it is! If you look into it, there's so much evidence. We've been lied to."

"Stop," I said. "You're smarter than this."

"But—"

"Really, Kit," I said, firmly now. "If Mum heard you saying things like that . . . It's disrespectful to Stephen's memory."

Your eyes filled with tears. "I didn't . . ."

"I know you didn't mean it like that. But this stuff . . . it's delusional."

After a final look at the screen, you closed the laptop lid. "Okay. Sorry."

We went down to dinner together after that, and I thought, I suppose, that was the end of it.

15

Max

"Killer Kate"

LET'S NOT BEAT AROUND THE bush: this wasn't my first conspiracy rodeo. I'd spent a lot of time on the Rabbit Hole before, and back then it'd been far more personal. In the grim early days of 2020, I'd been put on our Covid coverage, running the liveblog in the first few months of lockdown, going to the press conferences, rounding up all those eerie images of empty public spaces around the world, and generally trying to be a voice of calm and reason in what felt like an unprecedented shitstorm.

It hadn't taken long for the conspiracy theorists to surface. Posting comments under my articles, sending threats to my work email. People calling me a traitor, a stooge, a puppet of the cabal. I was told I should be lynched, executed for war crimes. My habit of periodically googling myself started turning up results on sites like the Rabbit Hole. Users posting about whether I was being paid or blackmailed or whether I was even a real person, long discussions about how I should be punished for peddling my lies about the virus, the vaccine, the hospitalization rates.

Then someone shared my home address on one of those threads, and I stopped finding it mildly amusing and started feeling fucking unnerved. I wrote a complaint to the email address that was listed for the moderator—as if anyone were actually monitoring that place—and the post got taken down a couple of days later. It didn't make me feel much better, wondering how many weirdos had made note of it before that, and I started checking the thread obsessively. I even thought about calling the police, asking for advice; spent weeks with one eye on the street while I was working at my desk, Anya and Albie oblivious in the other room. Long nights wondering if anyone out there actually believed the things they were saying about me and the other journalists whose blood they were baying for. Eventually I confided in Anya—the bare minimum, leaving out the fairly crucial fact I'd been doxxed—and asked her to lock down her social media.

I kept reporting. It was my job, and then, more than ever, I took it seriously.

Eventually the world started opening up again, and I went back to my proper role as crime and court correspondent, happy to forget I'd lifted the lid on that particular infested hole of the internet. Yet now here I was again, that old feeling of dread back as I opened the home page of the site, typing your name instead of my own into the rudimentary search bar. *katiekat*, you'd called yourself, a helpful bit of intel from Hasan. Very sweet. I watched as a list of all your comments unfurled down the screen, going all the way back to 2015, when you'd have been, what, fourteen, fifteen?

I clicked on the first thread, which was one of hundreds about 9/11 being faked. That old chestnut.

i can't believe they lied to us, you'd written. *i can't stop watching it.*

I clicked on the video in the original post, a slo-mo clip of the planes striking the towers, with shitty graphics flagging the supposed inconsistencies.

That post, that conspiracy theory, had been your gateway drug. As I clicked through page after page, I could trace your journey from 9/11 to JFK, the Illuminati to chemtrails. I remembered myself at that age, the kinds of things I got worked up about: global warming and Rwandan genocide and Kurt Cobain dying. And there you were, spending hours in the middle of the night chatting to some nutjob in Plymouth who'd decided Theresa May was actually a pair of twins from Russia.

I finished one coffee and made another, clicking away from the Theresa thread (it seemed you'd had trouble swallowing that one). I read through the notes I'd made, processing this unexpected new link between your story and mine. Reassessing the kind of person you were. *Nothing Kit does shocks me*, your brother had said, and maybe now I understood a little more what he'd meant. You weren't exactly what I expected when I thought of the tinfoil hat brigade on that site, and I wondered what other surprises you had in store for me.

We were pretty limited in what we could print about you right then, with the criminal proceedings against you active—we'd already run an article about your arrest in which we could state where you'd lived and the facts of your employment at the club, a couple of choice quotes about the shock that members of your local community were feeling. But a couple of days later, a preliminary hearing was held, and we all knew it would mean a surge of public interest in you, a timetable decided for your trial.

You appeared via video link from HMP Peterborough with your head bowed, a prison guard in shot behind you. You had on a baggy gray sweatshirt and your hair scraped back in a ponytail. You looked rough, Kate. Hard faced. Not much like the smiley girl in the park.

You spoke only to confirm that you were indeed Katherine Anne Cole. You had a babyish voice, didn't really look at the screen as you spoke.

The judge, McQuilliam—a battle-axe who already looked pissed off with the whole thing—set a date for your plea hearing and a provisional date for your trial, and I scribbled them down and underlined both several times, mentally blocking out my calendar.

Back at my desk, I rushed out an article: "IN THE DOCK: Waitress Kate Appears in Court for March House Murders." You were just Waitress Kate for now. Neutral, factual. But if you were found guilty, those headlines would change. I could already write it in my head: "KILLER KATE: Waitress Sentenced to Life for March House Murders."

We got the court artist's sketch of you from the hearing to go with my write-up. A smudgy portrait in shades of beige and gray, your face shadowed and tired looking. One of the subs chose another old picture from your social media to go alongside it: you blonder and bouncier, beaming at the camera as you held up a bottle of champagne on a rooftop somewhere.

I found Popov's widow, Clara, on Facebook and sent her a polite, fairly formal message that I then copied and pasted and sent to Ainsworth's wife. Harris Lowe and Lucian Wrightman had several wives and ex-wives between them, but also adult kids—and that felt like a more interesting angle to pursue. They were around your age; it'd be a poignant parallel to draw, and I was proud I'd thought of it. I found one of Wrightman's sons, Hunter, on Instagram and sent off something a bit friendly to him, along with Lowe's eldest daughter, Tiffany, and his son, Ollie.

Back trawling Google, I found another picture from when you were even younger, maybe sixteen or seventeen. Dressed in skinny jeans and a band T-shirt, you were posing awkwardly outside your sixth form's library. It had been taken by a local newspaper to go with an article about the new computer banks that had been funded by a lottery grant, and though you were smiling with the other gangly teenagers who'd been herded into the shot, you looked like you'd rather be anywhere else.

16

Gabriel

"K. C."

WE FINISHED SCHOOL AND STARTED sixth form and our A-levels, and I was mostly pretty happy with how that all turned out. People were nice and the teachers were nice and the tuck shop in the sixth-form common room sold Tangy Tom's crisps, so life was good.

Sometimes I'd see you in the common room too. I liked the way you dressed—flowery dresses with those black biker boots, or jeans with battered Keds and old T-shirts cut and stitched into new shapes, your wrists loaded with silver bangles and at least two necklaces round your neck. Your hair wasn't straight or curly, waves of blond and brown that you played with when you were thinking, or twisted up into a knot on the top of your head when you were serious about work or a conversation you were having. You weren't part of the cool groups, but you weren't a nerd, either—you were just kind of . . . *you*. You hung around with a girl called Megan sometimes, or just by yourself reading a book or writing on your laptop, and you never seemed to care at all what anyone else was doing around you.

I'd sit there watching, daring myself to go and sit next to you. It had been over a year since you'd saved me, and although sometimes when you passed me on your way in or out of the common room or the canteen, you smiled or said hi, I wasn't even sure if you remembered me at all.

A week before my seventeenth birthday, I'd had a cold that turned into a chest infection, as was my body's custom, and I had the morning off for a doctor's appointment. As I walked through the playground at lunch, I heard two girls saying your name.

"She's *insane*," one of them was saying. "I wouldn't mess with her."

"You could take her," the friend said, and both of them started laughing as they disappeared into the canteen.

Bart was waiting for me in the common room, a baguette in his hand and mayonnaise on his chin.

"You heard about the drama?" he asked, before I'd even sat down or gestured at him to wipe the mayo off, and I shook my head.

"Katie Cole, your favorite," he said, eyebrows waggling. "Punched Heather Spencer in the face in the middle of history."

"What?" I took my own lunch out of my bag. I wasn't hungry at all, but I had to take my antibiotics and doing it on an empty stomach made me feel properly puke-on-my-desk sick.

"Yep." Bart took another ambitious mouthful of his baguette and talked right through it. "Apparently Katie started crying in the middle of a video about the Blitz—like full-on panic attack—and Heather laughed at her." He chewed too fast, then swallowed. "Heather's nose is broken. And Katie told her in front of everyone that next time she'd push her head through a *window*."

I unfolded the foil on my sandwiches, thinking about that.

"I told you," Bart said, leaning back in his chair, crossing one ankle over his knee. "Trouble," he said, with a single nod like punctuation.

I thought it sounded kind of amazing.

17

John

"Kit-Kat"

YOU HIT A GIRL AT school and were handed an immediate two-day suspension. A zero-tolerance policy to violence, we were told when, shell-shocked, we tried to protest. You had never done anything even remotely like that before, and we were sure you'd been provoked, that there had been some kind of misunderstanding.

"She deserved it," you told us, taut with anger, when we collected you. When we got home, you stalked upstairs to your room without a word, and your mum and I looked at each other, stunned.

"I'll speak to her," I said, and your mum shook her head, went through to the kitchen, and poured a glass of wine.

But when I tried, you turned your back on me. "I don't want to talk about it," you said. "Just ground me and get it over with."

A week later, you cut your hair, left the clumps of it scattered on the bathroom floor. Your mum, once the calmest person I knew, hit the roof. The argument that followed was the first in a long string of huge rows that seemed, sometimes, to begin spontaneously, with none of us sure what had provoked them. Your retorts to the simplest of requests were often vicious. Curfews were missed, chores ignored. You and Bobby could argue over anything: food, the TV, who'd been in the bathroom longest, and who was right about any topic or opinion.

You started to even pick fights with me. Ignoring me when I asked you to empty the dishwasher or take Wilbur out, rolling your eyes if I pulled you up on it.

"You do it," you said, more than once, and you almost looked pleased when I finally lost my temper and sent you to your room.

"What's going on with you?" I asked you later, when you came downstairs and I thought we'd both calmed down. "This isn't like you."

"Isn't it?" you asked as you stalked past me and out of the house, slamming the door behind you.

18

Tarun

"Katherine"

AFTER YOUR FIRST HEARING, I phoned Ursula. The cogs of my brain had begun turning again, seeking comfort in the familiar, practical steps of forming a defense case.

"I'd like us to find our own digital forensics expert, and someone who specializes in online radicalization."

"Good thinking. I'll make a list of suggestions."

"Will she agree to seeing an independent psychiatrist?"

"I'm not sure—perhaps you could—"

"Try and persuade her," I cut her off. "I'm not sure we have any hope of pursuing a diminished responsibility defense, but we should cover all bases."

"She says she didn't do it," Ursula reminded me.

"Yes, well." I opened my own laptop, ready to begin work. "We should cover all bases."

Ahead of previous trials, I had often visited crime scenes. Even when months or years had passed since the crime had occurred, I had always found it useful to put myself into the scene, to view it from every possible angle. To visualize events exactly as the Crown's case described them, in order to spot those tiny details that didn't fit. I have even accompanied juries to crime scenes, to locations where bodies were found or lives were taken, stood in rain and sun as the most unexpected piece of evidence—a single degree's difference in the angle of a wall or a line of sight—laid bare a lie that had been told inside the courtroom.

It felt important to do so with your brief. Important that I do everything right.

Tucked away in a quiet corner of Mayfair, Dexter Square was a lush expanse of green behind ornate railings, a residents' garden shrouded by neat box hedges and towering trees, a climbing rose trailing over the gate. I walked round it, the first spots of rain darkening the pavement, and crossed over to the quiet mews where March House was hidden.

A four-story building in classic red brick, the club was at the center of the short terrace, private residences on either side. Discretion was valued highly by its patrons, and the only security camera in the building was located at the front door. I stood on the pavement outside looking up at it, mentally flicking through the images it had captured of you and the victims that were now included in the CPS's disclosure.

In the wake of the murders, the decision had been made to close the club. The front door, famously difficult to gain access to, now stood open, men carrying dust sheets and clipboards traipsing in and out. I rang the bell anyway, and stepped into the lobby to wait.

It was a grand space, with black-and-white floor tiles and a high ceiling, one wall and the elevator doors a solid block of gold leaf. I turned slowly, studying it, then stepped back out onto the front step, checking the angle of the camera.

"Mr. Rao?"

I turned and saw a woman in a silk blouse and well-tailored trousers, her hair swept into an elegant chignon. "Camilla," she said, a manicured hand tapping her own chest. "We spoke on the phone."

"Thank you for agreeing to let me visit."

She gave a terse nod. "I can let you have twenty minutes. I'll be locking the place up after that."

I thanked her and took the elevator to the first floor. The inside of it was gold too, the fixtures elaborate and ornate, like stepping inside a Fabergé egg.

On the first floor, the doors opened with a soft ping, revealing an oil painting of a hare. The first in a long row of paintings that lined the wood-paneled corridor, a grandfather clock ticking softly.

The club lounge was framed on two sides by large bay windows, which looked out over the rooftops of the houses beyond and the trees of Dexter Square. The bar stood in one corner, a vast rosewood monolith with stuffed hares in glass bell jars standing sentry at either end. The room was furnished with leather booths along one wall, the other tables accompanied by leather chesterfields and velvet armchairs, now in the process of being draped in cream dust sheets.

I wandered back down the corridor, noting where the kitchen, staff room, and toilets were, the fire exit at the end. I put a hand tentatively on the push bar, checking behind me before opening the door. Not alarmed.

Stepping out into the stairwell, I leaned over the rail. As I'd suspected, at the bottom were two doors: one that led outside and one that led to the private dining rooms on the ground floor. I took photos on my phone, slid it back into my jacket pocket before returning to the hallway.

I took the elevator downstairs to the lobby again, this time stepping through the door marked discreetly with a gold plate listing the names of the dining rooms: Voltaire, Descartes, Socrates. The corridor inside was cool and quiet, the wait station a vintage bureau with a mounted tablet I assumed you had used for putting through orders. A hatch in the wall beside it, when I tugged up the wooden panel, housed a dumbwaiter that ran up to the kitchen.

I strode to the end of the hallway and tried the fire door there, again stepping out into the stairwell. I opened the external door and poked my head out into the small courtyard, noting as I did so a discarded wedge of cardboard on the floor near the jamb. At some point, the door had been wedged open, and I wondered how regular an occurrence that might have been—and whether it had been the case at any point on the tenth of August.

The courtyard was cobbled and small, a seven-foot wall surrounding it, a gate at its center. I crossed the cobbles to look at it; it appeared secure, and a code was required to gain access from the street. The camera angled at it, according to the police report, had been out of action for several months. A fact that was inconvenient for you, but might capture the imaginations of the jury.

I turned and looked back at the club. Beside the fire door was the private entrance to the apartment that occupied the top floor of the building. Hunter Wrightman, Lucian's son, lived alone there, according to police records. He had an alibi for the night of the murders, had been at a party across the city with many witnesses, but I took photos of the gate and apartment entrances anyway, keen to remind myself of the various ways in which it was possible an unknown party could have entered March House.

I went back into the ground floor corridor, taking a perfunctory look at the other private dining rooms, the Descartes and Socrates Rooms. Finally, I let myself into the Voltaire Room, mentally placing the crime scene images I had seen. It was dark, mahogany paneling on the walls, the windowless room lit solely by an ostentatious chandelier—a spiky, modern-looking thing—that hung from the high ceiling. The table was bespoke, handcrafted from an ancient oak felled by a storm on the grounds of a stately home, its chairs upholstered in burgundy leather, and a statue made by a recent Turner Prize winner stood in one corner, an antique cocktail bar in the other. I avoided touching any of it, the fine trace of fingerprint powder still coating the surfaces.

Taking a slow circuit of the table, I mapped out the crime-scene images in my head. Placing where each of the men had been found and then, rewinding, imagining them alive. Eating, drinking, oblivious to what was about to befall them. As I reached the door again, I stopped and conjured you. A shadow in the background, fetching, serving, and then fleeing.

I watched you all in my mind's eye for a moment longer, and then I turned and left the club.

19

Gabriel

"K. C."

I WENT TO THE CINEMA with Bart one Friday night at the start of summer, a lame shark film we were repeating all the cheesiest lines from as we walked home along the dune path. Halfway down the beach there was a group of people having a party with a bonfire burning and music playing. It was usually something I'd give a wider berth than norovirus, but Bart stopped to look and spotted some people from our year.

"Let's go over," he said, eyebrows up all excited like the McDonald's arches.

I stared at him like he was proposing we go bull running or naked firewalking, but he was already strolling off across the sand like Super-SocialMan, and then, at the edge of the group, I saw you.

You were wearing a big jumper over shorts, with your hair all down and wavy and blowing like a model's in the wind. You turned as we were walking over, and my whole body went hot, then cold.

"Hey," you said.

"Hi," I said back. After a quick brain malfunction, I remembered something to say next: "How are y—" But you were already brushing past me, taking the beer your friend Megan was holding out to you.

I watched as you drained it in three long gulps. You went over to your bag, took out a bottle of vodka. Megan laughed, but kind of nervously.

"Take it easy," she told you, but you just shrugged and drifted away again, sipping straight from the bottle.

Bart started talking to some girls from his maths class, and I hung around awkwardly at the edge, trying to laugh in the right places and to not look like I was paying way more attention to the conversation you were having in the group a few feet away.

"I'm going to Peru first," you said. "Then maybe Mexico. Then to the Great Wall of China, then Bali. I'm not sure after that, there's just too many things I want to see."

"Yeah, okay," Megan said. "How are you planning to pay for that?"

"I have money," you said, but Megan rolled her eyes and started talking to the boy next to her about a band I'd never heard of.

As the night went on, I noticed the way you laughed sometimes when you were uncomfortable. The way you frowned when other people found something funny. I liked that your face was backward that way, liked trying to unlock its secrets when you didn't know you were being watched.

When everyone sat down, you kept losing the games people started, kept choosing dares instead of truths. You flashed your boobs when Alex Evans told you to, downed a drink when Bart got to pick your dare. You laughed each time, but later, when it was fully dark around us, you started crying. You were sitting by me then, your face in your hands, and everyone went quiet.

"Don't worry," Megan said, rolling her eyes. "She does this."

Someone suggested night swimming. It was late and not that warm anymore, but no one seemed to care. You stopped crying and watched as they all stripped off, started running into the sea in their underwear. Megan was already halfway into the shallows, and you looked unsure, your hands going to the bottom of your top like you were going to pull it over your head.

"Don't," I said to you, over the splashes of everyone else. "You don't have to. It'll be cold."

I was scared you were so drunk you'd drown.

"Okay," you said, and you sat back down beside me with a thump.

Something shimmered on your wrist, and I reached down without thinking and held it up to look at it properly. A tiny silver silhouette of a cat threaded on a thin chain.

"Oh," you said, looking down at it. At my rough hand, the fingers stained with ink, almost touching you. "From my dad. He calls me that: Kit-Kat."

The one beer I'd drunk must have given me a buzz of confidence because I said, "It suits you."

"You reckon? My brother says I look like a mouse."

"What's wrong with mice?" I asked.

You smiled, looked away. "You're right," you said. "What's wrong with mice?"

20

Tarun

"Katherine"

I BEGAN PREPARING FOR YOUR Plea and Trial Preparation Hearing, working through the summary of evidence provided thus far by the prosecution, along with the notes Ursula and I had both made after conversations with you. My clerk had also passed me a fraud brief, something with enough technical jargon and complicated financial details to keep me busy, and I started to enjoy the familiar routine of traveling into chambers, working methodically through files, with little time to allow any anxious or intrusive thoughts in.

On my way into chambers one day, I stopped by to speak to Ruth, the junior who had been assigned to assist me on your brief. I was pleased to be working with her. I'd been told by a colleague that she'd been indispensable on an assault case he'd prosecuted a couple of months earlier, and I felt relieved to have a capable pair of hands on the team. Her desk was meticulously organized, and she was hunched over a laptop, typing earnestly as I arrived.

"Could you work through the transcripts of Miss Cole's activity on the Rabbit Hole and add every post to the spreadsheet I sent over?" I asked.

She nodded. "Already started."

"Excellent, thank you. Do you have a number for Harry Wise? We'll need to speak with him about the forensic evidence at some point."

"Oh, Harry retired." She frowned. "About six months ago now. Didn't you know?"

"I didn't. I had some time off last year," I said. A little more curtly than I meant to. "Well, let's discuss some alternatives this afternoon."

I went to my office, closing the door so that I could make the call I'd been putting off for several days.

Elliot was the political editor at a broadsheet with an excellent reputation for its investigative work. We hadn't spoken since he moved out, and I found my mouth was dry as I listened to the phone ringing. I cleared my throat as he picked up.

"Tarun. This is a nice surprise."

This was a kindness that was typical of him, and I sank into my chair, leaning my head back to study the yellowing ceiling, trying to squash down a wave of longing.

"Are you well?" I asked.

"I am. Are you?"

It was a question that was still difficult to answer. "Getting there." I cleared my throat again. "It's a business call, I'm afraid. What do you know about Dominic Ainsworth?"

There was a brief silence, and when he spoke again, his tone was wary. "You've got the Kate Cole case."

"Yes."

"That sounds like a lot to take on."

I scratched behind my ear, swallowed dryly. "It's what I do."

He hesitated again. "You need to look after yourself."

"I will." I was irritated now. "I am."

He cleared his throat. "Well, to answer your question, Ainsworth went to Oxford with the PM. Studied PPE. Brief and largely uneventful career as an MP and then got his junior minister job once the PM was elected. Apart from the complete bin fire of his breakfast TV appearances during the pandemic, he's coasted along nicely until the last year or two."

"And then what?"

"There were rumors of him lobbying colleagues in the cabinet on behalf of business associates, but no one here had found enough to make those accusations stick."

I considered this. Ainsworth certainly wouldn't have been the first government minister taking clandestine payments in order to advance an associate's—or their own—interests, contrary to Parliament's code of conduct, but I wasn't sure where a new sleaze scandal of that nature would fit into your defense. It seemed unlikely to have provided someone with a motive for murder.

"Any idea why he might have been dining with Lucian Wrightman?"

"None. But I can look into it."

"Thank you. That would be really helpful." I paused, not wanting to end the conversation.

"We should—" he said, at the same time as I tried, "I'd like—"

He laughed. "It's nice to hear your voice."

I put the pen down. "Yes," I said. "I . . ."

There was a murmur in the background, someone asking him a question.

"One second," he said to them, with an affection that told me it was not a colleague, that he was perhaps at home, his new home, and not at his office. "Sorry, T—"

"I'd better go," I said. I hung up and returned to my notes on you.

21

Gabriel

"K. C."

WE SPENT A LOT OF that summer sitting on the dunes, listening to the waves while you quizzed me endlessly about myself and the things I liked.

"If you were a type of cereal, what would you be?"

I looked at you, panicked, like I'd never seen a box of cereal before. "I . . . I don't know. Weetabix?"

Said literally no one ever. You carried on while I quietly and painfully died inside.

"Would you rather be able to control time or fly?"

I frowned at that, looking out at the sea. "What kinds of parameters are there on the time thing?"

You groaned. "Come on, tell me about yourself."

"What do you want to know?" I asked, embarrassed. "Date of birth, star sign? Height and weight?"

"No, no, no," you said, rolling your eyes and nudging my foot with yours. "None of that boring stuff. Tell me something *important*. Your worst fear. The best thing that ever happened to you. Come on, I love this game."

I could feel my ears getting hot. I swallowed. "I guess . . . my worst fear is all of us getting wiped out by a nuclear bomb."

"No it isn't," you said.

I shrugged. My whole face was lava hot by then, and I tried visualizing milk, cold and white in the fridge, and then a polar bear in the arctic, because I read one time that helps.

"You don't have to tell me yet," you said. "So what's the best thing that ever happened to you?"

I thought about it, plucking at the marram grass beside me. "Moving here," I said eventually, already cringing inside. I turned to you before you could reply. "What's yours?"

You leaned back on your elbows.

"Any day now," you said. "I'm ready for it."

We started messaging all the time too, and we talked about everything, stuff I never imagined saying out loud. I told you about how ill I'd been as a kid, how sometimes I had nightmares that it had happened again, that I couldn't get up or walk or do anything but lie there, my whole body hurting.

I told you how my dad had left when I was five and lived in America now, with a new wife and twin girls who he put photos of in the birthday cards that arrived each year. No money, no proper message. Just *Happy Birthday, Love Dad* and a picture of their big white smiles, their shiny blond hair.

How I worried about how hard my mum worked and how sometimes I wished I'd turned out better for her.

You were so kind to me, always. You listened. You understood. You never made me feel stupid or wrong or embarrassed. *Your dad sounds like a total douche canoe*, you wrote, and made me laugh. *I bet your mum feels so lucky she has you*, you said, and it made me glow inside. I replied with a funny dog video so you wouldn't think I was a total sad-sack loser.

But you shared things too. You talked about your brother and how much it still hurt when you thought about him. You told me you had nightmares too. That you were watching him from the car, waiting for the bomb to go off. Beating at the window with both your hands, trying to warn him.

You told me that sometimes you dreamt your mother told you she wished it was you who'd died. That sometimes you agreed.

We talked about the world too. About true crime and wars and nuclear weapons and space travel. One night, you watched a documentary about Jimmy Savile. It made you so angry. *How do they live with themselves?* you wrote. *All of those people who let it happen?*

I told you I didn't know. I told you I never stopped being surprised by how fucked up the world could be.

There's this website, you wrote one day. *Have you seen it?*

The Rabbit Hole. I opened the link, even as another message dropped down from you: *It's so crazy,* with a head-exploding emoji.

I started reading, only stopping to send you a row of head-exploding emojis of my own.

22

John

"Kit-Kat"

YOU WORKED HARD DURING YOUR final year of A-levels. You spent hours at your laptop, always looking up, surprised, when one of us came to knock at your door to tell you dinner was ready or that you should go to bed. *Just studying*, you'd say.

You and Bobby began to rub along together a little better too, or ignored each other's existence for the most part, and I noticed that you and your mum began spending more time together again, doing the things you had when you were small: reading in the garden together, sharing a Kit Kat. Watching old reruns of *Friends* and laughing at lines you'd laughed at a hundred times before.

You were still our Kit. Lying on the floor with Wilbur, stroking his belly while his tail thumped the carpet. Stealing crisps from my plate as I made a sandwich in the kitchen, saving articles you thought your mum would be interested in.

The day of your final exam, she got up early and made you your favorite breakfast, blueberry pancakes. You looked so genuinely happy when you came down and saw them that for a second, I pictured you at seven years old again. Standing on that same spot in the kitchen, tossing blueberries into your mouth as you laughed at something Stephen said.

"Thank you," you said, wrapping your arms around her, your face pressed into her back. "This is so lovely, thank you."

Neil arrived the following day for your mum's birthday, bringing with him a battered bunch of flowers and a foul mood.

"Rory's buggered off without notice," he said, the latest of his farm-hands to disappear. "Got another sow down sick as well."

I poured him a drink and willed him to stop. Your mum felt constantly guilty that we'd moved so far away from the farm, that she didn't pull her weight, and I didn't want us to argue about it on her birthday.

But she was too busy frowning at her phone to listen to Neil's latest catalog of woes. She handed it to me without saying a word, and I looked down and saw an email from Julia. She and Peter were moving back into the village.

23

Gabriel

"K. C."

YOU BUNKED OFF SCHOOL A lot in our last year, when no one seemed to notice or care where we were anyway, and when I asked you about it, you told me that you liked to go to the beach, or to the woods, or to Bristol or Exeter on the train. That sometimes you did the work we were supposed to and sometimes you didn't, and that you liked to take your sketchbook and your laptop and draw clothes and make plans, and that you were waiting, always waiting, for the day that school would be over and we could start living our actual lives.

This was a wild thought to me, one I hadn't really gotten round to considering, and every time you told me about the places you wanted to go, the people you wanted to meet, I felt like someone had just turned the color up on the world.

I tried to keep up with revision, but a lot of the time I just wanted to message you. We'd stay up late, swapping posts from the Rabbit Hole, talking endlessly about flight MH370 and the moon landing hoax, and sometimes I'd find myself sitting in my exams, remembering things you'd said instead of where I was or what I was supposed to be doing.

"He's got a girlfriend," Aunt Shelley said to my mum one day, holding my chin between her thumb and forefinger like she was actually reading it on my face. "Christ alive, he's in love."

"Leave him be," my mum said, swatting her with a tea towel and passing her a Cinzano.

"I'm not," I said, going bright red. "I'm really not."

But secretly I thought maybe one day I could invite you round, that maybe it actually would be fun for you to meet my mum.

I hate exams, you wrote that night. *I know I've failed them all.*

You don't need them, I replied. *You've got bigger plans!*

You sent a row of smiley faces. *You always make me feel better.*

And I felt like *I'd* just walked on the moon.

Then at almost eleven you texted again: *I need to talk. Can you meet me at the beach?*

You were sitting at the top of a dune when I arrived, your knees pulled up to your chest, your arms hugging them tightly. You looked wound up all tight, anxious and angry and nothing like your normal self, and I wanted to put my arm round you, tell you everything was going to be okay.

"A few years ago," you said, "there was this guy."

You told me the story about the man who'd owned the gym and how no one had believed you.

"And now he's come back," you said, "like none of it happened. Like he has every right to be here, when everyone hates me."

"Everyone doesn't—" I started, but you shook your head.

"He shouldn't be back here." You looked up at me.

We walked through the dunes, my trainers sliding on the cold sand, the grass whispering in the dark. "In my head, he's a monster," you said.

"Maybe he is," I said. "They don't always look how you expect them to."

When I snuck a glance at you, your jaw was clenched tight. "I can't believe he came back here," you said, as the lights of the town loomed ahead of us.

Later, maybe as we watched the fire catch and go wild, smoke filling the sky, or as we ran away, our lungs burning, I remember that one of us said, *He deserves it.* But to this day I can't remember if it was you or me.

24

John

"Kit-Kat"

THE FIRE BEGAN IN THE middle of the night. I stopped to buy milk on my way back from a run the next morning and overheard a conversation between the shop assistant and the woman in front of me. A terrible thing, they said. The owner had been lucky to get out alive.

I thought nothing of it. Showered and dressed for work, passing your closed bedroom door on my way out.

Mrs. Pollock and her ancient Persian cat, Bitsy, were my first patients that day, and she had, as always, heard the news. "It was your friend," she said, smacking her lips as she searched for the name. "You know, whatshisface Walters."

"Peter," I said, a shard of ice in my stomach.

"Unlucky timing for them," she said, cheerful now. "Not back five minutes, and the whole place up in smoke."

I murmured in agreement, busied myself checking Bitsy's heart rate. Ignoring the slow climb of my own pulse.

I'd said goodbye to Neil that morning, expecting him to have left long before I got home. But when I came back from work, his bag was at the foot of the stairs, and he and your mum were sitting at the kitchen table.

"Have you heard?" your mum asked.

"The fire?" I nodded. "Have you spoken to Julia?"

She told me that she had. "The police are saying vandals," she said.

"There was that summer house that got burned down in Willsham a few months ago."

"I heard one of the nurses talking about that," I agreed, and then your mum pushed a hoodie of yours across the kitchen table to me.

Before I even picked it up, I could smell the smoke on it.

"Taken up a pipe, has she?" Neil asked.

I put the jumper down. "You surely don't think . . ."

"I don't want to." Your mum gave me a plaintive look.

"Sarah," I said, pulling out a chair. "This is really serious. I can't—"

"What's really serious?" You'd breezed through the open front door, a half-eaten apple in hand. "Is that my hoodie?"

"Yes." Your mum got up, held it out to you. "I'm wondering why it reeks of smoke."

You shrugged, took a bite out of your apple. "Does it?"

"*Yes*," your mum said again. "It reeks of smoke, and someone tried to burn Peter and Julia's house down last night."

I studied your face for a reaction, saw none. It gave me that terrible cold feeling again.

"Tell us the truth, kitten," your uncle warned.

"I saw the fire," you said. "I walked past, okay?"

Your mum shook the hoodie at you. "You *saw* it. You just happened to walk past?"

You rolled your eyes and turned away. "I can't believe this."

"Don't roll your eyes at me!" She grabbed you by the shoulders and slammed you against the wall. "*Answer me.* Did you do it?"

You looked stunned, a kind of half smile caught on your face. We'd never been physical with you—never smacked or even threatened it, never dragged you from a shop when you were throwing a tantrum.

"No," you said. The word came out harsh, mocking, your faces inches apart. "Happy now?"

"Sarah . . ." Neil said, but she ignored him.

"I don't believe you," she said to you. She had shocked herself, became teary as she released you.

"Then *don't*," you spat, your voice thick with emotion too. You rubbed your arms as your eyes fell on Neil's holdall in the hallway. "I can't stay here," you said. "Can I come with you?"

"Kit, come on . . ." I tried, but it felt as if the room were still reverberating with the thud of your back hitting the wall. And I'd just sat there and let it happen. I felt numb.

"Maybe that'd be a good idea," Neil said. He gave me a look I couldn't read.

There was a moment's pause as you looked at your mum. But she, breathing hard, didn't look up or speak.

"Fine," you said.

25

Max

"Killer Kate"

CHECKING TWITTER, I WAS GRATIFIED to see my article about your hearing being reposted. Shocked emoji after shocked emoji. *Can't believe this*, one guy had written. *She looks so sweet*. Someone else had stolen an old school photo of you from somewhere—pink cheeked and cheesy-smiling with your hair in a perky little ponytail—and drawn in devil horns and red eyes. Further down my feed, a woman had posted an angry video of herself talking to the camera. "I'm sick of all these *poor Katie Cole* comments, like she's too cute and young to have done this. She's been charged! They don't do that for nothing. She did it. Evil has many faces, people." The first reply, from @kcv7945320191, read *And what a lovely face it is*. Someone else had written *Maybe the men were the evil ones, ever thought about that?* The likes on that one were steadily growing. And every time I refreshed my feed, new posts appeared.

It was starting. Just like I'd known it would. And this was before anything had come out about you and the Rabbit Hole—a new side to the story I knew I had to be the one to break.

My office door opened, Albie peering round it. His little mouth pursed into the cheeky pout he did when he knew he was doing something he wasn't supposed to be—which, in this case, was breaking a rule Anya had put in place after he'd wandered in on me looking at autopsy photos on Reddit.

"I lost David," he said.

"Uh-oh." I wheeled my chair back, got up. "Backup is on the way."

I checked the living room, where Albie's schoolbag was open on the sofa, the rest of its contents lined up carefully on the cushion beside it.

"Bedroom?" I asked.

"Checked."

"Let's check again. Just to be certain."

He hared up the stairs ahead of me. "I did check," he said, already bounding into the room and kneeling down to look under the bed.

"Not with my special X-ray eyes," I said, lifting the pillow where Albie always put at least one of the many hideous plastic spiders he'd collected before he went to sleep. I suspected *Spider-Man* had started it; Anya was sure it was *Charlotte's Web.*

David, a particularly lifelike rubber Halloween prop, eyed us both from under the pillow.

"He stays in your bag," I warned, as Albie snatched him up and hurried back downstairs. "Remember what Miss Taylor said!"

I went back to my office, where Anya was putting down a cup of coffee for me.

"I don't deserve you," I said, dropping into my chair. "When do we start worrying that this spider thing *isn't* a phase?"

But she was frowning at my laptop screen. I realized too late that I'd left the Rabbit Hole open. I glanced up at her.

"Just background," I said. "For the Kate Cole story."

She shook her head at me, pressed her lips together.

"Please," she said. "Don't get involved with that site again."

I raised an eyebrow at her, closed the window. "Just background," I said firmly. "I'll see you later."

After they'd left for the day, I made my first call—to Reginald Winters, one of the paper's major shareholders and my editor's godfather, who I'd met at several events and who'd been a member of March House for over a decade. He was an oily old git, avoided at said events by all the female staff, and he answered the phone with a racking cough that made me hold the receiver away from my ear.

"Thanks for taking the time to speak to me," I said.

"Of course. Terrible thing, what happened to them. I can't quite believe it."

"Did you ever meet Kate Cole?"

"She seemed a sweet little thing." He coughed again, phlegm rattling. "Lovely smile."

"So you were surprised to hear she'd been arrested, then?"

"Very." He sniffed. "Sweet little thing," he said again. "You never can tell, can you?"

"Did you know the men well?"

"No, no," he said dismissively. "Lucian, of course. I attended a few of his dinners, back in the day. But I rather keep myself to myself these days. Which I suppose I ought to be grateful for now."

"What was he like, Wrightman?"

He snorted. "Oh, he could ruffle feathers, when he wanted to. You know the second wife, Mimi, was married to his best friend before?"

"I didn't."

"Stiffed him on a deal as well, just to really put the boot in." He laughed. "But you don't get to where Lucian was without cutting a few throats. I liked him."

"The others?" I asked, scribbling notes.

"Harris was friendly enough. I didn't know the Russian. As for Ainsworth . . . Bit of a wet weekend, that one. Bloody useless MP." He chuckled. "Don't quote me on that. Rather in poor taste to say now."

I thanked him and hung up, then headed for the Briars, a vast country estate in Sussex, where I'd made an appointment with Harris Lowe's older sister.

She was a horsey-faced woman with overbleached hair and a distinct air of eau de gin. The conservatory the housekeeper had shown me into—the morning room—was cold, the view through the glass walls of rolling green fields and topiary hedges. Hettie Lowe was sitting at a glass-topped table, ignoring the tea set that had been put out for us.

"I'm very sorry for your loss," I said. "Thank you for agreeing to speak with me."

"Harris was the most wonderful man," she said, fretting at one of her earrings. "It's a terrible loss for all of us."

"Of course." I busied myself getting out my notebook and phone. "Please pass on the *Herald*'s condolences to the entire family."

She nodded. Outside, a man in a waxed overcoat and baseball cap let himself through one of the gates in a paddock, a shotgun cocked over one shoulder.

"My nephew," she said, noticing me looking. "Ollie. Hasn't left my side since we heard."

"Harris's son?"

"Yes." She reached for the milk jug, poured way too much into both teacups. "The apple of his eye."

I watched her adding tea from the pot, the liquid in the cups turning an unappealing shade of dishwater.

"Was Harris good friends with Lucian Wrightman and the others?"

She pursed her lips, the pale pink lipstick on them already worn off in patches. "I've no idea. Harris had lots of friends, lots of associates. He was a social creature—isn't that the point of joining a club?"

"No enemies that you know of?"

She looked up sharply, crumbs of makeup at the corners of her eyes. "None," she said, shoving the cup and saucer across the table to me.

"Had he ever mentioned Kate Cole?"

She made a face. "He made a comment once about one of the waitresses, a new one, flirting with Lucian. I assume that was her."

I made a note of this. Surely it wasn't going to turn out you were a jilted lover?

"Nothing else? No reason she might have had a grudge against the four of them?"

"A grudge?" She put down her cup with a heavy chink. "What happened to him, to them, was unimaginable evil, pure and simple," she said.

I murmured sympathetically, taking a biscuit from the bone china plate, and asked her if I could quote her on that.

26

Gabriel

"K. C."

I WAS LYING AWAKE THAT night with my mind racing as usual, every worry I'd ever had come to visit me like old friends crowding round the bed. I rolled onto my side just in time to see my phone light up with a message, and when I grabbed it, your name was right there like I'd magicked it out of my head and onto the screen.

I've gone to stay with my uncle for a while, you wrote, and then you put a sad face.

Before I could reply to ask you why, you added, *But we can still talk.*

K, I replied, and this time you sent a happy face.

27

Tarun

"Katherine"

AN ADJOURNMENT HAD BEEN GRANTED in my fraud case, an important witness unavailable, and the next possible date was months away. I'd been preparing myself for my return to court all week, the nervous energy I'd built up now with no target at which to direct it, and so I was wired and jittery when I met Ursula outside the prison for the conference she'd organized with you.

"Ready?" she asked.

I nodded, and we headed for the entrance.

"There's possibly an angle with the conspiracy website stuff," I said. "With the right experts, if I could find a precedent . . . if we could persuasively portray it as an extreme kind of brainwashing . . . but it would be radical."

Ursula frowned but didn't say anything, and I found myself growing more irritated.

The feeling changed as we went through security, a tightening in my chest like a slow-moving vise, a tingle in my hands and lips as I grew lightheaded. The first sign of an anxiety attack I had had in months. I willed myself to breathe slowly and deeply, to remember that it would pass, as my heart started to race.

"Okay?" Ursula asked me, her voice light, once we were through.

"Fine," I said, still concentrating on the belly breathing a therapist had taught me, waiting for the diazepam I'd taken outside to kick in.

She nodded, shoving her hands in her pockets as we followed the guard to the private room assigned for us.

You seemed on edge as you came in and perched at the edge of your chair, your hands clasped on the table in front of you.

"Why is it taking so long?" you asked. "How much longer will I be in here?"

"Well, next is your Plea and Trial Preparation Hearing," Ursula said gently, as the first waves of diazepam blissfully began to settle over me. "That will be your opportunity to enter your plea for each count on the indictment, after which arrangements will be made for us to proceed to trial."

"That is *if* you enter a not-guilty plea," I put in. "Should you plead guilty, a date would be set for your sentencing instead."

"But I'm *not* guilty," you said hotly.

"We just want to make sure you understand every option available to you," Ursula said, though she also shot me a look, surprised, perhaps, by the direct tone I had taken with you.

"If you enter a not-guilty plea for any or all of the charges," I continued, "it's possible that we could pursue a partial defense of diminished responsibility, if we were able to persuade the court that you were not of sound mind at the time the killings took place. Alternatively, that you suffered a loss of control. Either of those defenses might see you found guilty of manslaughter instead, which would carry a lesser sentence."

You looked at me, appalled now. "But that's still saying I'm guilty."

I met your gaze. "Yes."

"No." You shook your head, as if for emphasis. "No, I'm not doing that."

I felt reassured by the strength of your reaction, though an unwelcome thought surfaced almost immediately: *Perhaps she's just a good actress.*

"Then we focus on your defense," I said. "That someone else could have, and did, place that bottle of brandy in the room."

You seemed relieved, your shoulders sagging slightly.

"It was there when I started my shift," you said. "Right there with the wine Camilla had decanted for them."

"Ms. Johnson said in her statement that it wasn't there when she left the room after setting up for the dinner. That's a short window for someone else to have entered."

You chewed at the inside of your lip. "If she's telling the truth."

I searched your face again for any sign that you were not.

"Your behavior after you left March House will form a key part of the Crown's case against you," I said. "That you ran away immediately after the brandy was served—"

"I didn't realize," you said, your voice growing plaintive. "I swear, I just wanted to get away from them all."

"Where did you go?"

You frowned, as if you disliked the question. "I went to visit my brother's grave," you said, like it was none of my business.

"When you were arrested, you said they deserved it," I said. Beside me, Ursula coughed, again uncomfortable with the combative turn the conversation was taking.

"I told you I didn't mean that."

"Well, that's not going to cut it, I'm afraid. It was a callous thing to say, and a jury will want to know why anyone would think those men might have deserved what happened to them."

"I don't . . . I didn't hear . . ." You were angry now, frustrated as you stumbled over your words, and I had an undesirable insight into how you might perform under cross-examination. "I *didn't mean it*," you said, through gritted teeth. "I don't think they deserved it."

"Katherine—"

"Why are you calling me that?" you cut in. "My name is Katie."

I thought about the flurry of headlines, the way you had been re-branded. Waitress Kate, a cold-blooded killer hiding in plain sight, the pretty blonde holding a champagne bottle aloft on a London rooftop, now sketched scowling in the dock. I had to make you palatable to the jury. You would be Katherine, barely more than a schoolgirl, someone from a loving, respectable family.

"Not in that courtroom," I said. "You'll have to trust me on that one."

You raised an eyebrow. "I don't," you said.

28

Conrad

"Wildcat"

YOU WERE A BOMB GOING off in my life.

It was all going to plan. I was within touching distance of a promotion, the regrettable circumstances of a few years prior finally disappearing in the rearview mirror. I'd paid my dues, worked my arse off, and I'd got the results to show for it.

I had Molly. A girl too good for Hinge and for me, and I'd wasted no time at all in locking her down. We'd moved in together after six months, I'd proposed on our one-year anniversary—a walk along the beach in Cornwall, with her dream ring and a wanky speech I'd written on my phone that morning. We had a flat, were talking about getting a dog.

I was doing just fine.

Then there was you.

I'd been operations manager at Potbellies for two years, one shy of the number I'd been promised would see me progress into a director or head of operations role. It was a small company and there were bits of the job I liked: strategy meetings with the MD, sweet-talking the trade customers. Completely overhauling some of the archaic processes that had been in place when I joined.

And there were bits of it I hated, namely the site visits that came from overseeing the entire production process. My predecessor had told me I'd never eat a sausage again once I'd toured an abattoir or our factory, but he was a pussy, ended up signed off with stress. I had a much stronger stomach. What I *did* hate was trekking to the arse end of nowhere to stand around in the reek of pig farm for hours.

Godfrey's Farm was my least favorite of all, because it meant going up to Scotland and staying overnight in the local shit-box hotel, and because, frankly, your uncle Neil was a miserable git who made me feel like half the time he'd happily chuck me into the abattoir line too. But I turned up that day, and there you were, standing at the gate. White T-shirt sliding off your shoulder to show freckled skin. Cutoff jean shorts frayed against your thighs, your legs long and pale. Your blond hair was all tangled from the wind, and you brushed it away from your face as you smiled at me and opened the gate.

"Nice clipboard," you said.

Your uncle came out behind you, ruddy face creased into a smirk. He was broad, his big hand rough as he gripped mine in an obnoxiously firm handshake.

"Journey all right?" he asked.

"Yeah, fine, thanks," I said.

"Want tea?"

Looking at the dreary little farmhouse with its mossy, sagging roof and graying white walls, I wasn't sure I did, but I said yes anyway.

"Go on, kitten," he said to you. "Fetch the man a brew."

You gave him a mock salute. "Yes, sir." A quick side-eye at me.

"My niece," he said, once you were out of earshot and we were walking up toward the barns. "Visiting for the summer."

I let him show me round the farrowing paddock, the fields beyond where the new litters were grazing and rooting around, and I pretended to be interested.

You arrived with my tea. A chipped mug with a whiskey brand's logo on it, faded from too much washing. The tea too strong, not appealing in the gray afternoon light.

I thanked you. "My pleasure," you said. Holding my gaze for several seconds too long.

"Come on," Neil barked. "Let's get all yer boxes ticked and get you on yer way."

Charming.

When I looked back, you were watching me. Leaning on the wall to the paddock, that smile on your face.

Later, on my way out, you were waiting by my car.

"What do you think?" you asked. "Did we pass?"

"Of course," I said. Thinking: if I never see another pig farm, organic or not, it'll be too soon. I unlocked my car, waiting for you to move out of the way.

"Take me with you," you said.

I laughed, not sure if you were joking.

"Where are you staying?" you asked. "Somewhere fancy?"

"I wouldn't call it that."

"Somewhere fun?"

I looked at your lips, the pale skin of your neck. Your bra visible through your T-shirt.

"Not fun so far," I said.

"I could help with that," you said.

29

Max

"Killer Kate"

BACK IN MY STUDY, I returned to the Rabbit Hole.

Your posts on the site quickly became angrier. It was the raison d'être of the place, a fetid little fury tank, and you were easily spurred on by every new poster. *this makes me so mad*, you wrote on one post in 2019, with a GIF of a dancing cartoon panda I thought you must have added by accident. *how can they get away with this?* you wrote on another, this time with a GIF of Daenerys from *Game of Thrones*. You liked adding her, I noticed, and I wondered if you wanted to be her. There'd definitely been at least one poisoning in the show, the little shit-weasel king—I found the scene on YouTube and made a note of the parallel. The internet always loved a headline about kids being turned evil by TV shows and video games.

The topics you took an interest in ranged from the bizarre—the leaked texts of a celebrity Scientologist, which all of you spent hours poring over for coded satanist messages—to the truly brain-dead—a completely made-up report about a mysterious new medication being developed in Tasmania that aided mind control. But most often you returned to the group of truthers still hung up on 9/11 and to a stubborn bunch of people speculating endlessly about missing flight MH370.

It was all much of a muchness, wasn't it? Every theory coming back to the same central tenet: that the world was being controlled by a secret group of powerful people who were bending events to their own nefarious will, usually while drinking the blood of children or wanking each other off over a pentagram. That didn't seem to make any of it less convincing to you.

i'm realizing there's so much i didn't understand, you wrote once, at gone two in the morning. *this place is opening my eyes so much.*

I almost felt sorry for you, you sounded so taken in by it all. Naïve beyond belief. And then I remembered why I was reading your posts in the first place. The sympathy vanished.

In 2020, about five years after you'd joined the site, a user started posting, someone who called themselves Mr. E.

It's a really shit name, you have to admit.

That first post had been cryptic:

A reckoning is coming. Justice will be done.

Keep watching.

The first few replies had been taking the piss, but people were interested, especially when, five minutes later, Mr. E was back:

It's time for The Group to pay.

That got a bit more attention, sparked a wave of replies asking who he was talking about.

They're the people with all the power, and they're laughing at you.

So far, so vague. It tantalized you all, though—among hundreds of comments, there you were, katiekat: *tell us more. who ru?*

They call their meeting place Olympus because they think they're gods.

Sacrifices are made at Olympus. Lives taken to further The Group's dark deeds.

A reckoning is coming. Keep watching.

He disappeared after that, leaving you all behind to discuss exactly how much shit he was full of.

But the next night, there he was again:

It's dangerous for me to be writing here. But the world should know. They're running the show, pulling all our strings. They've made their fortunes out of wars and pandemics and they won't let anything stop them.

Over a hundred replies to that one, and not all of them cynical. A stream of questions from users: Who were the Group, then? Was this the cabal by another name? How were they pulling these strings? What did they want? Who had been sacrificed?

Is Olympus Bohemian Grove? someone had asked, referring to the weird Californian wilderness estate where a load of rich old men supposedly went and performed drunk rituals in the woods to ensure their stratospheric success.

Mr. E was noncommittal: *The Group are everywhere.*

You're not answering our questions, one of the most frequent posters, gabe333, replied. *This is bullshit,* someone else put, though it seemed like the other users who'd started sending Mr. E hearts and were already speculating about the Group didn't agree.

In the months after that, Mr. E started to enjoy himself. His claims got wilder. He confirmed that Covid had been designed and decided over a dinner at "Olympus," just like every war and disaster before it had been. That we were all being monitored in our homes by our Alexas and our smart TVs, our phones, all because of the Group's dark and decidedly vague plans. (*What do you think happened to BlackBerry?* he wrote, a detail I did appreciate. *They wouldn't go along with it so The Group sank them without a trace.*)

Whenever anyone asked for more specifics, he'd go back to vague catchphrases: *Trust nobody. Question everything.* Everything except him, it seemed.

I realized I'd started gritting my teeth, the hours spent trawling through that place triggering way too many memories of the months when they'd all been talking about me.

But I kept reading, watching as Mr. E's following kept growing, the number of likes on his posts ticking up into the thousands, the comments becoming increasingly chilling: *We'll be your army,* someone wrote.

Eat the rich, posted someone else, generating hundreds of their own likes and heart emojis.

A month later, Mr. E was back: *The Group met at Olympus tonight. They drank champagne and ate steaks from a Parisian butcher that's the most expensive in the world while they made plans for the underground bunkers they'll hide in when the end comes.*

That really triggered a whole bunch of you. *They're planning for the end???* someone wrote.

Always, Mr. E replied. You posted an angry face emoji.

A week later, in November 2021, a new post: *Activity at Olympus today. A world leader and a Royal both showed up to kiss the feet of The Group.*

Two months after that: *The Group are watching you. Olympus is watching.*

Let's burn it all down, one user posted, *we'll do whatever you say, Mr. E.* I screenshotted it all, made pages and pages of notes. I felt angry, Kate. Angry at how fired up he'd got you all, how easy it had been. I wanted to know who this guy was, whether he'd had any idea how dangerous it was, messing with the kinds of people who hung out on that site.

And then, most damning of all, came a post from early 2022, six months before the murders. *Another dinner at Olympus tonight. New plans ready to be put into action. Something is coming. Question everything - E.*

Underneath it, one of the first comments read, *I think Olympus is a club called March House.*

30

Conrad

"Wildcat"

I LEFT THE HOTEL THE next morning still drunk, still replaying the night as I drove away from Comrie and back toward the border. I turned up my music, smiling to myself as I thought about the way you'd looked when you slipped out of my bed to retrieve your clothes.

As the hangover faded, reality kicked in. I realized what I'd done.

I'd told myself I'd be different this time. That having Molly would make me different. I'd told myself that being with someone like her, being able to introduce her as my wife, was everything I'd ever wanted. And now, at the first opportunity, I'd fucked it. I stopped at a service station and drank a coffee, felt like throwing it up. Stood with the wind whipping the shit out of me, like that might remove any lingering trace of you.

I thought about the way you'd leaned over that gate, the coy sideways glances. The way you'd said, *Take me with you*. I couldn't believe I'd fallen for it.

I got back in the car, panic turning to anger. Why had I done it? Why had I let you into the car? Why had I let you come back to my room? I started replaying it again, torturing myself with the moments when I should've said no. Should've stepped back from the brink.

But as the drive went on, one long stretch of road after another, I started to calm down. Nobody had died. Nobody had been hurt. This didn't have to be the end of anything.

By the time I joined the M25, I could reason with myself: We all make mistakes. Do things in the heat of the moment. Things that happen four hundred miles away from home, that mean nothing. Nobody needed to know. I could just chalk it up to a temporary slip, giving in to you, and forget about it. Go back to being the better person Molly was supposed to make me.

She was there when I walked through the door, the kitchen immaculate, the table laid. "I made that chicken you like," she said, wrapping her arms round my neck and leaning up to kiss me. "Thought you deserved it, after that long drive."

I kissed her back and thought: this is it, this is my life.

But there you were, every time I let my thoughts wander. Standing by the car, smiling at me, while Molly blow-dried her hair in our bedroom, talking to me in the mirror. Leaning in to kiss me, your cheeks pink, while she was showing me her latest work campaign or telling me about a new podcast she thought I should listen to. Each time, I felt like a rabbit in the headlights, like she'd be able to see the whole thing written right across my face.

I got better at it as the days went on. Better at putting you into your own little pocket in my head, where I could take you out at will, allow myself the luxury of remembering the way you smelled, the little whimper you made as you came.

But it had its own texture, the memory, became slowly distant, like a film I'd seen instead of something I'd done, and that felt safe.

Safe. It's laughable, when I think of it now. You're many things, wildcat, but safe has never been one of them.

31

Tarun

"Katherine"

AS OUR CONFERENCE DREW TO a close, Ursula excused herself to use the bathroom, and you and I eyed each other across the table, like two people set up on an unsolicited blind date.

"I'm telling you the truth," you said eventually. "I didn't kill them."

"Good."

You leaned forward, your elbows on the table. "You don't like me."

I looked up, surprised by your frankness. "I don't need to like or not like you. My job is to represent you. This is a professional relationship."

You nodded and were quiet for a moment. "I'm trying," you said eventually.

"Trying?"

"To trust you."

You and me both, I thought.

Afterward, as we left the prison conducting a cursory debrief, Ursula paused at the entrance to the car park. "It went well," she said. "I'll be in touch with Ruth ahead of the hearing." She gave me a final, searching look. "You're okay?"

I stiffened. "Fine."

"Because I'm here, anytime you need to talk. I know it might feel significant, the first murder—"

"It may be my hundredth murder," I said tartly. "I've actually lost count. We'll speak soon."

Ursula nodded, accepting the dismissal. "Want a lift?"

"I'll take the train. I have some work to do." I raised a hand in farewell and headed off, walking faster as I tried to shut out the inevitable thoughts now surfacing.

As I sat in the deserted train carriage, I allowed myself to remember the first time I'd read Marla's brief. She had been accused of murdering her husband's mistress, a younger woman who had been brutally stabbed at home. It had been immediately obvious to me that, just as in your case, Marla's guilt had been clearly presumed, right from the first stages of the investigation, without the possibility of other suspects ever being properly pursued.

Her alibi had been regrettably absent, that much was true. Her phone, thrown at a wall during a moment of anguish, offered no cell site analysis to confirm her claim that she'd been at home on the morning Tilly Edwards had been killed. But though there was no evidence placing her at the marital home, there was also no real evidence placing her at the victim's house. The murder weapon was missing. DNA traces found in Marla's car could just as easily have been left there by her husband, who often borrowed the vehicle, leaving his own sports car under its cover in the garage. A witness who claimed to have seen Marla in the area did not, in my opinion, provide a reliable enough account for the case to hinge on.

Over the weeks of the trial, I found myself growing closer to Marla. We'd both studied at the same college in Cambridge, though she'd graduated five years before me, and our conversations moved from the professional to the personal. She confided in me about the pain of her marriage ending, the shock of the betrayal. The fear she felt, each night in her cell, that she'd never leave that prison. I found myself opening up to her about my relationship with Elliot, his frustrations with my commitment to work and the arguments between us that had grown too frequent, too bitter. She was a good listener, kind. When, after a final, explosive fight, Elliot told me he was leaving, she offered me the name of her therapist, told me that I would be okay. I threw myself into work, into dismantling the prosecution's case, piece by piece, and I believed her.

She was calm on the stand too, poised and polite despite her obvious distress. Stabbing is a crime of passion, messy and uncontrolled. It did not fit, and when the jury's not-guilty verdict was returned, a little over a day after their deliberations had begun, I felt only the faint pleasure of an obvious answer being confirmed. We stood together outside the courthouse, and I gave a brief statement to the press. Justice had been served, I told them, as cameras clicked endlessly at us.

A little over a month after Marla was released, she invited me to dinner. She cooked the filet steak she'd once told me she dreamt about in her cell, and poured glasses of a Barolo she said had been served at her wedding.

We made small talk about the friends and family she'd made plans with, about the holiday she wanted to take. I complimented her on the food, told her how much I was enjoying the wine. She asked about the case I was working on, a GBH trial where my client, the defendant, was accused of battering a colleague with a length of steel pole during an argument over a parking space. He'd pleaded guilty, as I'd wanted him to, and so I felt at ease talking to her about it.

"It's frightening," I said. "He got back in his car and drove away. Went shopping, as if nothing had happened. How do you collect yourself after violence like that?"

"It's easier than you think," she said. "Almost like stepping back into a room you'd temporarily left."

I stared at her, saw her expression change as she realized what she'd just said. She paused. Moistened her lips.

"Not that I'd know, of course," she said, placing her knife and fork together neatly on the plate, the meal over.

"No," I said, the word coming out weakly.

"Well," she said, smiling at me over her wineglass. "As you said. Justice served."

In the weeks that followed, I became unwell.

It had been building for a long time. I can see that now. I had taken on too much, had worked myself into the ground. I'd bought my flat a year earlier, with a mortgage too large to be sensible, and my father had been moved into a care home, the cost for which I had offered to cover, not wanting my mother to sell their house. I had been unable to give Elliot the time he needed and deserved, and the guilt of that added another pressure, my GP prescribing me stronger migraine medication for the terrible, pulsing headaches that each new week seemed to bring and that had only made our arguments worse.

But after Marla, I felt as if something had come loose inside me. That some crucial seam or seal had burst, some core bit of me now untethered, so that I began forgetting things, making mistakes. Lying awake for nights on end and then sleeping so heavily I missed entire weekends, could barely string sentences together when I finally dragged myself from bed. I tortured myself with the thought that I had pushed Elliot away in order to defend someone who was guilty all along, and yet I was so full of self-loathing that I couldn't reach out to him, couldn't attempt to make amends.

I found myself at my desk in chambers often staring endlessly into space, unable to pick up the next brief, or searching through old notes on cases long forgotten, reevaluating them as my faith in my own instincts disintegrated.

"You're spiraling," Ursula told me once, as I railed about it to her over a lunch I couldn't bring myself to eat. "You have to stop. You need to speak to someone about the way you're feeling."

But I wouldn't listen. Not at first. Not when I had a panic attack on the Tube and was finally forced to sign myself off work. Then another struck, and then another, until they got so bad I thought I might actually be having a heart attack and took myself to A&E at St. Thomas's.

Those had been long, dark months. I stopped answering calls, stopped leaving the flat. Spent hours searching through social media posts about my old cases, all of the people out there who had believed I was doing something wrong, that the person I was defending deserved to rot in a cell. And without realizing it, I took their place as a prisoner. Locked myself away, sentenced to the relentless punishment of endlessly circling thoughts, medication tamping down the worst of my anxiety but leaving me beneath a thick fog, the outside world held safely away.

Therapy had forced me to work through the feelings, had taught me techniques to cope, and eventually I felt strong enough to face the world again. To begin rebuilding my faith in the justice system I had poured my entire life into. To return to work, to the only thing I had ever been good at.

And then I met you.

32

John

"Kit-Kat"

BOBBY SET OFF ON A planned six-month trip to Australia the day after you left with Neil, and your mum and I were alone. The house felt so quiet that the few words we exchanged each day seemed to echo for hours afterward.

When you were little, you liked to look at pictures of us when we'd first met. Me with a full head of hair, the same sandy brown as yours. Your mum with her sailor collar blouses and '80s shoulder pads, laughing in almost every photo.

I still remember it so clearly; walking into the barn at Godfrey's Farm as a student vet, hungover and nervous, your grandfather smoking a Woodbine and the sick pig I'd come to visit grunting anxiously in the end stall. And there was your mum, sitting there in the stinking straw with the pig's head in her lap, her sleeves rolled up and her jeans filthy.

She looked up at me, scrutinizing me with my pale face and foppish haircut, my clean shirt already sweat stained. Rolling her eyes, she gestured at the straw beside her. "Are you waiting for an invitation or what?" she asked.

I fell in love with her there and then, though it took me a week to work up the nerve to call her from my student digs in Edinburgh. You loved to hear the story of our first date, a disastrous dinner in a cheap Greek restaurant, me scalding my mouth on the flaming cheese and your mum fishing the ice from her glass for me. The waiter who'd dropped an entire plate of pastitsio down her coat while it was hanging from the back of her chair. The shots of ouzo at the end of the meal and the drunken walk to the station afterward, your mum tripping on a curb and toppling both of us into a puddle. It was the best night of my life.

We spoke for hours on the phone, your granddad sometimes disconnecting the line in protest, and I've never tried so hard, or been so thrilled, to make someone laugh. I felt like I could say anything, ask anything. I was so caught up in an urge to know, to be known by this other person. By the time we were married, I felt I truly understood why we call that person *my other half.*

But so much had happened since then, and I could see it in her eyes each time we passed in the house: we were a mystery to each other again.

I tried to call you each day, and each day the call went straight to voicemail. I sent you a text: *We love you. Mum's sorry. We're here when you're ready to come home.*

You didn't respond.

33

Gabriel

"K. C."

I SENT YOU A MESSAGE checking you were okay the day after you left for Scotland, but you didn't reply. Every time I picked up my phone, I opened the thread again, staring at that last message, wondering if somehow it hadn't sent or if you didn't have signal or if you'd accidentally dropped your phone in a loch or had it eaten by a cow or sheep or llama or whatever your uncle kept on his farm.

I couldn't double text; that was the most important thing. I had to wait and be cool and definitely not text again.

I texted again. You didn't reply, and I died inside and then got on with my day.

A week later, I was washing up the dinner stuff while Mum was doing a night shift at the old people's home when I heard my phone vibrate on the desk in the other room. I ran to get it with my hands still all sudsy, wiped them down my front, already feeling stupid because it would obviously just be Bart or Papa Johns Pizza with a Friday-night discount for losers, but there it was, your name on the screen.

are you there?

I almost dropped the phone in the rush to type back. *Yep!*

thank god, you replied.

Are you okay?

no, you sent back, and then a sad face.

What's happened?

i've been ghosted by a guy and my uncle's a nightmare, you wrote, and I felt like all the blood dropped out of my body and through the floor and I was just there like a big hollow bag of bones with the phone in my hand and my thumb too frozen to type.

hello? you wrote. *are you still there?*

I sat down on the arm of the sofa, still staring at the screen. *Still here*, I put. *What's your uncle done?*

34

Max

"Killer Kate"

YOUR PLEA HEARING WAS HELD at the Old Bailey. The air in the courtroom was stuffy, and the judge looked like she'd rather be anywhere else. They were all there, your defense team. Your barrister with his round, clean-shaven face, his big belly. His junior was a woman in glasses who kept brushing the sweat from the back of her neck, your solicitor, five foot nothing, with cropped gray hair and the overall air of someone who could freeze a person solid with a single glance. They were in muttered conversation, while the prosecution—a female KC and her male junior—looked relaxed.

And there you were in the dock. Hair pulled back in a harsh ponytail, your shirt untucked like you didn't really care about making a good impression.

You stumbled over your words as you confirmed your name and date of birth. You looked bored as various administrative issues were addressed—though that I couldn't blame you for.

You hesitated again when they read out the first charge: the murder of Dominic Ainsworth. It felt like everyone in the court was holding their breath, waiting to see how you would plead.

"Not guilty," you said, and my pulse kicked up a gear. So there would be a trial.

You said it again as each charge was read out. *Not guilty. Not guilty.*

Not guilty. Over and over. And I watched your face and I didn't believe you. I've had a lot of practice at this, been up close with a lot of bad people who've done bad things, and I trust my instincts.

And then, in a rush, before anyone else could say anything, you leaned forward and said, "I love you. I'm sorry."

35

Conrad

"Wildcat"

ONE MONTH AFTER YOU'D LIT the fuse on my life, another explosion. An email received in the middle of the night, the first thing I saw when I woke up in the morning. The sender a name I didn't recognize, Rory Gunnell, but the subject line *Godfrey's Farm.*

My first thought: someone knew.

I ignored the urge to delete it unread, and clicked on it.

He was an ex-employee, one with a fuckload of axes to grind. Claiming your uncle regularly gave the pigs antibiotics and probiotics to promote growth—a clanging red no-no for the Soil Association's organic status and our entire brand—and that the welfare of the herd was poor, that farrowing guidelines had not been followed correctly, that the electric fencing to prevent escape was insufficient and in places dangerous. The list went on, saving the most damning for last: that meat withdrawal guidelines had been blatantly ignored, with medicated animals sent to slaughter and used in our products, sticking a finger in the face of the rules regarding organic status and creating a giant shitstorm for me to deal with.

I groaned.

"Everything okay?" Molly murmured beside me.

I wanted to throw my phone out of the window, pull the duvet over my head. Burrow into the warmth of her, let her stroke my head, my face, and make everything better, the way she always did.

I wanted to see you.

"So, what do you think? Genuine whistleblower or guy with a grudge?" Philip, my MD, asked, as we boarded the first train to Edinburgh.

"It's a very detailed grudge," I said.

I already felt sick as we sat down, wondered if I could claim noro or food poisoning and get off at York or Carlisle.

"If it leaks . . ." Philip said, and I felt like punching him. As if I didn't know this was the worst possible time for a scandal to hit us. Potbellies was just about to announce a partnership with a major supermarket chain, an exclusive new range of organic ready meals. A deal I'd been instrumental in for the best part of a year. The marketing materials were full of our usual obnoxious, wholesome, no-nasties-whatsoever spiel, and the meals had a corresponding price tag slapped on them. The whole thing had *Guardian* exposé written all over it.

"We'll sort it," I said, and I turned to look out of the window.

We both spent the journey glued to our phones. Philip looked up at me once, crumbs from his sandwich on his shirt.

"Damage limitation," he said. "That's what we do now."

And I thought: too late for that.

You weren't at the gate when we arrived, the sky miserable and gray. Our surprise inspection was received just as badly, your uncle defensive, defiant. "Who's been saying I don't look after my pigs?" he asked Philip, Philip shitting his pants on the spot.

"Nobody's saying that," he stammered. "We're just doing our due diligence."

He showed us round again, took pains to demonstrate each and every way his pigs were treated like kings.

"Nothing wrong with the fucking fences," he said, seeing us leaning in to check them. I noticed that in places they looked recently repaired.

"What about the use of probiotics and antibiotics?" Philip said, as we stood in the barn where the feed was stored, and your uncle pulled a face.

"Never," he scoffed. "When there's been sickness in a litter, maybe, but . . ."

"And the withdrawal period for the meat in those cases?" I asked, and his face darkened.

"There's the dimensions of the new farrowing areas to discuss too," Philip said, the sweat patches on his shirt growing. Your uncle looked like he wanted to rip his head off.

The smell of the place made me feel sicker. I stepped away, excusing myself to make a call.

You found me round the back of an outbuilding. It had started raining, and your hair was wet, your top clinging to you.

"You need a coat," I said.

A stupid thing to come out with, heat rising up the back of my neck.

But you were already kissing me.

"I can't," I told you.

You fumbled with my belt, pushed up the hem of your skirt.

"Stop," I told you.

Your hands closed around my wrists. Your skin like ice as I slid my fingers over your hips, dragged your underwear down.

You bit me that time. My lip, my cheek, my neck.

Feral, I called you afterward, and you laughed.

36

Tarun

"Katherine"

I THUNDERED DOWN THE STEPS to the cells, Ursula behind me. You eyed me as we entered, your expression guarded.

I love you. I'm sorry. Your words reverberating in my ears.

"What was that?" I asked, my pulse thumping. "Who were you talking to?"

You stared at me for so long that I thought you weren't going to answer. "My family," you said eventually, but your gaze slid away from my face.

You were lying to me. And it made me afraid.

At home, I found myself, in a moment of weakness, calling Elliot. I regretted it almost immediately, hung up after a couple of rings. I pushed the phone away from me, cringing, and opened my laptop in an attempt to distract myself with work.

I started working through the spreadsheet Ruth had made, detailing your teenage activity on the Rabbit Hole. I had believed you when you'd said you had only scrolled the site out of habit, but now, the hearing still fresh in my memory, I began to doubt my instincts again. Reading the words you had written as a teenager—*this place is opening my eyes so much*—put me on edge, and I closed the file and opened a different document, trying to ignore the feeling.

At your hearing, the judge had set the stage dates for both parties to serve their evidence. This meant that we would now prepare your defense case statement, including our disclosure requests for the prosecution. I began adding to my list: the Ring doorbell footage of the neighboring properties, including the street that backed onto the mews and March House's courtyard. The list of members' key cards that had been used to access the club in the week leading up to the murders, and any police investigation into a connection between them and the four victims.

This was better; it became easier to breathe, and my thoughts quieted as I mentally checked off each of the potential defense lines I'd been mapping out.

Then my phone lit up, Elliot returning my call, and my stomach dropped.

"Hi," I said, wondering whether to pretend my first call had been an accident, a pocket dial.

"Sorry I missed you," he said, his voice cheerful. "I actually meant to give you a call earlier."

"Did you?" A rather humiliating note of hope slipped out with the question, and I cleared my throat, hoping he hadn't noticed.

"So, look: I've been talking to the colleague who was tipped off about Dominic Ainsworth taking cash for access to the cabinet, and I've done a little digging of my own."

"Okay."

"And when I say digging, I mean shamelessly plundering my contacts list until I found someone who knew the secretary of one of the Wrightman Group's executive directors."

"Right." My pulse began to quicken.

"Looks like Lucian had decided to move into property. The Wrightman Group had been purchasing empty office blocks in the City, with a view to converting them to luxury accommodation."

I considered this. "Sounds like a wise investment, post-lockdown."

"Sure."

"Though presumably not that straightforward, planningwise."

"Actually it is, fairly, in some boroughs at least, under the current permitted development rights. But there would've been some urgency, because there's a bill in the pipeline that proposes giving local authorities the power to apply affordable housing obligations to commercial-to-residential conversions."

"Not in keeping with the luxury market."

"Exactly. I imagine Ainsworth was offering his expertise on ways around that."

"For a consultancy fee."

"Precisely." I heard the hiss of him opening a can, the glug of him taking a sip. Root beer, I thought, his only vice. "I saw a chain of emails regarding the sale of one of Harris Lowe's properties, the Caledonia Building, to Wrightman. The first project of many, I think."

I got up and paced over to the breakfast bar. "I mean, it's not exactly a smoking gun."

He laughed. "We're in a major housing crisis, you know."

"Still. Assuming anyone knew about this, I can't imagine they'd be angry enough to kill them over it."

"It's a very angry time out there," Elliot said. "But no, I don't think we've stumbled across your motive."

"Thanks for looking into it anyway."

"No problem." I heard the ping of a microwave, a cupboard door being closed. "I remember what it's like at this stage. A lot of stones to turn, right?"

"Right." I glanced back at my laptop, the growing list. The stack of notes I was amassing in a paper file beside it.

"Well," he said. "Good luck with it. Sorry I couldn't help more, and sorry you had to chase."

"No, really . . ." I trailed off, too embarrassed to correct him. "I really appreciate it."

"Take care of yourself, T," he said, and then he hung up.

That evening, I ate a hurried dinner of buttered toast and an entire sleeve of chocolate digestives as I updated my notes with Elliot's information about Harris Lowe and Lucian Wrightman's new business venture. It felt like something of a nonstarter for our defense, but it was useful to know why the men might have been meeting for dinner, a box ticked in my head.

I googled Aleksandr Popov, whose presence was still a question mark—had he been there for business reasons, or was it purely a social occasion? Had someone wanted all four men dead, or was only one of them the real target, the others collateral damage?

Largely the search results were familiar information: Popov's various business holdings and the fortune he had amassed from his family's company, EPV Energy, and the controversy among some of the fans of the football team he and his brother had purchased early the previous year. I clicked over to the news tab, scrolling past all the coverage of the murders and then various articles about his football team's fortunes. Further down, a story caught my eye: a march to ban the use of fossil fuels, held that April, four months before the murders had taken place.

I studied the photo that accompanied the article. Popov was leaving the London HQ of EPV, a small huddle of protestors ambushing him as he walked through the revolving doors. Red paint had landed in an impressive arc across him and the glass, his chest taking the brunt of it. He looked furious, his handsome face twisted in an exclamation, splatters of red across one cheek.

I sent all of the photos from the article to print, added them to my file.

As I got ready for bed, I thought again about you that morning, the panicked way you'd rushed out the final words. *I love you. I'm sorry.* It felt as though there were pieces of the puzzle out of my reach, the story missing one or several links, and I was still afraid that you knew more than you'd told me. That the missing piece might perhaps be another person.

37

John

"Kit-Kat"

YOUR MUM WAS THE FIRST person Neil called. I came down to find her standing in the living room, her fingertips pressed to her mouth as she listened, the knuckles of the other hand pale as she gripped the phone.

"But why—" she started. "No, of course I'm not suggesting that—"

I could make out the angry buzz of your uncle's voice at the other end of the line.

"Well, what did they say?" she asked.

I waited as she finished the call. When she hung up, she shook her head at me. "Someone tipped off Potbellies that Neil's been breaching the conditions of their contract. And now there's an investigation into the pigs' welfare . . ." She stared at the phone as if hoping to see answers there. "If we lose that contract, I don't know what'll happen to the farm."

She sat down on the sofa beside me.

"Well, is it true?" I asked. "Are they being properly cared for?"

She recoiled. "Of *course* they are."

"Then does he have any idea who contacted them?" I asked. "That farmhand, the one who went off . . ."

"Maybe." She studied the floor. I put my arm round her and she sagged against me.

That night we slept in the middle of the bed instead of clinging to our separate sides.

But you rang early the next morning.

"Neil's gone mental at me," you said, sounding tearful. "He's accused me of getting him in trouble with the man from Potbellies, and he's been *awful*—"

Your mum, close enough to make out your raised voice, snatched the phone away from me.

"Sarah, don't—" I said, but she shook her head furiously at me, turned away and put you on speakerphone.

Behind her, on the mantelpiece, was a framed photo of the two of you. You were a toddler, standing on your mum's lap while she sat on a park bench. Your cheek was pressed to hers as you turned to smile at me and the camera. Your pudgy little hand splayed across her collarbone, your hair in the wispiest of pigtails. Both of you were beaming, the sky bright blue behind you.

"What's happened?" she said, and you repeated yourself.

"And did you?" she asked.

You laughed, a flat, bitter sound. "Is this how it'll be forever now? Anytime something bad happens, blame Kit? There was a flood in Wales last week. Did I do that too? What about that armed robbery in Manchester?"

"Don't be ridiculous," your mum said, but she was defensive now, irritated. "I had to ask."

"Did you?" you said, and then you hung up.

"I can't believe you did that," I said. "It's *Kit*, Sarah."

She stared back at me.

"Sometimes I wonder what it must be like to live in your world," she said, and she got up and left the house.

We slept on our own sides of the bed that night, the space between us a wider gulf than ever.

38

Max

"Killer Kate"

YOUR HEARING LIT A FIRE in my belly, I can't deny it. You telling someone you loved them—like that was the only thing that mattered when you were facing four murder charges and a life sentence—made the hairs on the back of my neck stand up. I wrote and rewrote versions of that scene, trying to get it exactly right. I knew it was crucial, a pivotal moment in your story.

I was sure that the person you'd been talking to was Mr. E.

I knew that this was it. My second book. It was so far beyond anything I'd imagined—we were talking modern-day Manson Family here, except Manson was just some anonymous guy posting on a forum. And you, a lone Manson girl—for now—had been so sucked in, so easily molded, that you'd thrown your entire life away and wrecked four families forever.

The next day, I got in my car and drove all the way to the place where you'd grown up. Three and a half hours on the road, Anya lighting up my phone with messages about the boiler needing servicing, could I pick oat milk up on the way home, how late was I going to be anyway?

It was a nice enough town. Neat little streets of terraced houses, cottages, and bungalows, a view of a measly strip of sea in the distance. I drove around a bit, negotiating narrow roads with cars parked like the residents were barricading against an enemy, and eventually left mine in the public car park at the entrance to the beach. Heading back into town on foot, I found a small high street with a few cafés and takeaway places, a couple of pubs. A surf shop and a bakery, a secondhand bookshop.

I went in that one first, thinking maybe I'd pick something up for Anya, something to soften the blow of me rolling home at whatever time that night. It was a little place, two narrow aisles stuffed with paperbacks, that musty smell of old books and damp. I walked up and down both sides a couple of times before picking up an old Pratchett I thought Anya would like.

When I took it to the till in the corner, a guy appeared from the back and nodded his approval.

"Good choice," he said, ringing it up. "One pound fifty."

I handed it over. "This your place?" I asked.

"Nah, a mate's." He flicked the till drawer shut. "I just help out every now and again."

"You're from round here, then?"

He eyed me over the top of his glasses. "Yeah."

"Did you know Kate Cole?" I asked.

"Oh. Yeah. We were in the same year at school." He shoved the book and a receipt in a paper bag, handed it over to me.

"What was she like?"

He pulled a face. "I didn't know her that well. She was close to my friend Gabe for a while."

"I guess everyone here must have been pretty shocked to hear the news."

"I don't know." He looked at me earnestly. "She was always kind of a magnet for trouble. If I'd heard *she'd* been murdered, I wouldn't have been, like, all that surprised, you know? But to hear she'd done that . . ."

He trailed off and I flagged that phrase in my head: a magnet for trouble.

"What kind of trouble?" I asked, aiming for a casual, gossipy tone that seemed to hit the mark because he leaned on the wooden counter, settling in. Enjoying it.

"She had a reputation," he said. "Supposedly she burned a house down, back when we were eighteen."

I froze at that bombshell. "Seriously?"

He nodded, eyes wide. "She disappeared right after that—that was the last anyone saw of her round here."

"Whose house was it?" I asked, racing to catch up in my head. Teenage arsonist to infamous poisoner—a new arc for you being painted in front of me.

At this, he became noticeably less comfortable. "It was a guy who owned a gymnastics place outside of town." He straightened up off his elbows and started fiddling with a pen pot beside the till. "How come you're so interested, anyway?"

"I'm a journalist," I said.

His eyebrows, bushy and expressive, took a panicked step up his face. "Oh yeah?"

"Don't worry. I'm not going to quote you or anything. I just want to understand what Kate was like. How she ended up in this situation, you know?"

He swallowed. "Sure."

"It would be really helpful if I could talk to your friend. Gabe, did you say?"

"Yeah," he said reluctantly. "Gabe."

"Do you have his number? I could give him a call."

He blanched. "I don't know about that."

I waited without saying anything, a tactic that works with maybe 70 percent of people.

"You could give me yours," he said, slightly dubiously. "I can pass it on. But I don't know . . ."

I gave him my card. "Just a chat, he doesn't have to commit to anything on record."

"Cool," he said, looking doubtful.

"And what was your name?" I offered him my hand, calm and friendly. "I'm Max, by the way."

"Bart." He shook it, then folded his arms across his chest.

"Nice to meet you, Bart." I tucked the book under my arm and headed out.

A week earlier, I'd found an account that belonged to someone else who claimed to have gone to school with you. Her name was Megan Baxter, and she had seventy-nine followers on Twitter and a profile picture of her with a puppy ears filter.

So sad about Katie C, she'd written when news of your arrest had broken. *Wish she'd got help when she needed it x.*

She'd stuck a load of hashtags on the end, inviting attention from a load of strangers who'd also been tweeting about you. When one of them replied, telling her exactly what they thought of you, she'd responded, *Thx for your opinion but I went to school with her so I think I know better lol.*

That had got a bit more interest, a handful of likes, and it had clearly spurred her on, because there were a few more from the past few weeks: *Katie Cole in the papers again. Wish I could say I can't believe it came to this but I totally can.* Obligatory sad face at the end.

I'd sent her a message, explaining who I was, and she'd happily given me her home address.

I found it easily enough, a two-up, two-down on a street a few rows back from the bookshop, a *Home Sweet Home* doormat outside the lilac front door. Megan answered the door in plush slippers and yoga leggings, a fleece and false eyelashes.

"I'm Max," I said, with my friendliest smile. "Sorry I'm late."

She showed me through to the tiny living room, a hellhole of velvet cushions, fluffy throws, and twee knickknacks. I looked around as I sat down, hoping to see your face in one of the engraved *Good Times* and *Making Memories* photo frames.

"I've been reading all your articles," she said. I couldn't tell if she meant that as a compliment or not.

"It must be difficult, seeing an old friend in the news like this."

She shrugged. "We haven't spoken in a while. I mostly feel sad for her family."

"In one of your tweets you said you can believe it came to this."

"Yeah." She picked at the edge of her nail, the same purple as the front door. "I think we all can."

"Why's that? What was Kate like, growing up?"

She thought about this, head tipped to one side. "I don't know the right word, really." A mean look snuck across her face. "A mess."

Some friend. "In what way?"

"One of those girls who cries when they're drunk, flirts with boys they don't fancy, always has some kind of drama going on . . . You know those girls who just lie about everything? Like they can't help themselves?"

I told her that I did.

"She could be sweet," Megan said uncertainly, maybe feeling guilty for putting the knife straight in. "But . . . I don't know. She had a temper too."

"I heard she burned a house down."

She seemed relieved that I already had this information. She tucked her feet up under her, getting comfortable now. "Yeah. Peter. He was lovely, him and his wife. They ran a gymnastics place just out of town. I had a birthday party there once."

"Why him?"

Her expression grew slyer. "Oh, you didn't hear that part? That was the first lie. When Katie was just a little kid. She told people Peter was some kind of pedo."

Stunned, I stared at her.

She waved a hand, rolling her eyes. "It was all totally made up; the police dropped the whole thing. Awful for them, though. I don't think I really understood at the time how bad it was, for someone to say something like that."

"You know for sure it was made up?"

"Well, *yeah*," she scoffed. "Ask anyone. Ask her brother, her mum. Trust me, if you knew Katie, you'd know. I'm telling you: she couldn't help herself. Lies were, like, her way of getting attention or something."

Well, you were certainly getting attention now.

"She feeds off it," Megan said, a little defensively. "That was what she was like the whole time we were teenagers. Making things up about boys who liked her or money she had or places she was going to go. She's a sociopath, isn't she? Or a narcissist. I always get those confused."

Every man and his dog seemed to be a narcissist these days, but I nodded. It was hardly the most surprising thing I'd heard about you.

"You said you haven't spoken in a while—why's that?"

She looked away, and I wondered again if she was starting to feel bad about the harsh way she'd spoken, a far cry from the performative, sweet little tweets about how sad she was for you. "She ran away after the fire," she said. "Maybe you heard that part."

"You weren't in touch after that?"

She shook her head. A cat jumped up onto the back of the sofa and strolled behind us, tail aloft. Megan scooped it up and put it on her lap.

"Are you going to write about this?" she asked.

"I'm not sure yet," I said. "It'll probably depend on the outcome of the trial."

Megan bit her lip. "I wouldn't want her to see my name involved," she said. "You know . . . if she gets off."

And I realized that she wasn't feeling guilty for what she'd said or sorry for you. She was scared of you.

After I left Megan's, I drove to the house where you grew up. I parked a little way down the road and took a proper look at it. A nice house, on a nice street. An apple tree in the front garden, the windows with neat net curtains and a Volvo on the drive. Like a sitcom version of a family home.

I got out of my car and walked up to it, wondering if you knew how lucky you'd been to grow up in a place like that. Trying to picture this new version of you walking down the garden path: liar, fire starter.

I'd thought that you were a naïve kid, sucked in by Mr. E, but now I could see that maybe you'd always been a different type of dangerous.

I reached your parents' front door and rang the bell. I never got nervous about interviews, even when I was doorstepping someone, but I could feel the adrenaline starting to flow, my mouth getting dry. I looked up at the house again, noticing a faded sticker on one of the upstairs windows, a miniature version of the cartoon house from *Up*, floating away with its thousands of balloons. One of Albie's favorites.

There was no answer, no twitch of the curtains or creeping steps inside. But I felt sure someone was in there, so I rang the doorbell again.

When five minutes passed, I had to give up. I got into my car, feeling unsatisfied, and scribbled a quick note on a page from my notebook, jogging back up the path to push it through the letter box.

I figured it was worth a try.

39

Conrad

"Wildcat"

WE MET IN THE BOARDROOM of doom, a windowless sweatbox at the back of our offices. Me, Philip, a lawyer, and our chairman, Joseph. Coffee going cold in the middle of the table.

"It's the timing," Philip said. "With the announcement ready to go . . ."

"There's no good time for a welfare scandal," Joseph said, looking at Philip like he'd just landed from Mars. "Or any question over the quality of our products."

"No." Philip deflated in his chair.

"My sister and I, we started this company with a clear ethos. With core values that are essential to Potbellies as a brand. That has been at the heart of every decision we've made, every expansion. It was a fundamental decision when we were acquired by Wrightman Foods, and I cannot let us lose sight of that now." He looked at me. "Conrad, I trust you. This is your call. Do we give Godfrey's Farm the benefit of the doubt?"

I tapped my pen against the notepad I'd brought with me, the page still entirely blank. I was torn. I hadn't seen any evidence of mistreatment on any of my site visits, but on the other hand, I'd never looked that hard.

And now I had an opportunity to impress the chairman and delete you from my life, in one simple move.

I put the pen down. "I think we have to take the accusations seriously."

"We're that farm's entire business . . ." Philip tried, his voice wavering.

"The principle of using ethically sourced and organic ingredients is *our* entire business," I said. "I say we find a new supplier."

Joseph smiled. "I agree. Thank you, Conrad."

Just like that.

I fired off the email to your uncle. Polite but factual, *I regret to say* and *We're sure you can understand why* and a *Kind regards* to close it off with no hard feelings.

Job done.

I felt light that night, as Molly and I planned a trip to Cork. We were going to visit wedding venues, and I found myself smiling as I watched her clicking through photos on the laptop, smiling each time she turned it round to show me. Smiling when I woke up to her face beside mine, the promise that I'd get to do that every day for the rest of my life. It was like Scotland was a nightmare that had never happened, and now I could shut the door on it entirely.

It probably reflects badly on me, that ability to compartmentalize. To detach myself from the bad things I've done. But it's a skill I learned long ago, and I'd be lying if I said it was difficult to sweep the last traces of guilt away.

A day later, you showed up.

You were waiting for me in the lobby at work, your hair all done, a low-cut summer dress on. You beamed as you saw me coming out of the lift, and for a second I was too shocked to react.

I almost turned and went right back up to the tenth floor.

You faltered then, seeing the look on my face. A deer in the headlights. You lifted your hand as if you were going to wave, left it hovering there halfway.

I noticed the way the receptionists were watching you. Barely hidden smiles, laughs bitten back.

I gestured for you to walk out with me. Kept my distance, even though I could tell you'd expected me to hug you, probably even to kiss you.

I tried not to sound annoyed as I asked you what you were doing there.

You looked confused as you said, "I can't stop thinking about you."

Everything was moving too fast, I could tell—your brain still not processing the way the scene had departed from the version you'd probably imagined as you'd traveled down.

"I thought we could . . ." you said, but fuck knows what you thought the end of that sentence was going to be.

"Come on," I said, feeling sorry for you. "Let me buy you a coffee."

I took you to a café round the corner, the shitty one no one from the office went to, and found a table for us near the back, away from the window. You asked for a Coke, and I got one from the fridge, ordered a green tea for me. I steeled myself and took the tray over to you.

It'll sound harsh, but I looked at you sitting there and was disappointed. Your makeup was too heavy, showed up the thinness of your lips, made your eyes look small and mean. In my memory, you'd taken on a hazy, pure quality, a perfume ad of a person. In the cold strip lighting of the café, you looked ordinary.

You looked younger than I remembered too. I felt a slight panic at that.

"Look," I said, and you flinched.

You were shrinking in front of me, and I tried to get it over with quickly for you.

"I had so much fun with you," I said. "But I'm engaged. I want to make that work."

You stared at me.

"You can't be serious," you said, your voice taking on a hard edge.

I found myself getting annoyed. I didn't feel like I'd made you any promises, given you any false hope. There had never been any suggestion that it had been anything more than sex. I could barely even remember your real name. You had come on to me—so hard, when I looked back, that in a way it was embarrassing.

I was embarrassed for you.

Still, I'm not totally heartless. I could see you were upset.

"It was great," I told you. "But it has to be a one-off. Like the best holiday romance. It was perfect as it was, wasn't it?"

If I'm honest, I felt like you were ruining it, tainting this thing that I'd been looking forward to keeping tucked away in its box. Something maybe I'd be able to look back on in years to come, when Molly and I had children, a fat mortgage, were stuck deep in the everyday rut of real life.

"I can't fucking believe this," you said. Volume rising enough that I saw the girl behind the counter glance over.

I kept calm as I said, "I'm sorry if there's been any misunderstanding." Playing it kind, reasonable. Defusing things before you could make a proper scene. I put a hand on your arm, gave it a gentle squeeze. "I didn't realize," I said.

You blinked a few times. "You said . . ."

But you didn't know what you'd thought I said. I capitalized as you stalled, leaning over to give you a hug. I hated myself, just a little, as I did it, and that made me want to get away from you.

"Let me get you a taxi to the station," I said. "Unless you have a place to stay?"

You shook your head. You were kind of pouting now, a spoilt-brat face that didn't suit you.

"Will you be all right?" I asked, in a way that didn't leave much space for an answer. I kissed you on the cheek and squeezed your hand.

"I'm sorry," I said. "In another life, maybe."

I think you were probably still looking at me as I left, but I didn't turn back.

40

John

"Kit-Kat"

IT WAS ME WHO ANSWERED the phone to Neil when he rang. "She's gone off," he said, gruffer than usual. No trace of apology. "Taken all her things."

I froze. "What do you mean, gone?" The farm was miles from anything.

"Stole my bike," he said. Angry again now. "Left it outside the bloody train station for anyone to nick."

I handed the phone over to your mum without another word. Tried to call you, over and over again, each time being sent to voicemail.

When a whole day passed without any of us being able to reach you, your mum called the police. But you were eighteen, were not considered vulnerable. We should get back in touch if we didn't hear from you, the officer who visited said, clearly irritated by this waste of his time.

It was late the following evening when we heard a key in the front door. Wilbur, who couldn't believe his luck, skittered stiffly from his basket to greet you.

"Kit," your mum said. "Where the hell have you been?"

I was looking at your bag, stained wet as if you'd dropped it in a puddle, your bare legs splashed with grime. Your makeup was smudged around your eyes, and you looked as if you hadn't slept in days.

"I'm tired," you said. You sounded utterly beaten. "Can I just go to bed?"

"No, you can't." Your mum moved to block your way. "You're going to explain yourself, right now."

You looked close to tears. "I haven't done anything wrong."

"We believe you," I said firmly.

"Potbellies have canceled the contract," your mum said.

"Why are you saying that like it's my fault?" you asked, eyes flashing. A spark ignited.

"Stop," I said. "We're all exhausted. Let's talk tomorrow. Kit, go and run a bath, and I'll make you something to eat."

You gave me a grateful smile and went up the stairs.

Your mum turned to me. "You can't keep doing this. You can't keep protecting her, ignoring everything . . ."

"She's my daughter," I said. "So yes. I can."

"For god's sake, John—"

"She said she didn't do it," I snapped. "So drop it. Drop it now, before we really do lose her."

When I came up with soup and some toast a while later, you were already asleep, your hair still wet from the bath. You were wearing an old pair of pajamas we'd bought you one Christmas, white flannel with penguins and snowflakes printed all over, and you looked so young.

Wilbur nudged at my leg and I opened the door a little wider and let him jump on the bed to sleep with you. He stayed guard there all night.

41

Tarun

"Katherine"

I ASKED URSULA TO ARRANGE another conference with you at the earliest possible moment. I had a new brief, this one prosecuting a serious assault case. I had to rush from a Zoom call with the client, barely making it onto the train before it pulled away from the platform. As I sat down, I glanced at my silenced phone and saw a new message from Elliot.

Hey, how's it going? he'd written, and when I opened it, I saw he was still online. For several minutes, I watched the text at the top of the screen: *Elliot is typing . . .* But no further message appeared.

Well, I typed, which felt an overstatement. I deleted it and wrote, *Fine, thanks. You?*

I regretted the stiffness, the lack of warmth, as soon as I saw the words appear in the thread. Elliot was no longer showing as online, and I waited for several minutes with no reply. I put the phone on the tray table, picked up my papers again. After half an hour had passed, I checked it, and seeing no new messages, I turned it facedown.

You looked pleased to see us when we arrived. You were dressed in clean clothes, your hair neat, and you smiled politely at the guard as he showed you into the room. You listened carefully as I explained that we would now begin preparing your defense case statement, pushing your sleeves up as if to show that you were ready to get to work.

"Okay," you said. "What do you need from me? What goes in it?"

"We will need to set out the elements of the prosecution's case we feel insufficient to prove your guilt; the most important of these are the fingerprint evidence and the digital evidence regarding the Rabbit Hole website."

You nodded slowly, picking at a corner of your lip. "Well, the fingerprints are obvious—I served them the drinks."

"Yes. And the lack of other prints to me suggests the bottle had been wiped at some point. I have a forensic expert witness we can call to support us there."

"The Rabbit Hole . . ." You looked up, anxious again now. "That's going to look bad, isn't it?"

"It's not ideal. But reading something isn't a crime, nor is it proof that you agreed with comments that were written there."

I waited, watching your face for a reaction. It remained what felt to me like a studious sort of blank, and I noticed that I'd begun to twitch my foot anxiously. I crossed my legs in an effort to stop.

"More importantly," Ursula said, "we can use your defense case statement to bring any other information we feel is relevant to the attention of the court, to encourage the CPS to pursue other lines of inquiry."

You looked up at me. "Other lines of inquiry?"

"Yes."

"You mean, finding out who actually did it?" There was a new energy about you now, a childish sort of hope.

"That would certainly be a favorable result."

You nodded again, sitting upright now. "What kind of information would we need?"

"Well, we'll be highlighting the window of opportunity another party would have had to enter the room before the dinner began. Camilla Johnson says the brandy wasn't there when she left the room at five fifty p.m. You say it was there when you arrived at six. You're certain about that?"

"Yes," you said, but then you paused, and I thought I saw a shadow of calculatedness pass over your face as you considered your answer. "No," you decided. "Not certain. But it was there when I came down from the bar with their first round of cocktails at about twenty past."

I didn't like that hesitation. Were you trying to choose the answer that gave the most space for someone else to have been responsible?

"Sorry," you said, your eyes searching my face as though you could read my thoughts. "I know I need to be sure. But it's hard to remember—I was late, so it was all a rush . . ."

"It's okay," Ursula told you. "Think about it. Come back to us on that one."

"If you ever observed any conflict between the men and anyone else at March House, that would also be useful," I said.

"Okay." Your lips pursed as you thought. "I hadn't worked there long, so I didn't know anyone that well . . ." You looked up at us, with what appeared to be genuine anxiety. "Sorry," you said.

"Don't worry," Ursula said firmly. "We'll keep working on it."

42

John

"Kit-Kat"

IN THE MORNING, YOU SEEMED to have a new purpose about you. You came downstairs while we were eating breakfast and poured yourself coffee from the cafetiere I'd left on the side. You'd put on makeup and a clean T-shirt and jeans, and Wilbur trotted along with you wherever you went, the most energetic I'd seen him in months.

You pulled out a chair and sat at the head of the table, looking from one to the other of us. Clearing your throat, you said, "I want to use the money in my fund to rent a flat in London."

"Absolutely not." Your mum picked up her coffee and took a sip, and I don't think you noticed the way her hand was shaking.

"Why not?" Your temper already ignited, volume rising.

"Why London?" I intervened.

You shrugged. "That's where I want to live."

"Well, what would you do there?"

"Design, maybe," you said. "That's what I'm good at."

"Then you need to study," I said, beginning to feel exasperated. I was trying to help you, but you weren't making it easy for me. "You can't just pitch up in a huge city and expect to walk into a job."

"Vivienne Westwood worked in a factory. And then on the side, she—"

"You are not renting a flat in London," your mum interrupted. "End of discussion."

"It's my money," you said. "Stephen left it to me."

"For something *real*," she retorted. "To go toward university or a house deposit. Not for you to just throw away on a whim."

We'd been so proud of him when he'd told us he wanted to nominate you for his death benefit. And when it was released, we'd chosen the best savings account we could find to keep it for you, had taken some small comfort that he would be helping you in adulthood, in the way I know he would have done if he had lived.

I thought of it all the time, a favorite daydream to torture myself with. Stephen teaching you to drive, helping you move into halls at university. Stephen and Bobby in the front row at your wedding day. All three of you in the garden, your children playing while you drank wine and laughed together.

"I'm an adult," you said, and I could see from the set of your jaw that you'd resolved not to lose your temper. "You can't dictate to me what I do with my life anymore."

"The account is in your dad's name," your mum said. She put the mug down. "And you haven't been behaving like an adult in the slightest, Kit. When you can do that, we'll start treating you like one."

"You have no right." You were the one shaking now.

"Be realistic, Kit," I said, hoping to reason with you. Wilbur retreated under the table to my feet. "If you want to talk about moving to London, that's fine. But you need a plan."

"Why?" you said, banging a hand on the table in a way that made Wilbur jump. "Hasn't what happened to Stephen taught you anything? Haven't you seen everything that's going on in the world? I don't want to *plan* my life. I want to go and live it."

"Don't do that." Your mum's voice was low and dangerous now. "Don't try and blame any of this on what happened to Stephen."

"Oh, I don't." You rose from your seat. "I blame you. And I'll never forgive you for it."

You walked out of the door before I could stop you, and it was several seconds before your mum took a big, gasping breath, like she'd been winded.

I dreamt about losing you all the time after that. Imagined you as a toddler in the supermarket—there in the baby seat in the trolley one second, gone the next. As a child, holding my hand as we walked down a busy street or beach, bolting as soon as I stopped to talk to someone or look at something. As a teenager, beside me on one of our meadow strolls, laughing at something I said and then, as I stooped to tie a shoelace, vanishing into thin air.

43

Max

"Killer Kate"

I GOT HOME TO FIND Anya doing Albie's bath with a glass of wine in hand.

"I'll take over," I said. "It's my night."

"Thanks." She kissed me, took the paper bag from the bookshop. "This for me?"

"Dad, where have you been?" Albie did his best to look stern with a Santa beard of bubbles on his face. David and a green plastic spider Albie had charmingly christened Bogey looked on from the edge of the bath.

"It was called Combe Little," I said, offering him a flannel. "I drove there and saw the sea."

"I did that," he announced. "I went there one time with Nanna and swam in the sea."

"I don't think Nanna's ever taken you to the seaside," I said, swiping wet hair back from his face.

"Yep. Last week." He handed me the flannel back. "I ate five ice creams and saw a shark."

This was a new thing I'd noticed him doing. Inventing things, making up stories and presenting them as fact. *Just a phase*, Anya had said, her answer to everything. Totally harmless, normal, experimenting with truth and fiction.

But that night, it made me think of you.

When Albie was in bed and Anya busy pruning herself in a bath of her own, I got out my laptop and started adding to my growing file on you.

I plugged "Peter gym fire Combe Little" into Google and quickly found the housefire both Bart and Megan had told me about. I read the local news articles, all thin on detail. The police had confirmed it was arson fairly quickly, but it'd been lumped in with a string of similar incidents in the county, and if they'd continued investigating beyond that, the news coverage hadn't. But now I had the guy's full name, Peter Walters, and so I searched a few combinations with that, trying to find any mention of your accusations against him.

Nothing in the mainstream news, obviously, but I found an old post on a local Facebook group. *Really disturbed about a rumor I've heard about Olympia Gym. Anyone else?* The first comment was immediately defensive: *It's disgusting. @Peter Walters is a pillar of this community. Can't believe someone's putting him and Julia through this.* There were more of the same; he'd definitely been popular. I wondered how your paths had crossed and what you'd actually said about him.

I thought about the friend Bart had mentioned, the kid who'd been close to you. Gabe. I opened your old Instagram account, trawled through your four-hundred-odd followers. Thankfully there was only one candidate, @gabe3s_, a weedy-looking kid listed as Gabriel S.

There were no pictures of you on his profile—no pictures of anything, actually, barring one kind of blurry one taken from the dunes near your hometown.

It was worth a shot, though, so I sent him a quick message, not trusting that Bart kid to pass my details on. *Be great to talk to you,* I wrote.

44

Conrad

"Wildcat"

YOU GOT MY WORK EMAIL from the company website. Added me on Instagram.

Hi:) you wrote on both platforms. When I didn't respond, another email followed. *I want to see you again.* Ten minutes later, another: *I miss you.*

I pretended I hadn't seen the friend request, replied to the email as carefully as dismantling a bomb: *It was really fun meeting you.* I added *Good luck with everything* as a closer, like you were one of our interns.

When you wrote again—*I keep thinking about what happened*—I was stressed. I deleted it, but when I went back to my inbox ten minutes later, there were two more. *I don't believe you don't feel the same!* A minute after that: *Remember how you called me wildcat;)*

Please stop contacting me, I replied, and sat there, panicked, after I'd sent it.

I started to worry there was something genuinely wrong with you. Because who could read so much into something that barely qualified as a one—okay, two—night stand? I didn't even know your last name, and somehow you'd imprinted on me like some deranged baby bird.

Don't do this, you replied. *I can come and see you again.*

A day later: *Why are you being like this?*

I started getting tension headaches at work, wondering what would happen if someone saw one of your messages. Some idiot in accounts had been fired the year before for sending a dick pic to one of the assistants, and suddenly I kept picturing the way the news would spread if I got hauled in and asked to explain what had happened.

But you were the niece of an ex-supplier, I reasoned, not another employee. It had been a work trip but not during work hours so: gray area?

I could spin it all I wanted. I felt it there: guillotine, right over my head.

A couple of days after I'd ignored your last email, there was still silence.

The relief. Knee shaking.

That same day, Joseph called me in, said he'd been impressed with my work, that he felt it was time I had a promotion. There wasn't a role at Potbellies right then, but he'd recommended me to another business in the Wrightman Group. If I was interested in that.

I was interested.

I went to the pub that night after work and drank five pints, felt like going out and buying a scratch card.

When I walked in my front door, Molly was sitting there on the sofa, looking like she'd seen a ghost.

Her laptop in front of her.

"You okay?" I asked. Like the answer to that wasn't obvious.

She pushed the laptop toward me, got up, and left the room. The bedroom door slammed as I glanced down and saw your name on the screen.

You'd found her online too, sent a long message. The last line caught my eye first: *I just thought you should know.* Panic making my vision dance as I scanned back up and read the rest. *Your fiancé is lying to you.* A long description of the things that I'd done to you. That you'd done to me.

I stopped feeling sorry for you then. Started to fear you.

45

Max

"Killer Kate"

THE NEWS CYCLE MOVED ON while we all waited for your trial, other people's crimes taking their turn in the headlines: a man accused of murdering his girlfriend in Dublin, a footballer convicted of a drunken hit-and-run. I got on with covering them, but I still kept tabs on the various threads on the Rabbit Hole that were discussing you like a hero.

Kate Cole struck at the heart of Olympus! read one of the typical comments. They were still all certain that March House really was the secret HQ of the Group that Mr. E had been talking about, and as he'd gone abruptly silent, there was no one around to correct them.

I went back to the original posts, the detective work they'd all done once they'd decided that they'd cracked Mr. E's code and found Olympus. The really obvious clue had come in the post claiming *A world leader and a Royal both showed up to kiss the feet of The Group*—the same user who'd first announced that it was March House had found a news article about the foreign secretary hosting the prime minister of Serbia at the club that day, along with a gossip site with photos of a Luxembourgian prince showing up for drinks with Aleksandr Popov that evening. Ding ding ding.

But there was other stuff that checked out too: Mr. E had claimed that the Group *ate steaks from a Parisian butcher that's the most expensive in the world*, which the denizens of the Rabbit Hole had found matched almost exactly a claim on the website of the club itself: *Our beef is sourced from Blanchet-Badeaux, the world's most exclusive butcher and boulangerie.*

So Mr. E knew that the most successful lies are always rooted in truth. He knew exactly what he was doing. And once he'd wound you all up and set you off, all he had to do was sit back and watch.

After checking out the Parisian beef connection for myself—and now hungry—I spent some time trawling through the club's website, clicking around the minimalist pages with all their airy talk of "a community of thinkers and game-changers," "a space to unwind, feast, indulge," blah blah blah. The photos of the stuffed hares on the bar and the art-filled walls and fussy furniture. The plates of poncy deconstructed meals with splatters of jus and shards of the bones of peasants or whatever accompanied the much-speculated-about filet steak on that day's specials menu.

It was wanky, sure, but no more so than some of the other clubs in London. It was when you started digging into the members themselves that things got interesting. I lost an entire afternoon to pages of search results for the club's name, scanning the headlines about politicians who'd been photographed coming and going, a Hollywood director who'd subsequently been arrested on sexual assault charges. A supermodel climbing the front steps on the arm of Harris Lowe a year before he'd gone into the club for the last time.

Not everyone was as paparazzi worthy; there were the billionaires you could walk past in the street without noticing, the tech guys and venture capitalists and pharma execs. I plugged their names into Google and Companies House and started down a whole new warren, eating up hours of time.

I'll be honest. The more I dug, the more I could see that there was plenty to question—to be angry about—when it came to March House, Kate. A handful of its members, when I really got into it, had donated enough to think tanks to influence much of the legislation introduced by the government in the past five years. Anti-protest laws that had punished radical environmentalists had been supported in Parliament with evidence from an "expert" body that existed on donations from an oil and gas behemoth—owned, as it happened, by the family of one Aleksandr Popov. Various tax breaks given to landlords and multiple-property owners had originally been suggested by the Clayton Economic Institute, a think tank whose chair had been photographed at events with various high-profile March House members, including Harris Lowe, who of course had made his money in—guess what?—property.

It was plenty shadowy and underhand and infuriating, I'll give you that.

But your Rabbit Hole crew were too busy fixating on your own fairy-tale monsters—not realizing that in the process, you'd become something far scarier.

That night at dinner, Anya was annoyed with me. Albie, oblivious, tucked into the fish and chips I'd gone out and collected in a rush, but I could feel the crackle of a mood from Anya's end of the table. I'd been supposed to cook Bolognese for us all; the defrosted pack of mince was still sitting accusingly in a puddle in the sink.

"I would eat chips for dinner every day if I was in charge," Albie declared, always my wingman.

"It's lucky Daddy's doing all this overtime, then, isn't it?" Anya pushed her own plate aside and reached over to refill her wine.

"*Very* lucky," Albie said, shoving the last two chips into his mouth at once and sliding off his seat. "Can I go watch *Ninja Kidz*?"

"For ten minutes," I said, grabbing him as he hurried past so that I could wipe his hands on a bit of kitchen roll. "Then we'll do some reading together."

"*Fine.*"

"I'm sorry," I said, when Anya and I were alone at the table. "I know I've been working all weekend, but it's important."

"The trial isn't for months yet," she said.

When I feigned ignorance, she shot me a look. "I can see our Google history too, you know. You're obsessed with March House and Kate Cole."

"This is a big story," I said, inwardly bristling at the word *obsessed*. "It could be a really important step for me. I'm thinking about another book."

She rolled her eyes and didn't say anything, instead glugging her wine.

Nettled, I said, "That's what you wanted, isn't it? For me to go back to investigative stuff? You're always on about how much you hate the *Herald*."

"I didn't mean you should go and drown yourself in something like this. Spending your weekends poking around horrible little corners of the internet after last time, instead of being with us. Your family."

"This is my job. I do it for you. *My family*. So we can live in this house and have nice things, and so that maybe, just maybe, by the time Albie's old enough, those *horrible little corners of the internet* might not actually exist."

"Very noble." She got up from the table and took the plates over to the sink. "Will we be invited to the palace when you get your knighthood or . . . ?"

"Don't be mean." I slid my arms round her waist and kissed her bare shoulder. "I just want to make you both proud of me."

She tipped her head against mine, relenting. Then swatted me with a tea towel. "You've got a Reading Record to fill out."

"And then film night?"

"It's a date."

That night, like he could read my mind, Albie chose *Up*. As Anya wept into her wine over the opening sequence and Albie set about repeating all of Dug the dog's lines, word for word, I thought about you. A little girl who'd loved the film so much she'd stuck a sticker of it in her bedroom window, now a woman on remand at HMP Peterborough.

Maybe it was the glass of wine I'd poured myself, maybe it was the way Albie, usually too cool and grown-up for cuddling now, leaned against me as he got tired, but that night, I felt really sad for you, Kate.

46

Conrad

"Wildcat"

YOU DISAPPEARED AFTER YOUR MESSAGE to Molly. Grenade thrown, no need to hang around to watch the carnage left behind.

I thought about lying. I knew she'd probably have believed me. Would've accepted a story about you being lonely, troubled, unhinged, the southern kid exiled to her uncle's farm, hungry for attention. The message you'd written, vicious as it was, might've played right into my hands, if I'd been able to persuade Molly not to write back, not to engage. Deny till you die, I might've told someone else in that situation. The only way.

In the end, I didn't have the stomach for it. Surprising, sometimes, finding your limit. How much easier it is, when it comes to it, to put your hands up. Confess.

Molly deserved the truth. She deserved better.

There was a point, in the middle of the storm, when I thought we might ride it out. That she'd forgive me. Moments during those tense nights when, sleeping on the sofa, I thought I heard her climb out of bed, tiptoe toward the door.

But then I'd catch her looking at her phone again. Your face on the screen.

47

Tarun

"Katherine"

THE MONTHS AFTER YOUR HEARING went far faster than I had expected. My assault brief ended swiftly with a guilty plea; the rescheduled fraud brief got underway and took up two long weeks of my time. I took another, a sexual assault, prosecuting this time, and then an aggravated robbery. It felt good to be in court again, to put on my wig and gown each morning, to transform into someone I began to recognize. Meanwhile, Ursula and I worked hard, fielding disclosure and discussing which evidence we would not be contesting, and which witnesses would be required to testify in court.

At home the night before your trial, I stood in my living room and studied the images and documents I had pinned over the wall. It helped me to think that way, to be able to physically move the pieces around in front of me as I shuffled them in my mind, ordering them into lines of reasoning, searching for any flaws I had missed.

I studied a still from the CCTV footage of you leaving March House in your white shirt and black waistcoat, neat black trousers and a black tie. The picture of professionalism, if one did not know what you were supposed to have left behind.

Beside it was the image that had been taken of you when you were brought into custody. Your hair falling out of its ponytail, your eyes staring. You'd lost the waistcoat at some point, the shirt rumpled and sweat stained. You looked angry, defiant. You didn't look like the person I had met, and I worried, still, which version of you was the real one.

One by one, I looked at the pictures of all four men arriving. Lucian Wrightman had been first, a yellow Selfridges bag in hand. Then Harris Lowe, emailing or texting as he climbed the steps to the club. Dominic Ainsworth had walked down the mews just as Aleksandr Popov, aviators on, had climbed out of a chauffeur-driven Rolls Royce, still idling at the curb as the two of them entered March House together.

I checked the list of evidence again, though I knew the words there by heart. Wrightman's shopping bag had been retrieved at the scene, a silk Valentino Garavani dress and a receipt for £3,450 inside. It was possible, of course, that it had also contained the poisoned brandy, but the question, when Lucian had been heading for his own club, with its extensively curated cellar, was *why?* And who would have given it to him?

I glanced at my phone and saw I had a message from Elliot.

Sorry I never replied. I'm good!

There was a minute or two of silence before he added, *Just wanted to check in. How you feeling about tomorrow?*

Nervous, I wrote, and then changed my mind. *I'm ready, I think,* I sent instead.

That's great, came the immediate response. *Am cheering you on from here.*

I stared at the words for a while. A thousand possible replies, and yet none of them felt quite right. As I watched, he went offline again.

I sank onto a stool at my breakfast bar and rested my head against the cool tiles of the counter. As welcome as the encouragement was, it was not helpful to think of Elliot right then.

And yet as I brushed my teeth, the thought of Elliot on a sunlit terrace, leaning against the stone balustrade with a bottle of beer in hand, surfaced so vividly I could almost imagine I was back there. The sounds of a friend's wedding in the ballroom behind us, the two of us—strangers then—both stepping out alone, seeking quiet and air. I remembered the way he'd pushed his sunglasses onto his head, appraising me. The way he'd nodded back toward the French doors, the crescendo of laughter from the speeches inside. "All that love," he'd said. "Very suffocating." A hand extended. "I'm Elliot."

I turned off the lights in the living space on my way to the bedroom, my eye catching on the wall of evidence as I clicked off the lamp. I remembered pacing in front of the one I'd built at the beginning of Marla's trial, Elliot in the doorway behind me where I now stood. *It's four a.m.*, he'd said. *This is insane. It's too much.* The cold way I'd replied, *Then go to bed and leave me alone*, not even turning to look at him.

The following evening, I'd forgotten to turn up to the belated birthday dinner he'd organized for me, a reservation he'd been trying to get for months.

As I got into bed, I pushed the memories away. Forced myself to think of you instead.

48

Gabriel

"K. C."

I DIDN'T HEAR FROM YOU again after that night, and I didn't contact you either. I spent a long time looking back over all our messages and realizing I'd been stupid, that I'd seen something, felt something, that wasn't there. And that made me feel scorched inside, like I wanted to claw the embarrassment out in a big, charred, toxic mess, so I played *Call of Cthulhu* and reread my entire collection of Hellboy comics and generally tried to avoid thinking about the whole thing.

The weeks went on and results day came and I'd done better than expected. Not amazing, but not as average as predicted, and I actually started to think that maybe I would like to go to university, and me and Mum talked a bit about what I could do and where I could go and the loans and how long it would take me to repay them.

"We'll make it work," she said. "I'll help you, if it's what you want."

"You don't have to do that," I said, feeling guilty about how hard she already worked to look after us both.

She ruffled my hair. "I do. How else will you afford the fancy retirement home I want?"

I got kind of carried away, thinking about it. Looking up different courses and apprenticeships, and doing calculations about how much I could save if I worked for a year, or two years, or three, or if I studied part-time. I pictured myself as a business guy in a great suit, or a teacher with elbow patches and possibly a stylish mustache. I even forgot to worry about you for a couple of days.

But then Bart showed up at my house one day with a bag of chips and a shaving rash, and he sat on the end of my bed and told me he'd heard you were living in London.

"I heard she burned Peter Walters's place down too," he said. "She's, like, on the run. She's a fugitive!"

"Don't be crazy," I said, and hated him.

After a while, I did start to miss you. I found myself spending more evenings on the site you'd sent me, the Rabbit Hole, and thinking about all the late-night conversations we'd had about the things we read there, wondering if you were still checking the posts too.

There was a lot of stuff on there that seemed too crazy to be true, but I still liked the way it all made me think.

Months went by while I started applying for temp work. Mum got me a job helping out at the hotel where she worked, just doing some pot washing and glass collecting, and I started applying for apprenticeships for the following year. Pootling along nicely, feeling pretty happy about where I might be going.

Then the first Mr. E post appeared.

A reckoning is coming. Justice will be done.

Keep watching.

I couldn't stop myself. I texted you right then with the link: *Did you see the new post on the RH?*

And straightaway, you started to write back.

49

Max

"Killer Kate"

YOUR TRIAL BEGAN IN A week of early sunshine, the sky a cartoon blue as I walked from the Tube to the Old Bailey. You were the must-see attraction, all of us packed onto the press bench like kids on a school trip. I sat next to the court reporter from the *Mail*. Smiled and said hi to a couple of others I recognized, knowing full well we'd all be competing bitterly for traffic, trying to make sure our coverage came top of the list for anyone googling your name.

The KC leading the prosecution was called Verity Naylor. Sour faced, a voice that didn't so much cut glass as laser it on sight. I crossed my arms and tried to stretch out my legs, already feeling restless and uncomfortable, as we listened to her opening speech.

She told the jury you were facing a four-count indictment, all for murder. She spoke about the "shock wave the killings had sent around our entire nation."

That was milking it, I'll be honest. The public were fascinated, sure, but I'd learned long ago that they were difficult to shock.

"When police arrested Miss Cole," she continued, "police bodycam footage will show you that she made a significant statement—that 'they deserved it.'

"During this trial, you will hear from witnesses who will testify that Miss Cole was a troubled teenager who became obsessed with conspiracy theories. Conspiracy theories that blamed a shadowy group of powerful men for 9/11, for Covid, for all of the world's ills, and that she decided to take matters into her own hands."

You didn't appear to be listening, your gaze flicking from the judge to the ceiling to the public gallery. You rubbed at the corner of your eye, sighed.

"You will hear that she pursued a job at March House specifically because of its connection to these conspiracy theories and that it was there that these four men—all of them fathers, all of them much-loved sons—were cruelly and senselessly murdered.

"You will hear that after those murders took place, Katherine Cole smiled to herself as she made her escape, knowing full well the carnage she had left in her wake."

I turned my attention back to you. The longer I watched, the more it seemed like your indifference was an act. Like it was a matter of pride for you to pretend you didn't care, that you weren't fazed by being in that wooden box in that big, stuffy room, all eyes on you. I could tell by the way you kept checking to see who was watching, the slightest flicker of a smile that kept crossing your face. I knew it then—it was all a show, and deep down, you were enjoying it.

50

Tarun

"Katherine"

WATCHING YOU IN THE DOCK, I felt worried. You were extremely nervous and had told me you felt like vomiting before we'd entered the court, but from a distance, you looked detached, calm. I had prided myself on being able to predict how a defendant would behave on the stand, on tailoring my questions to play to this, to calm those who became aggressive when stressed, to warm up those who might appear too cold or calculated to a jury. I couldn't read you, couldn't tell how you might react under cross-examination or even under my own questioning.

I was pleased we had Judge McQuilliam, who was patient and fair, always rigorously precise in her directions to the jury and her summing up. I was also pleased—or as pleased as one can ever be—with the jury we'd ended up with. Seven women, five men, a reasonable spread of ages, though I might have preferred a couple more on the younger end of the scale, in the hope that being closer to your age might make it easier for them to empathize with you.

I watched them during Verity's opening speech. The juror who'd been selected as foreperson, earnest faced and in his mid-sixties, was making notes and paying you little attention. The woman beside him, white haired and in a neat cardigan, looked faintly repulsed already, and I wondered if she'd be able to stomach the crime scene photos.

"On the night of the tenth of August, 2022, Miss Cole arrived at work prepared to make a quick getaway," Verity said. "Already stowed away in her locker was a backpack of clothes, a laptop, and, the Crown believes, the poison that would end four men's lives."

The juror at the end of the row was a young woman, perhaps late twenties, who hadn't taken her eyes off you since Verity's speech had begun. She was pregnant, a hand absent-mindedly rubbing the small bump beneath her cream blouse. A nurturing type, I might have hoped, though as she watched you, she looked afraid.

"It was a quiet night at March House," Verity continued. "Katherine Cole was assigned to the Voltaire Room, as was often the case during Mr. Wrightman's dinner parties. These dinners followed a typical pattern that would have been very familiar to Miss Cole, alcohol flowing, and this one closed with a bottle of brandy, a favorite of Mr. Wrightman's.

"It was in this brandy that a lethal dose of cyanide was delivered. The murders taking place as Katherine Cole left the club and boarded a bus at a little after midnight."

I returned my attention to you. Noticed the anxious way your eyes kept panning the gallery for your father. As Verity told the jury that "Miss Cole laughed as she did so, delighted by the four lives she had taken," you shook your head, a tiny movement, but perceptible all the same.

51

John

"Kit-Kat"

YOU LOOKED SO AFRAID IN the dock. Fidgeting, the way you always did when you were nervous or uncomfortable as a child. I felt sick for you, my legs shaky.

Murder. I still felt like it was a nightmare, like I might wake up at any minute. Be able to reach for my phone and text you: *I just had the weirdest dream.*

I saw the way your eyes scanned the public gallery, the relief on your face when you saw I was there. The way it disappeared as you realized that your mum wasn't.

She and Bobby were on their way to Scotland. The call had come early the day before. Your uncle Neil found dead in the farmhouse, his shotgun beside him. The end of a long, terrible spiral that had begun with the loss of the business.

It had been almost a year since my and your mother's divorce had been finalized, but still I'd been the first person she phoned. I think she'd expected me to go with her. She hadn't started crying until she realized I wouldn't.

As the prosecution barrister continued her opening speech, I watched the jury. Wondering what they were seeing. What they would think of you.

I tried to catch your eye, wanting to reassure you. Wanting you to know that I would be there each day, that I would make up for all the mistakes we had made.

Wanting you to know that I was sorry.

52

Conrad

"Wildcat"

IT TURNED OUT I WASN'T right for the new role, the big step up Joseph had recommended me for. But a week later, I got a call from the big *big* boss, who'd sat on the panel for my interview. He'd liked some of the things I'd had to say, he said. He was interested in talking to me more.

He was a nice guy, Lucian. Old-school. I ended up meeting him for lunch at Rules—steak and kidney pudding and a wine I didn't dare check the price of. As we ate, I clocked his suit, the Cartier cufflinks. His gray hair was suspiciously full; definitely plugs, I decided.

He expected me to be in awe of him, I think. Wrong-footed by the fact that he, founder of the Wrightman Group, was having lunch with little old me.

I'm not easily wrong-footed, though, and I knew that Lucian had a reputation for keeping an interest in all thirty-two of the companies owned by the group, big and small, and for dropping in to meet staff and invest in their career paths and lord it about in the way you're entitled to when you've turned your granddad's market stall into a billion-pound empire. I knew he'd done that exact lunch with a load of people who'd all ended up in senior roles in some of his best-performing companies, and so the only thing I was feeling was excited.

"You were disappointed not to get the operations director role at Feast, I imagine," he said.

"I was. But I know it was a competitive process."

He nodded. "I thought your answers were very good; I like the way you think. But the other candidate had more experience. A safer pair of hands, maybe."

"Fair enough," I told him.

"Mmm." He topped up both our wineglasses. "It felt like you made a bit of a sideways move when you joined Potbellies. You didn't see a path for progression at AGT?"

"I had a disagreement with my manager in that role," I told him.

"Ah. Dare I ask?"

Honesty was something I was trying out after everything that had happened with Molly, so I said, "I called him a prick."

Lucian scraped the last of his pudding onto his fork. "And was he?"

"I was hotheaded back then. But yeah, I still think he was."

Lucian laughed, put his knife and fork neatly down. "Well, then."

After that he asked if I was a football or a rugby man, told me his favorite book was *David Copperfield*.

On the way back to the Tube, I ducked into Waterstones and bought a copy. I checked my phone as I was paying and saw an email from his secretary, asking me if I could make a monthly meeting. A kind of mentoring arrangement. For now.

Too fucking right I could.

53

Max

"Killer Kate"

I POSTED MY WRITE-UP OF the first day of your trial at seven in the evening, and by the time I checked it at six the next morning, the first conspiracy nut had already come out of the woodwork. *Kate Cole knew the truth*, the comment read. *And Max Todd is a puppet of The Group.*

I knew from experience that more would come. But I refused to feel unnerved, told myself it would make a good sideline in the book—how in telling your story I became part of it. On the way into court that day, I started rereading *Helter Skelter* and wondering how hard I could push the parallels between Mr. E and you lot and Charles Manson and his Family.

Hoping that Anya wouldn't read the article and see that comment.

The first witness called by the prosecution was the bartender from the night of the murders, Sebastian Dwyer. He was giving his evidence via video link from Auckland, where he'd returned home after March House had closed its doors.

He looked nervous, straightening the collar of his pale blue shirt, leaning in too close to the camera. Naylor eased him in with softball questions, asking him how long he'd been working at the club when the murders took place and what his role encompassed.

"And what were your responsibilities on the evening of August tenth, when Mr. Wrightman's party had their booking?"

"I was running the bar in the club lounge, on the first floor."

"During a normal shift, what kind of interaction would you have with a private dining party, as bartender?"

"Not that much, especially when it was one of Lucian's dinners. He liked to be left alone, mostly, and he liked Katie to serve them."

"Why was that?"

He shrugged. "He had kind of a soft spot for her, I guess."

"What kind of interaction would you have with Katherine herself?"

"It would depend on what they were ordering—if they wanted cocktails, shorts, coffees, that kind of thing, she'd come and fetch those from me."

"But not other drinks?"

"Wine, brandy, port, the things that were in the cellar—they were the private dining host's responsibility to fetch and serve. It's supposed to be someone with sommelier training, but I got the impression she'd lied about that on her CV."

"What made you think that?"

He looked uncomfortable. "It was just . . . an impression I got. Gaps in her knowledge, the way she opened a bottle . . . I felt like she'd lied about the kinds of places she'd worked before."

I thought I saw the hint of a smile twitch your face again. After everything Mr. E had told you about the club, you'd lied your way in there—just like your childhood best friend had told me you always did.

Naylor seemed pleased with that detail too. "And on the night of August tenth, did Katie have occasion to come to the first floor bar where you were?"

"Yes. She collected a round of old-fashioneds at the beginning of the dinner."

"Did you notice anything unusual about her demeanor?"

A pause. "No," he said eventually. "She was a bit quiet, maybe."

Probably not the slam-dunk answer Naylor was hoping for, because she pushed him further. "A bit quiet—what was Miss Cole usually like at work?"

Dwyer hesitated again. "Um, Katie could . . . Katie had a temper, for sure. She's one of those people who kind of, you know, carry their own weather system around with them. Like if it's raining on her, you know about it. And if it's stormy, it kind of changes the atmosphere of a room."

I looked at you again. Your expression had darkened, and right then, it was easy to believe him.

54

Tarun

"Katherine"

"SHE HAD A TEMPER . . ." VERITY repeated. "And did that 'weather system,' those stormy moods, affect her work?"

He thought about that. "Sure, I guess . . . She could be short with customers, with me and Cam, tearful if things were going wrong . . . She was just unpredictable. And late a lot, like she always had something else going on."

"Was she late for her shift on August tenth?"

"Yes. Half an hour late, which meant that Cam, our manager, had to set up Voltaire for Lucian's party."

"What time was that?"

"The dinner was booked for six. Katie was supposed to start at five thirty."

"And that's when Camilla Johnson went down to set up the room in her place?"

"Yes. Around five thirty."

"How many guests were in the club lounge with you at that time?"

"A couple of tables, not many. It was quiet."

"How long was it before your manager returned to the first floor with you?"

"About twenty minutes, half an hour?"

"And how long after that did Miss Cole come up to the lounge to collect the cocktail order from you?"

"That was around six fifteen—she was still flustered from being late."

"During that time, Mr. Dwyer, did you notice any of the other patrons leaving the lounge?"

"Not that I recall."

I made a note, underlining it for myself three times.

"And after that, did you see Miss Cole again during the shift?"

Now he became more confident with his answers. "No."

"And what about the end of the shift? Can you tell us what happened as the evening came to a close?"

Though he looked like he'd rather do anything else, he nodded. "I started shutting down the bar around one thirty. But I thought I'd better check that no one in Lucian's party wanted a cocktail or anything to finish their night, so I went down to the ground floor to check in with Katie."

Verity nodded, waited for him to continue.

"She wasn't at the wait station where I expected her to be, so I assumed she was in Voltaire with them. I hung around."

"How long did you wait there?"

"Maybe ten minutes? But it was so quiet down there. And, like, it's meant to be quiet—the dining rooms are supposed to be private, you're not meant to hear people's conversations or whatever—but usually when a party's been drinking and having a good time for what, six, seven hours, you'd be able to hear them laughing and stuff. I started wondering if they'd actually left and Katie had forgotten to tell us." He cleared his throat, then took a sip of water.

Solemnly, he said, "I went and stood by the door and listened. And when I didn't hear anything, I knocked and went in."

As Verity painstakingly, apologetically, made him explain everything he'd seen inside that room, you closed your eyes.

55

Gabriel

"K. C."

AFTER THAT FIRST MR. E post on the Rabbit Hole, the scorched feeling went away, and I was glad we were kind of friends again. You sent me pictures of London—the deer in Richmond Park and the pelicans in St. James's, a mural in Shoreditch you liked, a band you went to see one night because you said the singer looked a bit like me, and a sandwich that you held in front of your face because it was bigger than your head. You told me about the places you found to stay on SpareRoom and couch-surfing websites, and I tried my best not to send back true crime podcasts and Reddit threads.

It felt nice, like a new chapter, the beginning of something good.

Then Covid hit and everything really did go to shit.

Lockdown probably shouldn't have been all bad for someone who was happiest socializing on anonymous forums, but I spent those first few weeks flipping anxiously between news sites and Twitter, finding threads written by preppers and watching *Contagion* and *Outbreak* on repeat like that wasn't the worst idea in the world. I couldn't concentrate on anything, and there wasn't anything to do anyway, except sit and worry and spiral.

You checked in every couple of days because you knew I was anxious, you knew how scary I found the idea of getting sick again. *This is all so crazy*, you wrote, but you made me feel better. You told me you were staying on a narrowboat on a canal with a girl you'd made friends with, sent me pictures of your bare feet hanging above the water and a video of the ducks and swans coming each morning for you to throw old bread to them. *Everything will be all right*, you told me, anytime I needed to hear it.

I miss you, I wrote late one night. I sat staring at the words for a few minutes before adding *being here* at the end and sending it.

I know, you wrote back an hour later. A sad face at the end. I waited as the dots that showed you were still typing flickered over and over.

I can't come home, you wrote eventually. *My uncle lost his business and they all think it's my fault.*

You told me how every morning, you walked along the canal and then cut through back streets until you got to the cemetery where Stephen was. *I sometimes wonder what he'd say about all this,* you wrote. *I wish he was here. He'd be making me bake sourdough and learn a language and do Joe Wicks videos every day for sure.*

My mum was like that, kept trying to make the best of things, even though the hotel was closed and she was constantly terrified of taking Covid into the old people's home. We watched box sets together, tried cooking new things, and while she was working, I found myself spending more time on the Rabbit Hole. Waiting for Mr. E to appear again.

You think this is bad? Soon will come the next stage, he wrote one afternoon. *Are you ready?*

I sat and watched TV with my mum that night, and the prime minister was making a speech. "Let there be no mystery about it," he said. "We will come back stronger."

I picked up my phone and texted you right away. *He said no Mr. E!!!!* I wrote, and then I logged straight onto the Rabbit Hole to check I wasn't the only one who'd noticed.

By the time the second lockdown ended, I got myself a shit job at a warehouse six miles from town, determined to get back on track. I packed boxes all day and slowly started losing my mind from boredom. It was all right for the first few months, when I'd listened to podcasts and music, but then they banned us from wearing headphones, and so I was alone with my thoughts for most of the day, buried in a fleece because it was so freezing in there.

I felt like an ant in that place. I kept thinking about that post. *Soon will come the next stage. Are you ready?*

56

Max

"Killer Kate"

YOUR BARRISTER WAS SWEATING AS he rose to cross-examine Sebastian Dwyer.

"Mr. Dwyer, you stated that Lucian Wrightman had 'a soft spot' for Katherine Cole. What did you mean by that?"

Dwyer looked a bit flustered. "Well, he liked her. He chatted to her when she was serving him, maybe more than he did the other waitstaff. And he'd started requesting her for his private dinners."

"Because he thought she was good at her job, didn't he?"

"I don't know . . . She was confident, I think. He liked that."

"And clearly *he* didn't think she had a temper, because he requested that she be the one to serve some of the most important members of his club—he'd never found her 'stormy,' or able to 'change the atmosphere of a room,' had he?" He heaped on the scorn as he quoted Dwyer's words back at him.

"I'm not sure," Dwyer said, wary now. "I guess not."

"In fact, none of the members of the club who gave witness statements described Katherine as anything other than polite, friendly, and good-tempered."

"Okay," Dwyer said, wrinkling his nose.

"Isn't it the case, Mr. Dwyer, that your recollections have been tainted, perhaps understandably, by the traumatic experience of discovering those four men dead?"

"I don't think so," Dwyer said, a weak answer, and Rao seized on it.

"You don't *think* so, but you can't be sure, isn't that right?"

Now he was properly flustered. "I don't know."

"And you also can't be sure how many patrons were in the club lounge during the time the Voltaire Room was left unattended, can you, when you were setting up for the evening shift alone?"

"I'm pretty sure," Dwyer said, but Rao ignored him, plowing on.

"Because as well as making drinks and restocking the bar, you were also taking the odd quiet moment to check your phone, weren't you?"

Dwyer looked injured. "I don't know," he said quietly. "Maybe."

"In fact, at five fifty-six p.m., you engaged in a seven-minute debate on Twitter with a user about which of Bob Dylan's albums was his best, didn't you?"

Dwyer, bright red now, looked down and agreed that probably he had.

"When you said that you couldn't 'recall' if anyone left the room during that window of time, it's simply not possible for us to trust that *recollection*, is it?"

He'd been a good choice for you, in some ways—kind of cuddly to look at, twinkly eyes in his round face, his own dark curls often poking free of the white wig in a disheveled kind of way. It was a nice balance for your coldness, even if Naylor's icy polish was more impressive.

I googled him during the lunch break and realized where I recognized him from. He'd represented Marla Davis, a woman accused of murdering her husband's mistress a couple of years earlier, a story I remembered covering. I speed-read through some of my old articles, the details coming back to me: the younger woman found stabbed in her kitchen, messages on her phone revealing that she and Paul Davis had planned to run away together. Messages on Marla Davis's phone between her and her best friend confirming that she'd learned of the affair, that she was angry about it. *I could kill them both*, she'd written, one night after two a.m. It was very grubby stuff, Kate. And yet your man Tarun had managed to get her off, calling it, in a statement to the press outside Cambridge Crown Court, "justice served."

He really had been a good choice for you.

That afternoon, the prosecution called the detective in charge of your case, Ross Bowen, Hasan's boss. He was a big guy, hair shaved short, shirt too tight across his chest. Roidy. But quietly spoken, very serious as he gave his name and explained that he'd worked for the Met for twenty years.

The jury was shown photos of the crime scene. The poor fuckers still sitting at that table; Lucian Wrightman with his head thrown back over the chair. Old heartthrob Popov facedown on the floor. Naylor directed the jury to a floor plan of March House, the lobby and the ground floor corridor with its three private dining rooms and a fire escape at the other end; the first floor with the club lounge and kitchen, staff room and toilets.

"DCI Bowen, could you tell us about your team's initial investigation, in terms of identifying a suspect?"

"We were told Miss Cole had been the person serving the party that evening and that she'd fled the premises before the bodies were discovered. That made locating her a priority. An alert was put out, and Katherine was arrested by officers at Paddington station at six thirty-two a.m."

Naylor announced that she wanted to play the bodycam footage from your arrest for the jury.

Everyone likes a bit of video evidence, so there was total silence as it began to play. The beginning was wobbly, the sound muffled, as whichever officer it belonged to ran through a crowd to catch up with you.

You turned at the sound of your name. Your hair was greasy and a mess, an old hoodie thrown over your uniform in a half-hearted disguise, your backpack over one shoulder. You looked stunned, like you couldn't believe you'd been caught.

"Katie Cole, you're under arrest," he said, as he turned you round, pinning your wrists behind your back. "I'm arresting you on suspicion of murder—"

"Get off me," you yelled over him. "That's too tight, you can't—"

"You're being taken into custody for interview," he continued, ignoring you. "You do not have to say anything. But it may harm your defense if you do not mention when questioned something that you later rely on in court. Anything you do say may be given in evidence."

Your face hardened. You looked right at him as you said it: "They deserved it."

Pretty damning, Kate. And straight from the horse's mouth.

While the video played, you looked at the courtroom door. Like you might make a bolt for it.

57

John

"Kit-Kat"

YOU LOOKED SO FRIGHTENED IN the bodycam footage that I had to force myself not to look away. You were thin, exhausted, disoriented. You looked helpless. I barely recognized you.

It was obvious to me that you were confused at first. That when he began to read you your rights, you panicked.

It was obvious to me that you would never have said *they deserved it* if you'd realized what they were talking about. That there had been some kind of misunderstanding.

While the video played, you kept looking toward the door. Like you were hoping for someone to arrive and save you, to stop this once and for all.

When the judge suggested we take a break, I went outside to get some air. It was another hot day, and I leaned against a wall and closed my eyes, letting the sun warm my face. I tried to ignore the image that immediately came of you growing older in a cell, turning your face up to the sky in a bleak prison yard.

When you were small, I imagined so many lives for you. You'd told me you wanted to be a vet, a hairdresser, a dancer. A singer, a pirate. Aged four, you briefly decided you wanted to be a postman after striking up a friendship with ours.

I'd never assumed anything about what the three of you might turn out to be, to do. But standing there, on that empty pavement, I began to grieve for all of the things that could have been and now never would.

It was pointless, and selfish, and I opened my eyes and steeled myself to return to the courtroom. A woman was standing in front of me; sleek blond hair and tailored dress, her arms wrapped round herself as if she were cold.

"You're her dad," she said. Her voice was trembling, and I was afraid, suddenly. I didn't reply.

"Alek was my husband," she said. "We have two children."

I had seen a picture of Aleksandr Popov's son and daughter in the papers; the boy perhaps ten or eleven, the girl younger, both grinning as he stood with his arms round them.

"I'm so sorry for your loss," I said. I wanted to back away, but my legs felt rooted to the ground.

"How am I supposed to tell them?" she asked. Her face had flushed. "How am I supposed to tell them that their daddy is dead and your daughter told the world he deserved it?" She started to cry.

"Please," I said. "I can't even imagine—"

"No," she said. "You can't." Someone had come out of the building looking for her, a woman, older, her face creasing as she saw us together.

"Clara," she said, putting a hand on her arm. She wouldn't meet my eye. "Come on. Let's go and get a coffee."

Clara was still staring at me. "You should be ashamed. You've seen it for yourself in there, and what do you think now? What do you think about that thing you brought into the world?"

I stepped away, blood thumping in my ears. "I'm sorry for your loss," I said again, and I put my head down and walked away, my heart raging with all of the things I wanted to say.

58

Tarun

"Katherine"

I CAME TO SEE YOU in the cells during the break. You were pale, sitting on the narrow cot.

"It's worse," you said. "The video. Seeing it again, seeing them watch it. It doesn't look like me. It doesn't look how I remember it at all."

I did not particularly wish to dwell on the bodycam video. It was perhaps the most damning piece of evidence against you, and I could only hope that when the time came for you to take the stand, you'd be convincing enough that the jury would believe you hadn't meant to say that the men had deserved it. That you were exhausted and confused about what was happening to you, which seemed obvious to me when I compared the you in front of me with the girl in the recording.

"Remember that the jury is always watching you," I said. "Even when a witness is speaking, they're looking at you. Their impression of you is important."

You frowned. "What does that mean?"

"It doesn't mean anything," I said. "I just want you to remember that you're on stage when you're in there."

"Noted," you said, as if this point were painfully obvious. You studied your hands.

"It's harder than I thought it would be," you said.

"It's all going well," I said briskly, and you nodded, your head slightly bowed. When I looked closer, I was surprised to find that you had become tearful.

"What is it?" I asked.

"The photos," you said. "That was . . . It was awful, seeing them like that. I can't stop thinking about it."

I was numb to the crime scene images by then, and I paused, surprised to see how affected you were.

"I'm sorry," I said. "I should have prepared you for those."

You shook your head. "It's fine. I'm fine."

But I paused on my way out, looking back at you again. Uncertain what to make of this new, softer side of you.

When I checked my phone before returning to court, I saw that Elliot had sent me a message: *Go get 'em.*

59

Gabriel

"K. C."

I STRUGGLED FOR A WHILE, even as the rest of the world started recovering. I was classed as clinically vulnerable, so I'd got my vaccine early, but I kept reading all this stuff about it on the Rabbit Hole and kept hearing how people got the virus anyway or how the virus wasn't even real or the vaccination was the actual problem or how chemtrails from planes were the things that would really kill us, and overall, it just felt like it was probably better if I stayed indoors whenever possible.

Then one night, you messaged. *There's a march this weekend*, you wrote. *You should come.*

The thought was wild, like you'd casually invited me to canoe to Alaska or ride a tiger to the shops. I stared at the message, trying to imagine getting on a train, getting on a Tube, standing in a crowd.

Come on, you sent. Like you could read my mind from all the way over there. *It'll be good for you.* A smiley face.

You met me at the station. You were leaning against a pillar and texting, a beam of sunlight catching you perfectly like a spotlight. Your hair was blonder, like you'd been outside a lot, and you were wearing a long black dress thing with a belt and loads of bracelets up both wrists. You looked up just as I came through the ticket barriers, and your whole face lit up with a smile that made me feel like my insides had turned upside down.

I knew I looked like shit. I'd put on weight, let my skin get bad and my hair grow too long, and I felt sweaty already, like I needed a shower. But you wrapped me in the biggest hug. "It's been so long," you said, squeezing me tighter. "I'm so happy you're here."

I hugged you back and hoped my T-shirt didn't feel damp where you were touching me.

"Let's go," you said, linking your arm through mine and guiding me through the crowds. Like you'd been living in the city all your life, like everyone would just move right out of your way.

"I can't believe you came," you said, turning back to grin at me as you led me onto an escalator.

Neither could I as I looked at all the people around us, all the masks and no masks and the grimy handrails and walls and the tunnel we were going into that really didn't seem like it was big enough for that many people to walk through, as I tried not to focus on the smell of food and sweat and dirt and metal and the sound of a million different conversations and headphone songs all at once.

"Of course I came," I said, like I was the easy breeziest. "What are we marching for again?"

You laughed. "It's about these new protest laws that are being proposed," you said. "I don't know that much about it, but Polly says it's a big deal. I told you about Polly, right?"

I nodded. Polly was the girl who owned or rented the narrowboat you lived on, and you'd told me that she cut your hair for you and left dirty dishes in the sink for days, that she microdosed ketamine for depression and sang country songs in the shower, and that you didn't know what would have happened to you in the city if you hadn't met her.

"She's *so* great," you said. "She's really smart. You'll love her."

You dragged me onto the Tube train just as the doors started beeping and slid shut. You found us two seats in the middle of the row, and we fell into them as the train pulled away from the platform.

The carriage was hot and busy, and we stopped in a tunnel for long enough that I started wondering how we'd get out if something bad had happened, but you didn't notice. "Rudy, that's Polly's boyfriend, will be there too, and probably this guy Mat and his girlfriend, Anneka, and maybe some others."

"Great," I said, letting out a sigh of relief as the train started moving again.

"But tomorrow we should go out and be tourists. What do you want to see?"

"Everything," I said, even though the truth was that all I wanted to see was you. I was nervous to move, like I might blink and you'd be gone, like this whole thing was happening in my imagination.

"I've missed you," you said, and everything else just faded away.

We got off the train at Embankment, and you walked so quickly through the tiled tunnels and up the escalator that I started to sweat again trying to keep up.

"Sorry," you said, turning to look at me and noticing. "I said we'd meet Polly outside, and I think we're late."

Polly did look kind of impatient when we found her by the entrance. She had hair the color of beetroot with this little fringe cut halfway up her forehead, and dark eyeliner that made her look sort of mean. But she hugged me tightly when you introduced us. "Heard lots about you," she said, then handed me a cardboard sign with brightly painted letters. *We Can't Be Silenced.*

You grinned at me. "I made that one."

"It's great," I said, and I looked at the one Polly was carrying. Big black letters on a red background: *The Rebellion Starts Here.*

"It's good, right?" she said, seeing me looking.

She had this nervous, jumpy energy, kept glancing around us as we joined the crowd headed toward Whitehall. "We're going to change the world," she said, putting an arm round both of us. Bashing me in the head with her sign in the process, but the sentiment was nice.

"We are," you said, smiling, and behind her back, you reached out and squeezed my hand.

All around us, people were holding hands, linking arms, holding up their homemade signs with messages like *Our Voices Will Be Heard* and *Protect Our Protests!* and *A Fair Free UK.* It made me feel like a part of something, and for a while, I was really happy I'd come. The sun was out as we walked along, and people were leaning out of windows and waving, and I saw a little kid at the window on the top deck of a bus that was stopped at some lights, and I waved at him, and you joined in too. Behind us someone started singing, and up ahead, a guy was handing out ice lollies, and the whole thing started feeling like a giant street party.

But the further we got, the more people there were, and the more police I noticed lining the edges of the road, these ones all kitted out with their riot gear. The singing stopped, and there was a kind of hush as we walked, getting packed in closer together, and Polly nudged you. "Ready?" she asked.

The crowd was so dense by the time we got to Parliament that we stopped moving, suddenly in a big knot of people. I looked around and saw that the atmosphere was changing. People wearing masks had started climbing the railings outside the House of Commons. As we watched, one of them got almost to the top and lit a flare, tossing it over so that it bounced onto the grass I was scared by then, but you just watched, your eyes wide like you were excited, and Polly started up a chant: "Kill the bill! Kill the bill! Kill the bill!"

In front of us, a girl pulled a baseball bat from her backpack, started carrying it in a loose grip by her side. Another flare flew out from the crowd behind us, disappearing into the lines of riot police who were getting into a tighter formation, shield to shield, ready to kettle everyone back.

"There's Rudy," Polly said, darting into a gap between the people in front of us. You were about to follow her.

"K," I said, reaching out to grab your arm. "I'm not sure if this is . . ."

You followed my eyeline to the police, saw the first surge of people rushing to meet them with bottles flying and everyone shouting.

"Let's go back," you said, linking your arm through mine. "I've had enough changing the world for one day."

It was almost night as we walked along the canal, lights coming on in the flats above us and the sky turning peach and purple and gray like a moody bruise. The boat was moored at the end of a long line, black and dark red with little round windows and a bike chained to the deck. You hopped on board and reached back to help me.

"Don't fall in," you said. "You wouldn't believe some of the things I've seen floating in there."

You made us tea and then we lay on the roof of the boat.

"You can't see the stars as well here as you can at home," you said.

I watched as a bank of cloud drifted over the moon. "It's not as dark here," I said. "It feels like tomorrow is never as far away."

"Only you could make light pollution sound poetic," you said. "Such a romantic, aren't you?"

"Am I?" I said, trying to sound sarcastic but secretly pleased.

"Have you been okay?" you asked, edging your head closer so you could rest it on my shoulder. "Sometimes, when we've been messaging, I've been worried about you."

My throat got all dry, so that I had to swallow a few times before I could answer. "I've found things kind of hard lately," I said carefully. "I don't really know why."

"Well, it's obvious, isn't it?" you said, rolling over to look at me. "You need to be here, with me."

60

John

"Kit-Kat"

BACK IN THE COURTROOM, NAYLOR said she wanted to ask DCI Bowen some questions about your arrest and time in custody.

"She was very quiet," he said. "Uncooperative."

They played the tape of your interview then. Showed you sitting with your hair tucked behind your ears as you picked at your lip, a nervous habit I hadn't seen since you were a child. You didn't respond to their questions until prompted by the duty solicitor to offer up a tiny "no comment" each time.

You must have been so scared.

"Fingerprints and DNA swabs were taken from Katherine when she was brought into custody," Naylor said. "Did those match any from the crime scene?"

"Yes. Which wasn't unexpected, obviously, given she'd been serving the victims all evening. But of particular interest to my team was a clear set of fingerprints retrieved from the bottle of brandy that had been identified as containing cyanide. These were a match for Katherine Cole."

In the dock, you clasped your hands firmly in your lap, as if to stop them from going to your mouth.

"Were any other fingerprints retrieved from that bottle?"

"One partial set, which belonged to Lucian Wrightman. The bottle had been found at his place at the table, which potentially indicated he'd poured a further round of drinks after Katherine had left the premises."

"Katherine also had a bag with her when she was arrested," Naylor said. "Members of the jury, you'll find a list of the items that were inside that bag on page seven of your bundle."

A rustle of pages being turned.

"A laptop and mobile phone were taken into evidence," Naylor said. "Were they examined at this stage?"

"Yes. When analyzed, both devices showed a considerable amount of time spent on conspiracy message boards, specifically a site called the Rabbit Hole."

"What kind of content had Katherine been accessing on this website?"

"The Rabbit Hole is a set of forums where users discuss and swap evidence to support a range of conspiracy theories. Of particular interest to us were posts Katherine had repeatedly visited, made by a user known as Mr. E. In these posts, Mr. E claimed that a sinister organization called the Group met at a secret location in London in order to manipulate the public for their own profit and power."

I felt sick. I remembered you showing me that video of the 9/11 attacks when you were a teenager and wondered if it was the same website. If I'd spoken to you properly then, instead of shutting the conversation down, would any of this be happening now?

Naylor nodded. "And why were those posts of particular interest?"

"Because users of the Rabbit Hole had decided that March House was that secret location."

My heart sank. You looked down at your feet.

"Were you able to track where the defendant went after leaving March House?"

"Yes, as part of our inquiries, we were able to locate CCTV footage of her boarding a bus."

The jury was shown a clip of that footage. You were sitting in a seat near the back, your face slightly turned toward the window, and you were smiling.

"Where did that bus take Miss Cole?" Naylor asked.

"Katherine disembarked at a stop near a military graveyard, where we discovered her brother is buried."

Stephen. The thought was a gut punch.

When I looked at you this time, you were already watching me. A terrible sadness on your face.

61

Tarun

"Katherine"

I ROSE TO FACE THE detective. I began my cross-examination by revisiting the list of your belongings that had been seized as evidence. The backpack containing your laptop, your phone, your clothes. A hairbrush, your sketch pad. An old tube of mascara and an open bag of jelly sweets.

"No poison," I said. "No vessel in which it might have been transported?"

"No," he said neutrally.

"And no such item has been retrieved during subsequent investigations, has it?"

"No."

I nodded, leaving a small pause before moving on. A kind of mental underlining for the jury: crucial evidence was missing.

"DCI Bowen, who would have been the person responsible for assessing Katherine Cole's mental state after her arrest?"

"That would be the custody officer."

I checked my notes. "Sergeant Rachel Peters."

"That's correct."

"It was Sergeant Peters's job to determine whether Miss Cole was fit to be detained and questioned, and to authorize her detention, wasn't it?"

"Yes."

I found myself settling into the rhythm of my questions. A kind of muscle memory kicking in. "And Sergeant Peters's assessment was that

Miss Cole was well and able to be interviewed, without requiring a mental state examination?"

He cleared his throat. "That's correct," he said again.

"Sergeant Peters isn't still in her role as custody officer, is she?"

Now he shifted his weight, looking warily at Verity. "Not currently."

"No," I said, pretending to consult my notes again. "Sergeant Peters is currently awaiting the results of an internal investigation after a formal complaint was lodged about her conduct. That's correct, isn't it?"

Bowen agreed that it was.

I asked for the video of your interview to be played again. You were staring at the wall, picking at your lip, your face. It was difficult to make out in the footage, but it looked to me—and I hoped to the jury—as if you were trembling.

"Do you know what a person who is in shock looks like?" I asked. "Or a person in a dissociative state?"

"I'm not qualified to make mental health assessments," he said, but he looked, as we all did, at your face paused on the screen, your eyes wide and dark and staring at the wall.

I glanced at you and saw you were also looking at the picture with interest. As if you were studying a stranger. It unnerved me, and I turned away quickly.

"It's a fact, isn't it, DCI Bowen, that Sergeant Rachel Peters was not up to the job she had been employed to do, and that given Katherine's behavior in custody, Sergeant Peters should have asked the force medical examiner for their assessment of Katherine's mental state before deeming her fit for interview?"

"I don't know," he said. "That was not my responsibility."

"No, your responsibility was to catch a murderer, wasn't it? And you were so certain you'd done that in record time, you threw all respect for due process to the wind."

His neck had started to become blotchy. "No," he said, with force.

"You didn't properly investigate any other possible suspects before charging Miss Cole, did you? You didn't even request the guest list for the tenth of August from March House until almost five p.m. the following day."

"I believe that's correct. But I have confidence we pursued all leads with every resource available to us."

"Really?" I tried to sound incredulous. "Well, I suppose that's true in one respect, DCI Bowen." I took a moment to page through my notes, as though I had all the time in the world now. My apparent confidence in a case can make all the difference to a jury. "You and your team have spent a lot of time reading the material on the Rabbit Hole, haven't you?"

"We have."

"What kinds of things do users on the Rabbit Hole have to say about the police?" I asked.

He licked his lips, cleared his throat. "They aren't our biggest fans."

"They don't trust you, do they?"

A nervous half laugh. "They don't."

I nodded. "In fact, the phrase 'don't trust the police' appears over five thousand times on the site, doesn't it?"

"I'll take your word for it."

"Don't trust the police, don't trust the media, don't trust the government. It's there time and time again, isn't it?"

"Okay."

"And it's likely that someone who has absorbed that message for years, since they were a teenager, would have an extreme reaction to being arrested by police officers, isn't it?"

He let out a long, displeased breath at that. "I suppose so," he conceded. "Yes."

"So it's possible that the kind of response you describe seeing in custody—quietness, uncooperativeness—might be caused by fear and distrust, rather than guilt, isn't it?"

"I wouldn't like to speculate," he said grimly, though of course I had already done that for all of us.

62

Conrad

"Wildcat"

AS OUR MONTHLY MEETINGS WENT on, I came to like Lucian. Sometimes we'd meet for lunch or a coffee; sometimes I'd be summoned to his office on the thirty-sixth floor of Wrightman HQ. He was all business for the first thirty minutes, wanting a rundown of everything I'd done, wanting to go through various performance reports for Potbellies to see what I thought about each set of results.

Absolute piece of piss. I'd been prepping for this since the day I'd started working there, could've done it in my sleep. Studying product lines and retail data, making sure I was confident each time I went in and told him I thought we should drop a range or that another supplier was cheaper.

"I'm impressed," he said to me once. "Philip needs to watch his back."

After a while, he started showing me the reports for other companies in the group: Martha's, the small chain of restaurants he owned, and Feast, the catering company. Not because he actually cared about my opinion but because he wanted to make sure I had one, that I understood the numbers.

Toward the end of each session, we'd talk about other stuff. At first it was the market or news from other parts of the group. Politics, sometimes, which took more prep work from me, given I had zero interest.

One day, a few months in: "You married, Conrad?"

A wistful smile from me. "Not yet, no." Deciding to avoid the whole Molly story.

"Enjoy the freedom," he said. "I'm on my third. Gets expensive."

It felt like a kind of friendship was starting. After that, he'd occasionally talk about one or other of his exes, the three kids he had between them. He had two, aged five and seven, with the new wife too—you had to wonder how he had the energy—and there always seemed to be someone, wife or ex-wife or offspring, needing his attention. With the younger ones, it was all badly behaved nannies or chicken pox or school fees. But the older ones were more trouble. His eldest, Violet, was at university and what Lucian referred to as "highly strung." That seemed to be code for "costs a lot in therapy bills." Her brother, Hunter, sounded like a complete fuckup. I showed up to the office once while Lucian was on the phone with him. Little shit had written off his Beamer while stoned out of his tiny mind and was calling from the police station.

I said nothing, of course. Acted like I hadn't heard.

The epitome of discretion. Of capability.

"I'm going to have to take a rain check," Lucian said as he hung up. "Let's get lunch next week. I want to talk to you about something."

That was at the beginning of 2021, and it turned out he had a promotion in mind for me: operations director at a business he'd just acquired, a liquor company called Kindred.

"It's small right now," he said, over another lunch at Rules, "but it'll look good on your CV. And it's a step on the right path."

"Thank you," I said. "I won't let you down."

Thinking: here we go.

I moved into a new place shortly after that, an apartment overlooking the water at Surrey Quays with a balcony and a huge master bedroom, a private gym, and a concierge service.

I didn't think about you for a long time—or at least if I did, it was a fleeting thought, tinged faintly with shame, regret.

Okay. I'll admit the memory still excited me too.

Each evening I scrolled half-heartedly through dating apps, and some nights I picked up girls in bars. I went through the motions of going on dates, but I guess a part of me still hoped that Molly and I might get back together. We still messaged every now and again—she'd send me an article she thought I'd be interested in, and I'd send her funny videos I knew she'd like. The thawing of the ice age you'd started between us, and maybe the beginning of us getting back to who we'd almost been.

It felt like everything was going my way.

63

Gabriel

"K. C."

MY MUM DROVE ME TO the coach station, and we sat in the car for a minute after she'd turned the engine off. I could tell she was trying not to cry. "I can finally turn your room into a yoga studio at least," she said.

"Charming."

"Take a lover."

"Gross."

"Take several."

"Sure, Mum."

She gave my shoulder a squeeze. "My boy, off to the big city," she said. "I feel old."

I got lost trying to find the address you'd given me. Took a wrong turn out of the Tube station and walked for twenty minutes in the opposite direction, the straps of my backpack rubbing painfully against my shoulders. I checked the map on my phone again, thinking I had to have gone wrong somewhere, because I was looking up at a grotty, empty gray office block that seemed like the place where happiness went to die. I read your text for the twentieth time—and when I looked up at the building again, there you were, waving at me from the fifth-floor window.

Wait there, you mouthed, and I almost dropped my backpack on the pavement in relief.

"Hello, friend," you said when you appeared a couple of minutes later, a beanie over your hair and big hoop earrings in your ears. You gave me a hug. "Find it okay?"

"Sure, no problem."

I followed you round the side of the building, wondering why you were ducking under some ancient-looking scaffolding and pulling open a cracked fire door.

"Hey, what is this place?" I called after you, and you just looked back over your shoulder and grinned.

"Keep an open mind," you said, holding the door for me.

The stairwell was dirty, full of plaster dust and crumbled ceiling tiles, and it smelled of spilt beer and piss.

"A really open mind," you said, and I clutched the straps of my backpack anxiously as we climbed up five flights. My legs were burning, and I started wondering where in my bag I'd put my inhaler.

"Home sweet home," you said brightly as we rounded the landing on the fifth floor. You put your arm round me and led me through the double doors, and I blinked as I tried to take it all in.

It was a big, open-plan space that had obviously been an office because there were still marks on the thin gray carpet where the desks and filing cabinets had been, a few sad-looking chairs wheeled off to one side. Someone had tacked string from some of the beams and hung fabric to make kind of curtained-off rooms around the edges, like the kind of fort my mum used to make me with a sheet and the kitchen chairs on rainy days. The whole place had a faint smell of smoke and weed and bodies, and in the middle were some old cushions and wood pallet sofas, where Polly and some others were sitting. I felt my face get hot, and you squeezed me closer.

"You remember Polly," you said, and I noticed right away that she was wearing one of your dresses.

"And this is Rudy." The guy sitting with Polly got up on long legs, pushing a hand through his wild hair. He had pale eyes and pointy eyebrows that made me think of a vampire. When he came over to shake my hand, his was dry and cold, which felt like further evidence.

"Welcome," he said. "Any friend of Kat's is a friend of ours."

"And this is Mat and Anneka," you said as another couple waved from one of the sofas. "And that's Jaz and Tom, and Leah and Grace . . ." I started panicking at all the names I had to remember, all the faces staring back at me, and stopped hearing what you were saying.

We all said hi, and I stood there kind of awkwardly.

"The others will be back later," you said. "Want to dump your stuff in my room?"

"Yeah," I said, relieved, and followed you over to a corner where two huge sheets of pink and purple fabric hung from the beams. They caught the sun as you pulled one back, sending literal rose-tinted light across all your things. You had a mattress made up neatly with blue sheets and a patterned throw with tiny mirrors stitched in. There was a threadbare old armchair and a coffee table, a stack of sketchbooks, and clothes folded on the floor beside the bed.

"This is really cool," I said, setting my bag down.

You grabbed my hand. "Come on—let me show you the best bit."

You dragged me out through a fire door at the back of the room and up another dark stairwell. "I hope you're excited," you said, but I was mostly trying not to trip on the concrete steps. You burst through the door at the top, letting in bright sunlight, and I felt kind of dazzled and dizzy as I stepped out onto the roof with you.

It was a flat, wide space with low walls that definitely did not seem to comply with any sane health and safety regulations, and beyond it, I could see what felt like the whole of London. Skyscrapers sparkling in the sun, a million buildings and roads tangled up for miles and the river in the distance.

"Welcome home," you said, spreading your arms to show off the view like you'd arranged it just for me, smiling at me as if I were the best thing you'd ever seen.

I felt so hopeful that day, so happy that you'd invited me. I felt like I'd do anything for you.

64

Max

"Killer Kate"

A WEEK INTO YOUR TRIAL, I checked my phone one morning and saw that overnight I'd finally received a reply from Hunter Wrightman. That perked me up. *What u want to know?* he'd written, a man of few words.

I wrote back quickly, still blinking away sleep. *I'd love to talk to you about your dad, what he was like.* Families tend to appreciate that approach—the chance to say nice things in public, a way to cancel out all the grubby, grim headlines that spring up round a trial.

He sent a single word straight back, no punctuation: *why.*

Bit of a weird question, but I couldn't tell if it was hostile or not, so I decided to answer it as if it were genuine. *It sounds like he was a good person,* I wrote. *He deserves the coverage, not his murderer.*

Laying it on too thick, probably, but he was a kid. Hook baited, I waited to see if he'd bite.

I checked my latest article about your trial: "Kate Cole 'Repeatedly Visited' Bizarre Online Conspiracy Theories About March House Before Murders, Court Hears." Not as dramatic as the previous day's: "Kate Cole Said Victims 'Deserved It.'" But still, the comments were racking up. I scanned them as Anya showered in the en suite, singing "Hotel California" to herself.

Not conspiracy theories, read the first one. *THE TRUTH.*

Max Todd choke on ur lies, read another, from someone with the username @MrEsCat.

Die u Olympus scum was a particularly charming one further down.

You're next was the last comment on the list, and I stared at that one for a while as Anya hit the chorus and an improvised key change, trying to push away the annoying creep of fear at the back of my mind. It made me angry, that feeling. It made me want to find Mr. E, to know who this person was, what they'd wanted to achieve. I wanted to rip the mask away, to show all of you, you gullible, dangerous idiots, exactly how stupid you'd been.

"Dad?" Albie appeared at the bedroom door, rubbing his eyes. One leg of his spider-patterned pajama bottoms rucked up to the knee, his hair standing up on one side. "I had a bad dream."

I flipped back the corner of the duvet, and he climbed in, tucking himself under my arm. Soft and warm and still so little—I forgot that a lot of the time. I locked my phone and tossed it onto the nightstand.

"Velociraptor in the kitchen again?" I was still in the doghouse for watching *Jurassic Park* with him six months earlier.

He shook his head. "Edward Scissorhands."

"Ah." Another error in parental judgment that I was glad Anya hadn't yet got wind of.

She came out of the bathroom in a towel then. "Good morning, pickle."

Albie pulled down the duvet on her side of the bed and she got in next to him. "I had a bad dream," he said, the snitch, but before I had to explain, her phone rang.

It was her sister, a perpetual disaster with an unrivaled radar for the most shit heel of men, and, predictably, it was a call that turned into an hour of murmured *I know*s and *Of course you didn't*s. That left me having to dress Albie and pack him off to school.

He was in a dawdling mood, with a hundred pressing questions to ask me, ranging from the contents of the lunch box I'd shoved in his backpack to why we didn't have a dog and how I'd survive a bear attack. By the time I dropped him at the gates, I felt like I'd been the one being cross-examined.

I made it to court just in time, hot and irritable and desperate for another coffee.

The witness called was Bianca Errani, a digital forensics technician from the Met, who looked nervous in her gray suit, fiddling with her engagement ring as she took the stand and stated her name and job title.

"And what does that role mean, specifically with regards to this case?" Naylor asked her.

"I examined a laptop and mobile phone belonging to the defendant."

"We've heard from DCI Bowen that these devices showed a significant amount of time spent on a website called the Rabbit Hole, and in particular to several posts referencing March House."

Errani nodded, dropping her hands to her sides. "Yes, the browser history and cache showed thousands of visits to that website, over a period of several years."

Naylor turned to the jury bench. "I'd like to direct your attention now, members of the jury, to pages ten to twenty in your bundle, where some of Katherine Cole's most-visited threads on the Rabbit Hole are reproduced."

First up were the various 9/11 threads you'd spent a lot of time on as a teenager.

My brother was killed in Afghanistan, you'd written in one of your early replies. *He died for this lie.*

You looked up at the gallery as Naylor read that one out, then down at the floor.

She moved quickly on to some of Mr. E's greatest hits, from that very first post about the Group to the posts that specifically referenced the attendance of a world leader and a member of the royal family.

"'They planned a pandemic and soon will come the next thing. Are you ready?'" She paused and looked up at the jury. "That's from March 2021."

Next came the one I'd been expecting: "'Another dinner at Olympus tonight. New plans ready to be put into action. Something is coming. Question everything. E.'"

"On this particular post," Naylor said, an elegant nail tapping her own copy of the transcripts, "we have the first occasion a user speculated that 'Olympus' might in fact refer to March House."

"That's correct. After that, March House was mentioned as a potential location frequently."

"Did Mr. E respond to these comments?"

"Mr. E upvoted several comments naming March House, which was unusual activity from that account. It caused a lot of excitement among the other posters."

"And in the months that followed, Mr. E continued posting references to events that had supposedly taken place at 'Olympus,' or, as Rabbit Hole users believed, March House." She turned the page and read out several more: "'A new swimming pool was built at the home of an MP today while he ate lunch at Olympus. A pool built on profits from selling our lives and liberties. Are you angry yet?'" and "'Three of the Group drank champagne at Olympus today while discussing the weapons technology they're exporting to Iran. Trust nobody. Keep your eyes open. E.'"

Naylor put down the page she'd been reading from and turned to Errani. "Katherine Cole began her job at March House two weeks after that, in May 2022. Based on your analysis, could one reasonably draw the conclusion that at that point in time, Miss Cole was aware of the connection Rabbit Hole users had made between these conspiracy theories and March House?"

Errani cleared her throat. "Those posts had been accessed on multiple occasions before that date, yes."

"And in the weeks leading up to August tenth, 2022, did Katherine Cole use either of her devices to look up information about any of the victims?"

Errani nodded. "There was search history regarding both Lucian Wrightman and Aleksandr Popov."

"The defendant had shown a specific interest in those men and their backgrounds, prior to the evening of their deaths."

"Yes."

The jury was directed to the page in their bundles where these searches were listed, an entry on August 8, 2022, two days before the murders:

Lucian Wrightman corrupt.

Aleksandr Popov evil.

If looks could kill, Kate, you would have added both Naylor and Bianca Errani to your tally right there and then.

65

Conrad

"Wildcat"

I WENT TO VISIT MY mum one Sunday about six months after I'd started my role at Kindred. I turned up with flowers, the same way I always did, wondering which version of her I'd get that day: apron on and dinner already in the oven, or three wines down and primed for some casual character assassination.

It was neither, that week. Though she poured the first wine before I'd even got my trainers off.

"You've not been round for a while," she sniffed. "I've been ill."

"What's been wrong?" I asked, curious which answer she'd choose from her usual lineup. Never *the mother of all hangovers*, which would have been the only honest one.

"Nothing." She lit a cigarette and brought the wineglass and bottle over to her armchair, so I got myself a beer.

"I was messaging Molly," she said. One of her little conversational darts; I didn't give her the satisfaction of reacting.

"Oh yeah?"

"Mmm. She's got herself a nice new boyfriend."

I won't lie. That one hurt. I took a slow breath, then said, "Yeah? That's great."

"It is. She deserves someone who treats her right."

"She does," I said. Thinking: I'll kill this fucking guy.

"You miss her, I bet."

"I do." Remembering Molly on the beach, the day I proposed. The happiest I'd ever made anyone.

"You'll be all right," Mum said. "Never lonely if there's a mirror at hand."

She started crying about an hour later, talking about this guy who'd dumped her three, four years earlier. "I gave him everything," she said, refilling her drink. "And what did I get back?"

I'd heard the story too many times but still hadn't found an answer she liked, so I stayed quiet.

"Pull that face all you want," she said. "You're the one who ruined my life. If I hadn't had you, I'd have been an actress. I'd have been famous."

"I know, Mum," I said.

Thinking: I'll give you the Oscar myself at this point.

That night you popped up in my message requests. Just a single word: *hi.* Followed by a smiley face.

And before I had time to stop the self-destruct urge pumping through me, I typed it right back: *hi:).*

66

Tarun

"Katherine"

YOU LOOKED ANXIOUS WHILE BIANCA Errani was on the stand, though you didn't seem to be paying particular attention to her testimony. I watched you scanning the gallery, your lips red and sore where you kept picking and biting at them. So different from the way Marla had sat, her posture elegant, her face immaculate, and yet it made me uneasy in its own way, your clear discomfort.

It made you look guilty.

I rose for cross, sweating beneath my robes.

"Ms. Errani, none of the victims were referred to in any of Mr. E's posts, were they? By name or otherwise?"

"No. Mr. E never named specific individuals."

"And they were never suggested by any users on any of these threads, were they?"

"Not to my knowledge."

"Nor were they, or March House, mentioned in any post from the account allegedly belonging to Katherine Cole."

"No," she conceded.

"In fact, it's the case, isn't it, that Katherine Cole hadn't posted about *anything* on the Rabbit Hole for almost eighteen months prior to the murders? That, as is often the case with teenage pastimes, she had grown out of it, lost interest?"

"She hadn't posted," Errani said calmly. "But she was still viewing the site regularly, including visiting the threads regarding March House."

I had succeeded in securing a defense witness who was an expert in online radicalization, planning to swiftly dismantle this as atypical of extremist behavior, so I moved on.

"It's hardly unusual for a young waitress, working in an exclusive establishment such as March House, to idly google some of the more famous patrons she encountered there, is it?"

"Your Honor, the witness can't possibly have knowledge of how 'idly' Miss Cole did anything," Verity cut in.

Judge McQuilliam raised an eyebrow at me.

"I'll withdraw that adjective," I said pettily.

"You can answer the question," the judge told the witness.

"Not especially unusual," Bianca said, more coldly now. "Though googling whether they were corrupt or evil doesn't seem that casual."

This had been a risk of raising the Google searches, and I feigned confidence as I said, "Really? In a luxury venue like March House, which prided itself on its extravagance, and where politicians and oil executives dined during the cost-of-living crisis, you think it unusual that someone might have questions about their moral fiber? That's not the same as wanting them dead, is it?"

Bianca Errani swallowed. "No. I suppose it's not."

"And there was no evidence," I continued, "found on either of the defendant's devices that suggested she wanted *anyone* dead, was there? She hadn't been researching cyanide or its effects? Attempting to purchase any kind of poisonous substance?"

Errani clasped her hands in front of her, shrugged lightly. "No. Not on those devices."

I thanked her and confirmed I had no further questions.

I looked at Ursula on the bench behind me as I sat down, and she smiled, gave me a flash of a thumbs-up, low down where no one else would see. I took a long, slow breath, replaying the conversation to myself, already analyzing each beat.

But when I looked at you, you were no longer looking anxious. For a second, I thought I saw a detached, cool sort of smile cross your face too.

That night, I found my gym clothes at the bottom of a drawer and dressed in them, ignoring the way the waistband dug into my gut. I took an old water bottle from the cupboard, found my AirPods. I picked up my phone, ready to head to the building's basement gym, a facility I hadn't used in at least two years. And then I sat back down, unlocked the phone, and called Elliot.

"Let me guess," he said when he answered. "You're about to resort to the treadmill."

"I thought perhaps the bike."

"Safer. You're not getting any younger."

"Hmmm."

"So it's been as smooth a return to work as could have been expected, then?"

"It's worse." I fiddled with my AirPods, tossing them gently in my palm like dice. "I don't think I'm rising to the challenge."

"I don't believe that." He yawned and I imagined him stretching, running a hand down the back of his neck. Sometimes when he was thinking, he pulled idly at the curls of hair there.

"I'm worried I wasn't ready."

"No you aren't," he said. "You're worried she's guilty."

I swallowed. "The thought has crossed my mind."

I got up and wandered the length of the living room, studying the coving and admiring the cobwebs that collected there. I needed to find a new cleaner.

"I'm not sure I'm really back to myself yet. After everything."

"Well," he said, voice gentle. "It cost you a lot."

"It cost me you."

"Please," he said with a tut. "I'm far more complex than that."

I was silent for a second, summoning my courage.

"I'm sorry," I said. "I was a terrible partner, I realize that now."

"No." The humor had gone from his voice and he sounded sad. "You weren't. It was just difficult to watch at times. Work—it just . . . It meant so much to you. Nothing else could compete."

"Look how that turned out."

He murmured sympathetically. "How are you feeling now?"

"Therapy helped. I think."

"Glad to hear it."

I let my gaze fall on the documents pinned on the wall. Wondering what my therapist would make of the display.

"And everything's okay with you?" I asked.

"All good here. Working on a piece about the subsidized catering in the House of Commons. Binging *Gilmore Girls* again. The usual."

The mental image produced an ache in my chest. "There are other shows, you know."

"Why would I need those?"

A photo pinned on the wall caught my attention, and I wandered over to it, leaning close to try and make out the detail at the edge of the frame.

"I read your profile of the new Green Party leader," I said. "I thought it was very good."

"Thank you." He sounded genuinely pleased. "That means a lot."

I plucked the photo from the wall and took it over to the counter, where the light was brighter.

"Give yourself a break on this one, okay? No treadmill. Maybe yoga. Meditation. One of those gong sound bath things."

I laughed. "Can you really see me at a sound bath?"

"I'd pay good money to."

I sat down at the breakfast bar. "I'm still wondering if there's something in the property venture," I mused. "A business contact with a grudge against the four of them because of it . . . But I can't find a way in."

"T, it isn't your job to prove who did it," he said, with kindness. "You only have to show that there's doubt that she did."

"I know," I said.

But I knew that, for me, that wouldn't be enough this time.

67

Gabriel

"K. C."

WHEN IT HAD BEEN OFFICES, the place was called the Caledonia Building, but now you all called it the Cally. Rudy had been the one who'd found it. He'd squatted in places before—an old hotel and then a mansion that belonged to some billionaire who didn't even notice for a year that twenty people had moved in.

"We had a pool in the basement," he told me that first night. "Four-poster beds, fur rugs . . . It became, like, this art collective, man. Painting murals all over the walls, turning it into this thing of beauty." He ran his hands through his hair, which I was starting to notice he did whenever he was excited about something. "You should've seen it. Actually, I think you *can* still see it—google 'Harris Lowe house takeover,' and there are photos."

He watched me with impatient owl eyes until I got my phone out and googled it. I scrolled through the photos of the giant entrance hall and bedrooms and massive dining room with their spray-painted walls— some cool things, like a lizard crawling up the banister and a whole forest of foxgloves and ferns around a bedroom, but mostly just a big smudgy mess of reds and blacks.

"Nice," I said.

"It's a housing rebellion," he said. "Need not greed, you know?"

I *didn't* know if I knew exactly what that meant, but I nodded along like I did.

"Check it out," he said, pulling his T-shirt down by the neck to show me a scar on his shoulder. "I got dragged out by the cops, and the fuckers did this."

I made what I hoped was the right noise and tried not to picture us all being dragged down the five flights of concrete stairs in the Cally.

I found it hard to sleep that night, even with you next to me. We didn't have a pool or fur rugs, but I kept imagining the owners coming to put all the desks and chairs back in, a load of people in work clothes queuing up the stairs with coffees and briefcases, waiting to get back to their places.

The next morning, when I got up, feeling shy, you were waiting for me with a cup of tea.

"You do get used to it, I promise," you said, rubbing my back and laughing when I yawned.

You were right. Everyone was so friendly, always offering food or drink or making space for me to join their conversations, that I started to relax and feel more confident. Leah liked Warhammer, and Jaz always had a million different books he thought I should read. Tom was into bird-watching, and I liked to go up on the roof and sit with him and learn all their different songs.

I guess I hadn't really realized how lonely I was until I wasn't anymore.

And best of all, I had my best friend back. Sometimes you came to sit on the roof with me and I could point out the things I'd learned from Tom, the see-saw-see-saw song of a great tit—*Always good to see those,* you said, and I blushed as I laughed—the rattling call of a magpie, the warbly whistle and twiddle of a robin. Once we even saw the bright green flashes of parakeets flitting between buildings. Sometimes you sat and told me stories about the café where you were working, where your manager was always drunk and making mistakes with the food and trying to feel up the waitresses and where you once put laxatives in his thermos of Malibu and pineapple juice.

"It kept him out of the way for the whole night," you said. "And we all got to actually keep our tips for once."

I thought you were a hero.

One morning I saw a post from Mr. E about the protest we'd been to.

The Group are angry about the marches in London last month. The people have a voice and that scares them. Keep fighting -E.

I felt happy, reading that. I felt like I was on the right side, that I was doing something good.

68

John

"Kit-Kat"

ALONE IN BOBBY'S FLAT, I lay down on the spare bed after I got back from court that afternoon, still in my suit, and thought about the computer forensics expert and the things you were supposed to have believed in so passionately that you had murdered four people. That you might spend the rest of your life in prison because of these stories—bad men inventing pandemics and wars, controlling us through radio waves—seemed unthinkable; as I replayed the day then, in the dim light of the small, warm room, it felt so surreal that I began to worry I was having some kind of out-of-body experience or total breakdown.

I fished my phone from my pocket and found your mother in my contacts, hesitating before I pressed call.

"Hi." She sounded drained, her voice flat.

"How are you?"

I'd stopped being afraid of asking stupid questions some time ago.

"I've spoken to the coroner, and I've made arrangements for the funeral." She gave me the details, neither of us acknowledging that this was not an answer to my question.

"I'll be there," I said.

"You don't have to."

The topic of Neil had started many arguments between us during the final days of our marriage. His mood had become increasingly dark over all three lockdowns, and each time she came back from what remained of the farm, the buildings slowly falling into disrepair, she'd been bitter about the world and our life, as if his outlook were catching.

"Of course I'll be there," I said.

There was a long pause before she asked, "Does she know?"

"I haven't told her." I stared at a mark on the ceiling. "I thought she had enough to think about right now."

She was quiet for a while. "The pictures they keep printing in the papers . . ." She swallowed.

"I try to avoid them."

"She looks so like my mother."

I drew in a breath. "Sometimes. Yes."

"It always terrified me."

"I know it did. But she isn't like her, Sarah."

Her voice was thicker when she spoke again. "I know you blame me—"

"I don't."

I had told this lie many times; in late-night arguments and counseling sessions, to our mediator and to your brother. It had always felt like a kindness—but whether it was for myself or for her, I'm still not sure.

I don't think she'd ever believed it. "I should go," she said.

"I'm here," I said. "If you need me."

She cleared her throat. "I'll be fine. There's a lot to do."

After we hung up, I lay there alone for a long time.

69

Conrad

"Wildcat"

I SHOULD HAVE PUT A stop to it. The morning after that first message, in the cold light of sober day, I should've blocked you. I'd already extracted myself once, and you'd done enough damage then.

What can I say? I kept thinking of Molly and the nice new boyfriend, and there you always were, so eager to please. With your sweet little questions about my day. Your compliments.

Your photos.

So: no blocking. I kept replying. I liked having you there in my pocket, so quick to respond whenever I threw you a bone—a *Good day?* or *How's it going?* Your replies running over three, four, five messages as if you were too excited to stop yourself pressing send before you'd finished typing.

It never took much to prompt you into sending another photo.

That body, wildcat.

I still think about it.

Lucian was pleased with me. In the post-lockdown world, a business bringing luxury booze to your door was still proving popular, and my first year's figures were stellar.

"I had a good feeling about you," he said, grinning at me as he ordered another martini to celebrate. "And I always trust my gut."

"Thanks for taking a chance on me," I told him.

That was me: flavor of the month, favorite child. Not that his actual kids were much competition. During lockdown, Leandro, fifteen, had confessed to blowing fifty grand on cryptocurrency and been suspended from school for circulating a photo of a fellow pupil's tits. The first part Lucian had told me; the second I'd gleaned from snatches of overheard conversations and texts I'd seen him exchanging with his second ex, Mimi. Violet had dropped out of uni for a second time and been packed off on some kind of luxury retreat, and Hunter, the car smasher, had thrown a party in his mother's Belgravia townhouse and caused hundreds of thousands of pounds worth of damage.

They made it easy, these kids. Easy for me to step up and be the son he'd always wished he'd had.

A week later, we were sitting in a cab, on the way back from a tour of Kindred's new warehouse, and he was busy scrolling through his phone—flicking back and forth between the FTSE and BBC Sport, occasionally opening a chain of text messages from his current wife, Ilse, about the summer home they were thinking of buying.

"I've got a meeting at March House this afternoon," Lucian said. "Are you a member yet?"

When I told him no, he nodded. "Let's fix that," he said.

March House had been on my radar for a while, a constant feature of Lucian's stories. I itched to get inside, to be someone who could drop it casually into conversation: *Oh, I've seen him around at the club.*

Did I have five grand a year to spare on membership? Maybe not, though I was certain the networking alone was worth far, far more. And for the status . . . Well, it's hard to put a price on that.

Did I let on that I'd been desperately hoping for that invitation for months by then?

No way.

"Thanks," I said, as casually as I could manage. "That'd be great."

70

Max

"Killer Kate"

I'D SPENT SO LONG LOOKING at photos of March House, in- and out-side of that courtroom, that turning up in person almost felt like arriving at a movie set. It was another miserable, rainy day but warm still, and I stood on the doorstep sweating under my Barbour—Anya had bought the three of us matching ones, another nail in my middle-class, National-Trust-patron coffin—waiting for someone to answer the buzzer.

I'd half expected Hunter Wrightman to send some kind of minion, but there he was himself, dressed in an old sweatshirt and jeans, hair messed up like he'd just got out of bed. When I looked down, he was wearing special-edition neon Air Maxes that probably cost more than my mortgage that month.

"Hi," I said, sticking a hand out for him to shake. "Max. Good to meet you in person."

"Hey." He shook it, looking dazed and like he wasn't entirely sure who I was. "Come in. We can go up, I guess."

I thought it was probably in bad taste to ask to see the Voltaire Room, where his father had been murdered, so I followed him into the famous gold elevator, thinking of all the stories about the club I'd read online. The parties that went on for days, the whole boar once roasted in one of the private dining rooms. The antique grandfather clock thrown from a window onto a black cab idling in the street below. The supermodel and the president caught having sex on the snooker table.

"What's going to happen to this place?" I asked Hunter. "Are there plans for it to reopen?"

He blinked at me. "There's a lot of arguing about it all at the moment." He waved a hand. "The estate and who gets what, you know . . ." He shrugged. "Having three wives makes it all kind of complicated. Everyone's fighting over the scraps."

Scraps was an unusual choice of word for the vast Wrightman empire, but I didn't pull him up on it.

"It must be difficult for you, being here," I said instead.

He shrugged. "I have an apartment upstairs. I didn't want to move out, so . . ."

I waited to see if there was an end to that sentence, but if there was, he forgot it. I followed him out of the elevator and into the hallway.

The place smelled musty as he led me into the club lounge, where the dramatic velvet curtains were half drawn, the light dim. Most of the furniture was covered in dust sheets, apart from a single table and two chairs.

"You want a drink?" Hunter asked, picking up an open can of Coke and sipping it.

"I'm fine, had a coffee on the way in," I said. I sat down, looking around at the grand room. Imagining you hovering in one corner in your little apron, watching the men with that cold smile I'd seen in court.

"Mind if I record?" I asked, holding my phone up to show him. Discomfort flickered across his face, but he nodded.

"Sure."

"Firstly, I'm so sorry about what happened to your dad. It must be really hard, having the trial going on and everyone talking about it."

He tugged off his sweatshirt, revealing a sweat-stained gray T-shirt. Round his neck were two silver chains, one thick and one thin, and his skinny arms were plastered with tattoos. "I try to avoid the news," he said.

"Understandable," I said. "Were the two of you close?"

He pulled another face. "We're very different people, and he left my mother when I was a kid," he said. "So not close, no." He looked down at the table, long lashes batting against pale skin and girly cheekbones. "Not that that makes it any easier."

"Of course." I ran a hand over the engraved arm of the chair, noticing the grimy marks on the table as I did. "What was he like, as a dad?"

He drummed his fingers against the table, like he was actually thinking about that. "Unique," he said eventually, and the way he looked at me made it feel like this was some kind of challenge.

"I'm guessing you were close as adults at least," I said. "Since he gave you the apartment upstairs?"

As in the Central London penthouse apartment, probably worth at least five million quid, I didn't add.

"Sure." Another incline of the head, a toke on his vape. "I was a problem child, and he liked to solve problems."

"You think he thought of you as a problem?"

As he inhaled on the vape again, my eye caught on the tattoo on the inside of his forearm, a sword or staff kind of thing with wings at the top, spreading out and under his elbow. Two snakes were wrapped around the length of it, fangs bared.

"Maybe I was," he said.

I left a gap in the conversation, but the tactic didn't work on him, the silence ticking slowly by in the dim room. "I guess you would have seen Kate Cole around the place," I said, changing the subject. "Did you know her?"

He waved a hand in the general direction of the lounge behind him. "There were a lot of waitresses. I never really paid much attention."

"Well, how do you feel about her now?"

He raised his eyebrows, a faux, cartoony kind of surprise. "How am I supposed to feel about the person on trial for murdering my dad?" He pouted, like he was thinking about that. Then, his eyes narrowing, he looked at me. "What do *you* think about her?"

"I think she was a very troubled young woman," I said evenly.

He nodded, leaning back in his chair and casting an arm across the frame. "I guess she'd have to be," he said.

I was starting to feel spooked. Maybe it was the Miss Havisham vibe of the room, with those yellow velvet curtains half tugged across, the whole place dusty and forgotten, and this kid rattling around in it like Richie Rich, the Tim Burton edition.

Or maybe it was just him. Because I've watched a lot of liars, Kate. And he was as bad at it as you were.

71

Gabriel

"K. C."

ABOUT A WEEK AFTER I moved into the Cally, you and I were sitting up on the roof. We'd just been to a fabric market you'd been excited about, and you'd helped me pick out some material, dark blue with silver shapes stamped along the border like some kind of excellent wizard cape, and then you'd stood on a chair to help me hang it so that I had my own room next to yours.

Now you were lying in the sun with the legs of your jeans rolled up and your eyes closed, a bag of fabric and your sketchbook next to you. I checked the Rabbit Hole and saw that Mr. E had posted.

Another secret report has shown what 5G masts are doing to our people. Cancer, tumors, memory loss. And. They. Hide. The. Evidence. Ask yourself why they needed a new network—they're going to use it to control us. Technology you can't even imagine yet. And who is profiting? The Group. One day they'll push the button and we'll be too late.

I scrolled through the comments, feeling sick. There were so many already.

The government amended the regulations about non-ionizing radiation six months before ours was erected, someone wrote. *Three cancer cases in my village so far. Coincidence?*

My phone had had a 5G icon at the top of the screen ever since I arrived in London, and I stared at it, feeling like it was almost pulsing there in the corner.

"Look at this." I held out the phone to show you the post. You were busy texting, and you only glanced at it, your eyes moving way too fast across the screen for you to be reading it properly.

"Crazy," you said, but I could tell you weren't taking it seriously. I started to wonder if it was a guy you were texting.

"Doesn't it scare you?" I asked. I was already reading the comments again.

You put down your phone. "I don't think it's true, Gabe. Remember a couple of years ago, when people were setting fire to the masts? And saying they caused Covid? Except there was Covid in places where there was no 5G, so that didn't make sense."

"But—"

You reached out and squeezed my hand. "I think it's probably best not to worry about most of the stuff people post on the Rabbit Hole."

It was a superpower you had, choosing what to worry about. It felt like most of the time, you chose nothing. Worries came for me instead, dug themselves into my brain. I couldn't stop myself reading about the pandemic, even while everyone else had thrown away their masks and got back to real life, because I was waiting to see what would come next. There would be something, the Rabbit Hole told me. Mr. E said that somewhere in the city, men in suits were planning it. And I felt helpless, panicked, wondering where it was all going to end.

One morning I slept late after being awake all night, and when I came out into the main room, I saw Polly and Rudy standing there huddled together with blood on their hands.

Rudy turned and saw me and grinned. "Want to get involved?"

"I . . . think I'm good," I said, still groggy. Blinking at the blood as it ran down their wrists.

Polly laughed, holding up the stage makeup bottle. "We're going on another march," she said. "Want to come?"

"Why are you wearing suits?" I was starting to wonder if I'd somehow gotten a contact high from one or all of the others while I'd slept, or if I was still dreaming.

"We're bankers," Polly said. Rudy held up a sign with the Earth painted on it, more fake blood dripping down.

"Know how many tons of carbon emissions are produced every year by the finance sector in the name of profit?" he asked. His fingers were leaving bloody prints all over the edge of the sign.

"Pass," I said.

"An unthinkable amount," he said. "Monstrous." I noticed he had dark finger marks through his hair as well. "Monstrous," he said again.

"We're going to throw blood at the Bank of England and the Stock Exchange," Polly said. "Come, it'll be fun."

I told them I had plans and would sit this one out.

That night, I couldn't sleep again. I'd been in London for a while now, long enough that I should have been finding my feet, doing all the things I'd imagined when you sent me pictures during lockdown. Eating all of the things algorithms kept sneakily dropping into my feed—roast dinner burritos in giant Yorkshire puddings, donut-topped freakshakes, and chicken wing challenges where I could get my name on the wall of fame. I should've been looking for a job. But London scared me. Trying to navigate the busy pavements and the Tube and the buses and the map on my phone scared me. The noise and the germs and the cameras everywhere scared me. I heard Mr. E's voice in my head all the time: *The Group are watching you. Are you ready?* I wasn't ready. I wanted to hide with the books Jaz gave me or the laptop you lent me for gaming or to lie up on the roof listening to the birds, leaving the sirens and the car horns and the angry people screaming into their phones or at each other far below.

I coughed and turned over again, trying to get comfortable, and you came and slipped into bed beside me.

"Hi," you whispered.

"Hi," I said back, more awake now than anyone has ever been in the history of the world.

"When I was little," you said, "and I couldn't sleep, my brother used to tell me stories. About this girl called Pancake and her friend Howard the bear."

"Did you come to tell me one?"

"You wish." You plumped up the pillow behind your head. "He'd send them on these adventures to all the places he'd been reading about, and there was a bird, the WotsitPotsit Bird, who was, like, their guide." You paused. "I think he actually stole that from *The Lion King*. Thingy, you know."

"Zazu."

"That's it. Zazu." You sighed. "I always imagined that it would be us, me and him, who'd go off on adventures one day. All the places he told me about Pancake and Howard going to, like Machu Picchu and the pyramids in Egypt and the Great Barrier Reef."

"Howard the bear could scuba dive?"

"Yes."

"Probably a polar bear. Although that would make Peru and Egypt a challenge."

"Well, now you're ruining it."

I rolled onto my side and looked at you. "He sounds like a really good person. Stephen."

"He was the best. The kindest and bravest." You turned so that we were facing each other in the dark. "You remind me of him."

I lay there soaking up those words for so long I was sure you'd fallen asleep. I turned carefully onto my back, listening to you breathing.

I'd just closed my eyes when you whispered, "Let's stick together, okay? Always."

72

Tarun

"Katherine"

I SAW VERITY ON THE way into court one morning, the two of us approaching from opposite directions. Her hair was loose, and she wore sunglasses, a Venti Starbucks cup in one hand. "Morning," she said. "Nice day for it." She held the door open for me.

"Still into rugby?" she asked. "We get tickets for Twickenham sometimes—Guy's company have a box."

"Yes, I still follow it," I said.

"I pretend to show interest." She took a sip of her coffee, nodded at one of the court clerks. "But it's not really my thing."

"I played," I said. "Long time ago now, but at university I was actually quite good."

"I was a lacrosse girl," she said. "Vicious, though. I didn't have the stomach for it."

"I find that hard to believe."

She grinned, offering her bag to the security guard. "It's good to have you back."

That day, she called Camilla Johnson as a witness. Camilla looked as elegant as she had when I'd met her at March House, poised in a sober dove gray suit. You looked very young in comparison, like you were playing dress-up in your navy one.

Verity asked about the date you'd started work, what Camilla's first impressions of you had been.

"Bright," she said. "Quick to learn. She was a little . . . unpolished, by our standards, but I could see why Lucian had seen promise in her."

There was a perfunctory back-and-forth about the club, and then Verity asked, "And in the weeks leading up to August tenth, did you notice anything unusual in Miss Cole's behavior at work?"

"Perhaps," Camilla said, her tone measured. "She could be sullen at times. Tearful. I wondered if there was something going on at home, as I noticed her bringing in a large backpack once, the kind you might use to go on a trip."

"Did you see Miss Cole collect the bag at the end of her shift?"

"I very clearly saw her leave without it. It stayed in her locker for the rest of the week."

"When was that?"

"The beginning of August."

Verity asked that the CCTV image of you boarding the bus on the night of the murders be displayed. "Is this the same bag?"

Camilla nodded. "Yes," she said aloud, when prompted by the clerk.

"So, as far as you know, it had been stored there the entire time, ready for the right moment—which arose, it turned out, on the evening of August tenth?"

"Yes."

You frowned at this, perhaps not unjustly; Verity's leading of the witness had aggravated me too. She began asking Camilla questions about that night, reiterating some of the points Sebastian Dwyer had made: that you were Lucian's requested waitress, that you had been solely responsible for serving the party.

"Did that include preparing the room for the dinner?"

"It should have. But Katie was late, so I set up the room and decanted the wine Lucian had requested—it needs to breathe for at least an hour, really, he was very particular."

Verity asked for another image to be shown to the witness, this time a photo, taken at the crime scene, of the almost empty bottle of Armagnac on the table. "Do you recognize this bottle, Ms. Johnson?"

She hesitated. "Well, I recognize the brand, of course. That was Lucian's favorite; he often liked to end his private dinners with it."

"And did this bottle come from the cellar at March House?"

"No." She said it assertively. "That bottle, that vintage, doesn't correspond with any we had in stock at the club. There was no bottle missing; it didn't come from there."

73

John

"Kit-Kat"

THERE WAS A COLDNESS TO the woman who had been your boss at March House. I noticed that she didn't look in your direction once.

You looked exhausted, like you wanted to cry, as Tarun began his cross-examination.

"Ms. Johnson, we've heard that you went down to set up the Voltaire Room at five thirty that evening."

"That's right."

"You went down to the cellar, selected the drinks that Mr. Wrightman had chosen, then on to the room."

"Yes."

"You decanted the red wine, chilled the white, dressed and laid the table according to Mr. Wrightman's exacting standards."

"Yes."

"Presumably you left the room to fetch the glassware, the table settings, and so on?"

"Yes."

"Was the room unlocked while you were doing so?"

"Well, yes, but for no more than ten minutes. At the very most," she said, flushing.

"Ten minutes during which someone else—any one of the various club members and staff we know to have been inside March House that night—could have entered the room alone, couldn't they?"

"I suppose so."

"And when you went upstairs to the lounge, having seen Miss Cole on her way up to the staff room ready to begin her shift, you again left the room unlocked, didn't you?"

"Yes, but only for a couple of minutes, barely that—Katie was back downstairs so quickly . . ."

"My point is, Ms. Johnson, that the room was not a vacuum. Katherine Cole is not the only person who could have brought the poisoned brandy into it, is she?"

I took a long, steadying breath. Surely the jury would agree, would see that someone else had done it.

"No, I suppose not," Camilla said.

"In fact, you were the person who was alone in that room for the longest, weren't you?"

"I'm not sure what you're implying." She seemed angry now, like she wanted to get down from the stand.

"Ms. Johnson, have you ever attended any kind of protest or rally?"

You looked surprised at the sudden switch in questioning. But Camilla had gone pale, and I felt a tiny flicker of hope.

"Yes," she admitted. "I went on a peaceful march about climate change last year."

Tarun smiled politely. "And that protest, held by Stop Oil Now, culminated at the headquarters of EPV Energy, didn't it? The company owned by Aleksandr Popov's family."

You looked up. Everyone in the courtroom seemed to have gone very still.

"Well, yes, but . . . Ten thousand people attended that protest. I went with friends. I had no idea Alek was anything to do with EPV."

"Really? You didn't recognize him as the man someone threw two liters of red paint over?"

"No."

"I find that very curious, Ms. Johnson, because on Instagram, you follow an account belonging to the influencer Lulu Price, a vocal supporter of Stop Oil Now, who regularly posts mocked-up mug shots of oil and gas executives, including the Popov brothers. You'd seen those posts, hadn't you?"

She gave a tight little shake of her head. "I don't remember."

"You didn't mention in your witness statement that you had political views that directly opposed those of one of the victims, did you?"

This time, the word came out as barely a whisper. "No."

"Because you knew that might make you look like you'd wish him harm, didn't you?"

For the first time, your manager looked at you, and suddenly it seemed as if she were the one who might cry.

74

Conrad

"Wildcat"

A MONTH LATER, I WAS joining Lucian at March House for a meeting. As great as I'd imagined: half-dark in the middle of the day, big grand ceilings, and the reek of money everywhere. I checked my reflection in the lift doors as we went up. Pleased to see I looked like I belonged. Pleased that, as we walked through the club lounge with people greeting Lucian like he was some returning emperor, they were all looking at me. Trying to figure out who I was.

Alek was already waiting at a table, a folded paper and coffee in front of him. He rose as we arrived.

"It's nice to meet you," he said, when Lucian introduced us.

As he shook my hand, I noted the Patek Philippe watch that poked from his cuff. A Calatrava, vintage. Forty grand, easily.

"Nice to meet you," I replied, casual, like I hadn't spent the car ride over googling his net worth.

We ordered coffees from the stunning blond hostess.

"Conrad here is someone I have in mind to run my new venture," Lucian said. "And I'm still keen to have you on board. I thought the three of us might talk it through a little more."

It turned out Lucian wanted to buy up empty office blocks whose previous occupants couldn't afford to keep paying for spaces their employees no longer wanted to use. Home working had been too much of a good thing for lots of people, and its effects seemed to be rumbling on even as the pandemic was brushed aside. Sections of the city, where previously you hadn't been able to walk a hundred meters without finding a packed Pret full of suits, were still ghost towns, even as Covid restrictions were lifted.

So: We'd turn them into luxury flats. For other people, on much better salaries, to do *their* home working in.

Lucian talked about getting Harris Lowe involved. I knew the name, mostly because of the diamonds, but I kept quiet and googled him later—diamonds turned out to be his family's game, but Lowe Estates was all about property.

Like all-the-best-squares-on-a-Monopoly-board levels of property.

I nodded in all the right places, asked questions to show my interest. Playing golden boy. Trying not to gawk at the level of investment Lucian was planning to raise, the numbers the two of them were casually throwing around.

All the while thinking: this is going to make me.

I got drunk at home that night, sat out on my balcony with a bottle of red. Looking out at the water, imagining myself on a yacht, in a second home. The warm glow of possibility giving me a high as the evening turned cold.

Then I opened my phone and saw that Molly had posted a reel of herself at Soho Farmhouse, her cheeks rosy as she walked through the grounds, as she sat in a hot tub and raised a glass of champagne to the camera. Two quaint little bicycles propped up on the porch of a cabin.

I drained the last of my wine and winced: bitter. Pulled down on the screen with my thumb to refresh my feed and make her disappear.

And there you were. Drinking on a rooftop in a skimpy top, grinning right at the camera.

It was so inviting, that photo. It felt rude not to send a quick hello.

75

Gabriel

"K. C."

WE WERE UP ON THE roof the next night when your phone lit up with a text.

I saw the way your face lit up too as you read it, and my heart sank.

76

Max

"Killer Kate"

I'LL ADMIT I WAS IMPRESSED by Rao's attempt to paint Camilla Johnson as some kind of eco-warrior terrorist—it was inventive at least. Half my office had gone on that march, though, most of them with cans of Pimm's and their kids in tow, and I don't think any of them would've done so much as push past Popov in the bus queue, let alone plot his murder.

An expert witness was called next, a toxicologist called Alana Martinez.

She walked Naylor through the lab report showing the lethal levels of cyanide found in the blood of all four men, also pointing to the high levels of lactic acid present.

"Lactic acidosis of this level would point to severe intoxication," she said, "a rapid deprivation of oxygen in the body."

After a brief but gruesome analysis of how quickly and painfully the men would have died, Naylor turned her attention to the poison itself.

"Where might one obtain hydrogen cyanide?" she asked.

Martinez shrugged. "Any number of places. It's used in lots of industrial processes—as a fumigant, a pesticide, a dye. But it occurs in nature too—cyanogenic glycosides are present in bitter almonds, apricots, and the cherry laurel, to name a few, and hydrogen cyanide can be liberated from these by a process of distillation."

"How difficult would that be?"

"Not particularly, if you knew what you were doing. Or had access to the internet."

And we all knew how much time you liked to spend on that, Kate.

As Martinez's testimony came to a close, there was a brief burst of noise up in the public gallery. I craned to see—a blond girl, maybe about your age, was trying to leave in a hurry. She had a hand clasped to her face, tears already falling, as she pushed past the others in her row—a man I recognized as Popov's brother, and Clara, his widow.

As Rao confirmed he had no questions for the witness, the girl made it out, the door swinging heavily shut behind her.

I wondered who she was.

77

John

"Kit-Kat"

I LEFT COURT IN A daze, lack of sleep finally catching up with me. I wasn't paying attention the way I usually did each time I arrived and left, and I didn't notice the man falling into step with me until he said my name.

I looked up and saw that he had his phone in my face, filming. "How does it feel?" he asked. "Your daughter's a hero."

"Please," I said. "Leave me alone."

"*Please*," he said, mocking me, and then laughed. "Don't be like that. We're on your side. We're Kate's army now. We'll finish what she started."

I shoved him, hard, and his mouth dropped open in surprise.

"Fuck you," he said, shoving me back.

"Stop!"

I turned, saw Clara Popov standing there. "I'm calling the police," she said, her phone pressed to her ear. "Is that what you want?"

"He's crazy," he said, but he stepped back, lowered his own phone.

The blood was still pounding in my head as I watched him walk away.

"Thank you." My voice sounded far away, black spots appearing at the edges of my vision.

Clara rolled her eyes, grabbed my arm. "Come in here."

She pushed open the door to a pub, a dingy little place that was thankfully empty. "Sit," she said, her voice tight. "It's the adrenaline. You'll be fine in a second."

I rested my head in my hands, trying to get the room to stop spinning. When I looked up, she'd fetched a glass of water and put it in front of me.

"You had a shock," she said. "You're fine."

"I think I've been in shock for the past year," I said.

She pressed her lips together and looked away.

"I'm sorry," I said. "I can't imagine how much worse it is for you."

"No." She looked at me in disgust. "You can't."

But she didn't leave. We sat together in silence for a couple of minutes.

"No one can," she said eventually. "Today, it's like nothing. This numbness . . . Like I've left my body. Like none of this is real. I could switch it off at any moment, like a TV show or video game or something."

I took a shaky sip of water.

"You didn't have to help me, then," I said. "Thank you."

She shook her head. "Alek always said I had a bleeding heart. That I'd get myself in trouble playing the hero one day."

The man had used the same word about you: *hero*. The thought made me feel sick.

"You must hate me," I said.

She raised her eyebrows. "Hate? No. I see you there, day after day, and I listen to what's being said, and . . . still you come. Every day. You come and you sit there. And I pity you. If it were my daughter . . ." After a pause, she gave a small toss of her head, her eyebrows raised, as if the thought were just too improbable to entertain.

"I know her," I said. "She couldn't have done this."

She shook her head again, exhaled sharply.

"My mother," she said eventually. "She read a lot of things during the pandemic, you know . . ." She blew out a heavy breath. "Posts on Facebook. Facebook! We thought she used it to find out all the neighborhood gossip, or to post photos of the children. But no. Suddenly she was telling me about lab leaks and vaccine conspiracies, how we were being lied to."

I shifted in my seat, wary again. "That's difficult," I said.

This seemed to irritate her. "It was insidious. On and on, every time we spoke. About elections, about catastrophes, about celebrities. Every-thing was fake news and I was a moron for believing it. I started dread-ing our calls."

I swallowed.

"She wasn't the person I knew," she said. "She became someone else. Perhaps that feels familiar to you."

I didn't dare move.

"Perhaps," she said, "understanding that might make it easier for you."

When I didn't respond, she rose from her seat. "You're wasting your time," she said. "That woman in there is not the little girl you loved. And I am sorry for you."

She left me there, and I drank the rest of the water, my hands shaking again.

78

Conrad

"Wildcat"

IT WASN'T MY BEST DECISION, put it that way.

I should've opened the apps, swiped till I found someone free that night. But you were right there, and the message was too easy to type.

Was thinking of you, I wrote, parroting one of your lines back at you. *How's life?*

I'd barely poured another drink before you replied: *I'm good!!! how are you?*

Ten seconds later: *what were you thinking about?*

At the end of the day, you were the one who suggested you come round.

Would be nice to catch up, you put, with one of your cringey little winking faces. As if we didn't both know exactly what that meant.

I sent you my address, and you were there less than half an hour later. I tried not to let it put me off, that stink of desperation.

But then you took off your coat, the T-shirt you were wearing so thin I could see the outline of your nipples through it.

"Shall we have a drink?" you asked, but I kissed you instead.

When you left the next morning, I could tell you were trying to play it cool. You'd figured me out a little more, wildcat, and it was sweet, in its way. You dressed and turned down my half-hearted offer of coffee, said you had somewhere to be.

You pulled on your shoes by the door, and I'll be honest, you looked good in that T-shirt, hair all tangled still.

"Thanks for having me," you said. Not forgetting your manners.

You'd almost made it out of the door before you added, "Maybe we can do it again?"

In the cold light of morning, I thought: I don't think so. But I smiled at you and told you, "Let's see."

And that, for you, seemed enough.

79

Tarun

"Katherine"

I'D BEGUN TO GROW IN confidence as the trial went on, to see the way forward for our defense, and to believe that I just might be able to get the jury on your side. Then Verity called Conrad Milton as a witness. I watched you meet his eye as he took the stand, and I felt a prickle of unease as I saw the expression on your face change.

You looked vulnerable.

He was dressed in an Ozwald Boateng suit, a crisp white shirt open at the neck, his face clean-shaven and his smile polite as he was sworn in. I looked at the jury and saw several of them watching him with interest.

He was exactly as I'd expected him to be, and I was not reassured by that.

Verity asked Milton how he knew you, and he told the court the same story that I had read in his witness statement: that he had been working for the company your uncle reared pigs for, and that he'd met you during a site visit.

"When I went back to my car," he explained, "she asked if she could hang out at my hotel with me."

"And you agreed?"

"Yes." A little shamefaced, a glance at the jury. A soft spot for me to work when my cross-examination began.

"You drove back to the hotel, and what happened while you were there?"

He cleared his throat. "We had sex."

"Who initiated that?"

"She did. She kissed me almost as soon as I closed the door behind us."

Verity carried on, her voice clinical. "And after you'd had sex, what happened?"

"I went back home the next day and didn't think much of it, really."

"Did you see Miss Cole again?"

There it was, the same ashamed look at the jury. "A month or so later, yeah. There was another inspection of the farm and she came and found me."

"Were the two of you intimate again?"

"Yes. She basically forced herself on me."

At this, your mouth opened as if you were about to interject.

"Was there a suggestion that a relationship might develop between you?"

"Not as far as I was concerned."

"But Miss Cole felt differently?"

I could have interrupted; it was another leading question, an increasingly tedious feature of proceedings that week. But I have learned over many years that juries grow tired of barristers jumping in to complain about every tiny this and that. They start to feel that perhaps you are suppressing evidence, sabotaging the opposition's case. I sighed and waited for Milton's answer, noticing that you had leaned forward in your seat.

"No . . . She came to see me at work. It was quite . . . It was over the top. A bit much."

"What did you do?"

He looked more uncomfortable. "I tried to let her down gently."

"Did that work?"

"Not really. She was very upset. She sent a lot of messages, both to me and my fiancée."

I'd been waiting for him to mention her, a convenient omission thus far, and with some pleasure, I saw the pregnant juror pull a face like she'd just tasted something sour.

"What was the content of those messages?" Verity asked.

"They were . . . spiteful. To Molly anyway. Torturing her with the details of what had happened between us."

You bit your lip and looked away. I wondered if it was remorse I saw crossing your face.

"And to you?"

"They were obsessive. Ranging from begging to angry, especially when I stopped replying."

Some of those messages had been printed out for the jury to read. I watched the clock as Verity directed them to the correct page, having already committed each word to memory: *u can't do this. please talk to me. DON'T IGNORE ME. i don't know what i'll do.*

Verity looked up at Milton, her voice sympathetic now. "How did that make you feel?"

"Frightened," he said. "Terrified, to be honest. It felt unhinged."

"How long did the messages continue for?"

"Not long. A couple of days, and then she gave up. It was a relief."

"And was that the last time you spoke to Miss Cole?"

"No." Milton cleared his throat. "We reconnected a couple of years later."

"How did that come about?"

"She messaged me." Since he'd begun speaking, he hadn't met your eye. "I think she regretted the way she'd behaved."

"And how did you feel about that?"

He gave a beseeching look at the jury. "Well, I felt a bit sorry for her. We've all done something crazy when we like someone, haven't we?" One of the older female jurors pursed her lips, the rest looking impassively back at him.

"And was that the end of the conversation?"

"No . . ." Another clearing of the throat. "We started to message a bit more after that. Just every now and again."

"You were friends?"

A slight flush of his cheeks at that. "I'd say it was more flirtatious by that point." He hesitated.

"So you were looking to rekindle something romantic?"

"I wouldn't put it exactly like that," Milton said, but this time, he shot a glance at you.

"Did you meet up in person?"

"Yes. Eventually we did arrange to meet."

"And was it a one-off, this meeting?"

"No." A glance at the public gallery this time. "There were several."

"Over a period of how long?"

Milton cast his eyes up at the ceiling. "A couple of months . . . three, perhaps. I can't be sure."

"You were dating," Verity said.

"Yes," Milton said. Like the word was a slug in his mouth.

"And where did you take Miss Cole for these dates?" Verity asked, and I watched your face blanch.

Milton looked at the jury this time. "March House."

80

Conrad

"Wildcat"

WE MET IN A BAR near my office the next time. You showed up in a short black dress with a denim jacket, bare legs I couldn't stop touching. I looked at you, and at first, I was into it, wildcat.

That morning, Molly had finally texted me. *I'm guessing your mum will have mentioned it,* she wrote. *But I'm with someone. I'm moving in with him. Just wanted to tell you myself.*

I checked her Instagram and saw a photo of her surrounded by moving boxes, posted two hours earlier. An open-mouthed smile, her face makeup free and model perfect. A house key held up for the camera. I went back to the message thread.

After you told the internet? I replied.

I owe you nothing, Conrad, she sent back, and then she blocked me.

"I'm happy you called," you said, halfway down your first drink.

"Me too." I leaned in to kiss you.

Not thinking about Molly, probably drinking champagne in her new boyfriend's Chelsea apartment. Putting on her silk pajama shorts and cooking in his kitchen or sitting on the edge of his bed, brushing her shiny hair.

"You're gorgeous," I told you, more to convince myself than you. But you plumped up with the compliment, squeezed my thigh confidently.

"I want to know more about you," you said. "Where are you from?"

"London." I wasn't particularly in the mood for small talk.

"Oh wow," you said, all wide-eyed and gushing. "That must have been cool. I'm jealous."

I doubted you'd say that if you saw the estate where I'd spent most of my childhood, but I smiled, humoring you. "Want another?" I asked. I'd drained my drink in half the time it had taken you.

You nodded, still all moon-eyed, and as I stood at the bar, I watched you downing the last of your cocktail as quickly as you could through your straw.

That was a mistake. You got drunk quickly, started talking too loudly, trying to join in the conversation of the group at the table next to us. When I suggested we move on, you leaned into me as we walked. Bambi on ice.

In the next place, I figured: if you can't beat 'em . . .

I did a shot of tequila each time you went to the toilet, soon got enough of a buzz to care less about the way you were slurring your words, laughing when things weren't really funny.

"I like it here," you said when you came back, flopping into your seat and looking around at the teddy bears hanging on the walls, the circus stripes on the ceiling. It was a hipster hellhole where the round had cost me over twenty quid despite the drinks being served in tin cans. I thought of Molly, sitting elegantly at a table with a crisp white tablecloth and candlelight. Or holding a gin and tonic at a country pub, cheeks pink from a Sunday afternoon walk.

"Not my kind of place," I said, making a face. "I only really drink at my club now."

"What club?" you asked.

I told you, and your face lit up.

"Well, why don't you take me there, then?" you asked.

I regretted it as soon as we got outside, the evening still light enough to see how young you looked, how cheap. You squealed as I showed you the mews where the club was hidden, the discreet black door. "So mysterious," you said, as I swiped us in with my gold key card.

You stood for a second in the entrance hall, looking down at the black-and-white marble tiles, up at the gold leaf wall. Pouting at your reflection in the gold elevator doors.

"I feel like a film star," you said. The doors slid open, and you stepped inside, stumbling on your heels as you turned and reached out a hand for me.

I felt a bit sick. Tequila and a faint sense of dread, hoping Lucian or Alek or anyone who might possibly know me wouldn't be there that night.

I asked the hostess for the booth at the back of the club lounge, where I knew we'd be hidden from view from most of the room. Acting like I was looking for somewhere private for us, like I just wanted the chance to feel you up under the table. You bumbled along, oblivious, sliding into the booth beside me with your dress riding up.

I ordered us a bottle of wine Lucian always recommended, mostly to impress Camilla, who was standing at the bar. I was annoyed that you'd cozied up close instead of taking the seat opposite like a normal person.

When the wine came, you watched as it was poured. Your eyes flicking too slowly across the room.

"Let's get some water," I said, though while you sipped yours, I put away a good amount of wine. Now safely seated, no Lucian in sight, I felt looser, that early hint of something wilder stirring inside me. I caught Camilla's eye across the bar, smiled at her.

"This place is really cool," you said. Running your hands over the leather booth, fingering the embroidery on a cushion. "Have you ever seen anyone important here?"

"More important than me?"

I was drunker than I'd realized.

"No," you said, smiling in a way I assume you thought was sexy. "Obviously not."

"I saw the prime minister once," I told you. "And I pissed next to the guy who directed Best Picture at this year's Oscars."

"You're so big-time. Your parents must be proud," you said.

"My mum says I'm her biggest mistake," I said. Thinking: Where did *that* come from?

You leaned against my shoulder. "I'm probably my mum's too," you said.

"Why?" I asked. "What did you do?"

You shrugged. "I never did figure that out."

I looked at my empty glass, picked up your full one.

"Why were you a mistake?" you asked.

"My dad cheated on her," I said. "Left before I was born. She thinks it was because she got pregnant."

"He just walked out on her?"

I drained your glass. "Yep."

"If someone betrayed me like that," you said, "I'd kill them."

In the morning, I watched you sleeping. Your hair was all mussed up, the night's makeup smudged around your eyes. Your mouth slack like a little kid's, your lips so inviting. You were naked, the covers pulled way down round your bum. The slope of your back so smooth, the curve of your breast pressed against the bed.

I had a sudden urge to touch you.

You opened your eyes and smiled.

81

Gabriel

"K. C."

I HATED HIM.

You told me about him one morning when it was just the two of us. You were sitting at the edge of the roof with your cup of tea, looking out at the city with this secret smile like there should have been cartoon hearts and lovebirds dancing round your head.

"He's the guy I met in Scotland," you said. "He was kind of a twat to me then, but . . . it's different this time."

I stuffed my mouth with toast and tried to swallow it down so I wouldn't have to answer you. But you didn't even seem to notice.

You changed after that. You really did. It was like you weren't even in the room with us most of the time. Every time your phone went off, you snatched it up like it was trying to escape and then you'd spend ages writing a reply, your face scrunched with concentration. Sometimes you even mouthed sentences as you typed them, like you were testing them out. You stopped wearing the things you usually wore, the shorts and T-shirts and leggings and dresses you made, and started dressing up. Putting on more makeup, brushing your hair until it was shiny and straight.

I guess I changed too.

When you came back from your second date, you told me that he'd taken you to March House. I couldn't even speak. You said you'd drunk wine and washed your hands in a sink painted gold and taken a selfie in the toilet mirror because it was like a piece of art. You told me that the way he looked at you as you came and sat back down made you feel like the most powerful person in the world.

"But that's the place," I said. I grabbed your phone from the mattress beside me and opened the Rabbit Hole. Showed you all the comments on some of Mr. E's posts about the Group. About their secret meetings in a hidden location in London. I scrolled down and showed you them, one after another.

It's obvious: March House, one read. *Every fucking politician and banker has a membership there. That's what Mr. E's trying to tell us.*

Big decisions are made in dark rooms in this place, someone else had written. *Stealing our freedom. Ruining our country. Taking us to war. All with a soundtrack of: ker-ching $$$.*

You looked at me and then you snatched the phone back.

"This is stupid," you said. "Don't you think this whole thing is stupid?"

I felt like you'd slapped me.

"I don't think it's stupid," I said. "I don't think you should go there."

"Mr. E is just a stupid little man hiding behind a computer screen," you said. You got up. "I don't want to talk about this anymore."

I sat there for a long time after you left, replaying the conversation. Feeling betrayed and sad and confused, and hating it.

I was so miserable the next day that I agreed to go with Rudy and Polly and chain myself to the headquarters of an oil corporation. I sat there listening to them all screaming about how the world was dying, and I thought, *Yep, sounds about right.*

"Direct action is all that's going to work," Polly told me. She'd painted tears down her cheeks in black eyeliner, but it was hot and we were sweating and they'd smudged a bit. Her arm was hot against mine and the chain wrapped round our wrists was starting to really hurt. "You know that, right?"

"He knows," Rudy said, those pale eyes narrowed. "He's one of us now, aren't you? Our very own Angel Gabriel?"

And I wanted that. I needed that so much, because I felt like I'd lost you.

82

Tarun

"Katherine"

DURING THE BREAK, I FOUND you pacing back and forth in the legal consultation room in the cells, your fists clenched.

"That isn't what happened," you said when you saw me. "How can he stand there and say that?"

"We'll be able to dispute his story when—"

You interrupted as if you hadn't heard me speaking. "He made it sound like . . . He's making me sound . . ." You let out a frustrated kind of growl.

"Calm down," I said, concerned you'd be unable to regain your composure when we were called back to court. "This is all—"

"He *used* me. And now he's out there—"

"He's out there showing the entire courtroom exactly the kind of person he is. I promise you that."

You sank onto a chair, put your head in your hands. "It's too hot in here."

It was an airless, miserable space. I sat down opposite you.

"He's fooling no one," I said.

"I can't believe he ever fooled *me*." You plucked at your shirt, fanned ineffectively at your face with both hands. "It's humiliating."

"I know his type," I said. "And I'd imagine most of the jury do too."

You stopped fanning your face.

"How could he tell it like that? Like . . . like it was all in my head, like he didn't lead me on at all. And he seemed to really *think* that."

"People tend to remember things in a way that suits them," I said. You closed your eyes, shook your head. "Now they all think it too." "Don't worry about him. I have it under control."

You opened your eyes and gave me an attempt at a smile, the effect rather pitiful. "Okay." You took a deep breath, smoothed your shirt down. "Thank you."

But privately, there was little doubt in my mind that Milton's testimony was doing us damage. That you might have used him to gain access to the club, the picture he had painted of you as vindictive, unstable—these were things that would strike a chord with a jury, far more effectively than me quibbling over your internet search history or the fact that you were not the only one who had had access to the Voltaire Room that night.

I excused myself to the bathroom before court was recalled, and took an extra tablet of propranolol, hoping to halt my own spiraling thoughts, the tightness in my chest.

83

Gabriel

"K. C."

YOU CAME UP TO FIND me on the roof one morning. I was lying on my back, listening to two different birdcalls and trying to work out which species they belonged to, when your face loomed over mine.

"I thought you'd be here," you said.

"I'm always here." *Chaffinch*, I thought. Then, a couple of seconds later, *Starling*.

"I need to talk to you." You sounded so serious that I sat up, crossing my legs to face you.

"I've been reading your posts on the Rabbit Hole," you said. "Gabriel, you're on there so much, and it's starting to really worry me."

I stared at you. "Why would it worry you?"

"Because . . ." You looked down at your hands. "Because the stuff they're all talking about isn't true, Gabe. And you're getting so angry about it."

You used to get angry about it too, I wanted to tell you. It was *our* thing.

"I just think you should maybe step away from the site for a while," you said. "We should go out more. Do some proper exploring, like we said we would? Why don't we get an open-top bus, be proper tourists for today?"

Like I was a little kid, someone you needed to babysit or make promises to.

"I'm fine here." I lay back down. "Maybe another time."

You sighed. "Suit yourself," you said, and I swear you rolled your eyes as you left.

It was obvious that guy was going to ghost you again. In the days after that, you were constantly checking your phone, your foot or your fingers tapping anxiously. Picking up books and putting them down, starting conversations and then abandoning them halfway through. Sometimes at night I'd see the glow of your laptop and know you were awake, but you didn't come to see me again.

One afternoon I was on my way to the roof when I caught a glimpse of you in the toilets, leaning over the sinks to get closer to the mirrors. I stopped and watched as you frowned and made faces at yourself. Like you were trying to see something there but were worried about what you were going to find. Like you were worried there was something wrong with you.

I felt angry with you then. That you'd let someone, some stupid dick-head who didn't deserve you, do that. That you weren't who I thought you were.

84

John

"Kit-Kat"

WATCHING CONRAD MILTON AS HE reentered the witness box, I felt like I might jump the rail, grab him by the neck. You sat there, looking utterly crushed, and I felt like I could kill him.

He had met you at the farm, just as I had met your mum, and I wondered if you'd imagined you were writing your own version of that story you loved so much, a story you would in turn tell all of us.

Instead, he had canceled the farm's contract, causing untold harm, and rejected you.

I wondered if it had been loneliness that had made you respond when he got back in touch. Loneliness that had been our fault, and that had led you to that club.

The prosecution barrister began her examination-in-chief again.

"So, you began taking Miss Cole on dates to March House, where you were a member."

"A couple of times," Milton put in.

"Whose idea was it to go there?"

"Hers."

"And did you introduce her to anyone else at the club on those occasions? Friends, colleagues?"

He looked disturbed by the idea. "I mostly kept a low profile when we were there. Until she met Lucian."

I saw the foreperson of the jury look up from his notes, a couple of the others leaning forward with new interest. I felt a lurch of nausea.

There was a kind of showmanship in the way Naylor leaned forward too and said, "Tell us about that."

85

Conrad

"Wildcat"

I ENJOYED IT. I'M NOT going to pretend I didn't. The way you listened to everything I said like it was the smartest thing you'd ever heard, laughed at any quip I made. The energy you always put into trying to impress me. To please me.

You never expected me to take you out, though if I ever said I felt like going for sushi or Vietnamese or pizza, it was all *God, me too* and *You read my mind.* Did you fancy a beer? Of course you did. Had you seen this film? No, but you definitely wanted to. Could I take your clothes off? Always.

Low-maintenance. Enjoyable. For a while.

The hungry way you looked at me, though . . . that quickly started to feel suffocating. The way you started to talk about *we*: all your *we should go to* or *we should watch* or *we should do that sometime.* My skin crawling a little more with each one. The way you'd turn up with pastries from the bakery I'd mentioned in passing once, or a bottle of aftershave I'd once posted on Instagram, saying it was my favorite. "You don't have to do stuff like that," I told you, cringing at the thought of you handing over your shitty little cash-in-hand wages from the dive bar you were working in.

A shrug of your shoulder, an embarrassing little wink. "You deserve nice things," you said.

I started to wonder what the fuck I'd been thinking. Realizing that the bunny-boiler act probably wasn't something you'd grown out of. I was annoyed with myself for being so stupid, and that made me annoyed with you.

I'd flick through the apps again, even while you were asleep next to me, feeling slightly repulsed by the way you slept with your mouth open, the edge of a snore on each breath.

I went on a date, didn't call or reply to your texts the next day or the one after that. Made it almost a week and thought maybe you'd disappeared again—until you turned up one night at my apartment with a cheap bottle of wine and no underwear on.

"What are you doing here?" I asked.

You grinned and pushed past me. "What do you think?"

I watched you helping yourself to glasses, pouring a drink, and realized you'd gotten far too comfortable.

I started leaving your messages unanswered for longer, inventing reasons I couldn't meet. Edging you off me, one finger at a time. A slow fade was kindest, easiest.

I think about you all day, every day, you wrote one night. *Do you think about me?*

Maybe not that slow, I decided. I ignored that message entirely, left the one after that unread.

At work at least, things were moving in the right direction with the new company. Harris Lowe came on board, and Lucian took me to the club that night for a drink to celebrate.

Harris was short and broad, his hair and beard bristly. The definition of grizzly compared to Lucian's slick. "Good to meet you," he said as I stood to greet him. His grip unforgiving, skin rough, like shaking hands with a tree.

"Conrad's my new protégé," Lucian said.

"I prefer right-hand man," I said, and Harris laughed.

"We all need one of those." He ordered a whiskey, patted Camilla's arm when she was the one who delivered it. "You're looking well," he told her, which was one way of putting it. She was poured into a black pencil skirt and tight sweater, a single diamond nestled on a silver chain between her collarbones. "One of ours?" Harris asked, gesturing to it.

"Oh, I wish," she said. She smiled at me.

Lucian raised his glass. "To old and new friends."

"To new friends," Harris said, chinking his glass against mine. "Looking forward to working with you."

When you called, I silenced the phone, put it facedown on the table.

When I checked it five minutes later, there were seven missed calls from you.

Ten minutes later, Camilla came over. A kind of apologetic look on her face. Said she was sorry to interrupt, but my guest was waiting downstairs for me. A Katie Cole.

Lucian laughed, asked if I'd forgotten I had a date. And I couldn't do anything but laugh too, say you must've got the times wrong. Reluctantly, I told Camilla they could send you up.

You were wearing the short black dress again, with grubby trainers this time. You slid into the seat next to me, stuck your hand out to Lucian as you beamed at Harris.

"I'm Katie," you said. "So nice to meet you."

"Charmed," he said. "Can we get you a drink?"

Without looking at a menu, you asked for the wine I always picked, Lucian's favorite, and he gave me a knowing smile.

You turned to me. "You didn't answer the phone," you said.

"My fault," Lucian said. "I've been keeping him busy. I apologize."

You smiled so sweetly. "Work comes first," you said.

Lucian smiled. "Not on my watch," he said.

Your wine arrived, and you took it without looking at Camilla or thanking her, your eyes flicking between Lucian and Harris.

"Conrad's told me so much about you," you said to Lucian, which was a lie. I could count the serious conversations I'd had with you on one hand.

"All good, I hope."

"Of course," you said, taking a big glug of your wine. "You're his Mr. Miyagi."

Lucian chuckled, practically in full twinkly-eyed-granddad mode, and I realized, with growing horror, that he liked you. I watched, half-impressed, half-irritated, and wondered how to make you go away.

I think you could tell. You could read me better than I realized, wildcat; that's the thing I can see now. Because you shot me a look, your eyes narrowed.

"My boss is horrible," you said. "I'm always jealous when I hear about you."

"What do you do?" Harris asked. He, at least, seemed bored of you.

You sighed, looked down. Pretending to be shy. "Just waitressing. The owner is a total sleaze, and the pay and hours are awful."

Lucian tutted. "Well, we can't be having that. Not for a friend of Conrad's."

I felt like the world had gone into slow motion as I watched him tell you he was sure they could find you a job at the club, no problem.

And you smiled, like a little kid at Christmas. "That's so kind," you said. "Thank you."

86

Max

"Killer Kate"

I WAS IN A GOOD mood that night, despite a relentless interrogation from Albie on topics including how I'd survive a killer bee attack and whether ghosts could poo. The Milton thing was all great copy—we couldn't identify him, but I could write about the jury being told you'd had an obsessive relationship with a member of the club that had resulted in you wangling yourself a job there. "Kate Cole's March House Lover Was 'Terrified'" made a perfect little headline, one that got an accordingly tasty wave of traffic to the site. On the second day: "Kate Cole Used Lover to Get Job at March House." Social media was going mad for all of it, your name trending every day.

"I think they *can* poo," Albie mused on the sofa beside me, the iPad I'd given him not enough of a distraction from this burning thought.

"Me too," Anya said, coming in. "Come on, bedtime." She handed me a beer. "Can you sort out the rice?"

"On it." I took the iPad from Albie and kissed him good night. As they went upstairs, I glanced down and paused the video he'd been watching—some kind of unboxing crap, his fascination with watching other kids open and play with toys seemingly never-ending. I scrolled idly through the videos the algorithm had gathered as suggested next watches for him: a weird combination of *Ninja Kidz*, *Bluey*, and Mr. E content, united at last. I'd need to clear the cache, start remembering what Anya had said about only letting Albie use his own tablet and the YouTube Kids app.

Near the bottom of the list was a video, titled "Dispatches from Mr. E #33," and I clicked it, noticing that it was part of a series, and that the user, DeeDee19, had nearly half a million subscribers.

"We have a new post from E," a blond, mildly unhinged-looking woman announced gleefully. "Let's dive right in."

The background behind her—her dining room, by the look of it—switched to a screengrab of the Rabbit Hole and Mr. E's post. It was the one about an MP having lunch at "Olympus" while a new swimming pool was being built at his house. As the woman read it in voice-over, various words and phrases were highlighted.

Images from Greek mythology flooded the screen, layering over each other with cheap effects—a bearded god with a lightning bolt, Poseidon Ursula-Andressing his way out of the sea, a winged staff with two snakes wound round it, an urn, a shield, Mount Olympus itself—as DeeDee recapped everything Mr. E had already said about the Group and Olympus.

She appeared on-screen again, using a natty little split screen to show a paparazzi shot of an MP, Grahame Wood, leaving March House on the same day the Mr. E post had appeared. Confirmation, again, that like all good con artists, Mr. E knew when to season his bullshit with fact.

"I checked the planning applications for that area, and it's true," she squealed. "Grahame Wood is having a pool built at the back of his giant house, with money he earns by going for long lunches at the heart of evil when he's supposed to be serving us." She took a sip from a hot-pink Stanley cup. "Am I the only person who feels completely, entirely *enraged* by this?" she asked the camera, long nails clicking as she clapped her hands together. "Am I the only person who wants to hear from Mr. E about what he wants us to do next?"

According to the comments beneath the video, she was not the only person. Not by a long way. And one of them caught my eye: gabe333. I stared at the username for a second, then checked back on the Rabbit Hole and saw that I'd remembered rightly—he was one of the frequent posters there as well.

I thought about that childhood friend of yours, Gabe, my spidey sense tingling. When I went back to his Instagram, his username had a three in it too: @gabe3s_. Not an exact match, sure, but enough of a coincidence.

If your childhood friend had been a Mr. E follower too, was he still? Did he know who Mr. E was? And what might you have confided in—or, even better, planned with—him?

87

Gabriel

"K. C."

I PASSED THE BATHROOM AGAIN a couple of nights later, and you were in there getting dressed up. You'd put on a tight black skirt and a shirt, and you were looking in the mirror again, putting on lipstick like it was war paint.

"Where are you going?" I asked you as you headed for the stairs.

"Work," you said. "I'll see you tomorrow, okay?"

You'd never dressed up like that for work before, and I wondered if you were meeting *him* afterward. But in the morning, you were there. Yawning and making tea and talking to Leah about a dress you were making for her, like everything was back to normal.

That day we sat on the roof together, and you sketched, and I read and listened to a house sparrow chirping from a chimney a few buildings over. When a little black-and-white pied wagtail hopped across the concrete near our feet, you stopped moving.

"It's so cute," you said. "And monochrome, very classy."

"They're my favorites," I said.

You were drawing a dress, and you put down your pencil and picked a skinny marker out of the huge box you had, started shading in black on the body and the skirt.

"I'm sorry I haven't been around as much," you said, without looking up. The wagtail flew a couple of meters and landed on the edge of the roof, looking back at us.

"Don't worry about it," I said, easy breezy again as I turned the page, but inside, my heart was going mad.

"I just . . ." You recapped the marker and chose another one. "I had some things to figure out."

"And did you?"

You looked up and smiled. "I did. I'm feeling a lot better now."

We stayed up there until the sun set that night, lying on our bellies to watch it come down in a big, showy fuss of pink and orange and red, and it seemed like everything would be okay again, it really did.

But a couple of nights later, you left a key card by the bathroom sink. When Polly came in holding it up, her face was all tight and weird, her mouth screwed into a line. "Why do you have this?" she asked. "When have you been to March House?"

You blushed. I'd never seen you do that before. "I work there now," you said, and I felt like someone had dropped an anvil on me, like I was a cartoon squashed flat to the ground.

"You work at March House?" Polly said, her voice getting loud, and it was like I couldn't breathe suddenly, like inside I was still peeling myself off the floor. "Are you serious?"

"Yes." You straightened up, like you were trying to make yourself taller. "It's good money."

Rudy put down the bottle of rum he'd been trying to open with a penknife. "You know the kind of blood the members of that place have on their hands? The damage they've done?"

You rolled your eyes. "I don't talk business with them, I just take their drink orders."

"The guy that owns that place, Wrightman, is a climate change denier." Polly sounded like a cartoon too now, all squeaky and fast. "Have you seen the things he's said about it? Do you realize how much forest has been destroyed by the companies in his group?"

"What do you want me to do about it, Poll?" you asked, and I could tell you were getting annoyed now. "Magic the trees back? I just want to earn some money."

"I don't know, Kat," Mat said. He held up the paper he'd been reading, the headline on the front page some big scary shouty one about the next huge rise in energy bills that was coming. I looked at the two men on the front cover—one the prime minister, the other a tall guy staring at the pap taking the picture. He was named in the caption: *Aleksandr Popov and the PM leave March House on Wednesday evening.* "Is this really the kind of person you want to cozy up to?"

"Why?" you asked. "What's he done?"

Mat raised his eyebrows. "He's making millions out of the energy crisis."

"It's a national fucking emergency," Polly said. "A catastrophic social disaster, and no one gives a fuck. People are going to genuinely freeze to death this winter, or aren't going to be able to feed their kids. And Popov and the fuckers like him are all sitting there wiping their fucking arses on *our* money." She lit a cigarette, took a drag. "Wiping their fucking arses and tipping *you* with it."

"Oh, have a day off," you snapped, rolling your eyes again. "I know what I'm doing, okay?"

Polly looked like you'd slapped her. Rudy folded his arms, the penknife still open in his hand.

"Someone who lives here, in this community, can't be associated with a place like that," he said.

You laughed, but as you looked around, none of the others met your eye. "This is ridiculous," you said. You looked at me, but I still couldn't breathe, and right then, in your shirt and skirt, you looked like a stranger.

When I didn't say anything, you laughed again.

"Fine," you said, and you turned on your heel and left.

88

Tarun

"Katherine"

I MADE SURE I LOCKED eyes with you as you entered the dock that morning. Nodded to you: now we would get our turn. You seemed to get the message, because you gave me a small nod in return as you sat down.

Milton was wearing another expensive suit that day, this one charcoal gray. He'd cut himself shaving, and I focused on that small imperfection as proceedings began.

Verity resumed her examination-in-chief.

"After Miss Cole began working at March House, what was your relationship with her?" she asked.

Milton's mouth set in a hard line. "I tried my best to avoid her," he said. "Which proved difficult."

"You were no longer exchanging messages?"

"I was no longer responding to hers."

"And how did Miss Cole react to that rebuff?"

I made a face at that, hoping the jury might notice.

"She persisted," Milton said. "And when she stopped, I began to receive awful messages from an anonymous email account, really vile stuff."

"What was the content of those emails?"

"Telling me I'd pay for what I'd done, that I'd wish I was dead. It was terrifying, and because of the timing, I can only assume they were from her."

I rolled my eyes, pretended to make a note. As Verity wound down her questions, I hoped no one could hear the anxious gurgling of my stomach.

"Any questions for the witness, Mr. Rao?" Judge McQuilliam asked.

This had once been the kind of moment I relished in a trial, the part I was good at, and I felt a strange sort of anticipation as I stood. Milton watched me warily.

I chose a conspiratorial tone as I said, "You have no evidence that those anonymous emails were from Katherine Cole, do you?"

"They were exactly her style," he said. "And I had no reason to suspect anyone else."

"I'll repeat the question: You have no evidence they were from Miss Cole, do you?"

He made a sour face. "No."

"Mr. Milton, how old was the defendant when you first had sex with her?"

His expression hardened. "I believe she was eighteen. She didn't tell me that at the time."

"Eighteen." I nodded, let that settle with the jury. "And how old were you?"

He had the decency to sound sheepish now. "I was thirty-two."

"Thank you." I paused as if collecting my thoughts. "You were thirty-two years old, and she was barely beyond the age at which she could legally have sex. There's an obvious imbalance of power in that relationship, isn't there?"

There was a clench in his jaw as he answered. "It didn't feel that way at the time."

"How did it feel?"

"It felt like she was doing all the chasing. Like she knew exactly what she wanted."

I raised an eyebrow in the jury's direction, leaving that comment to fester in the air between us.

"Isn't it true, Mr. Milton, that you invited Katherine Cole to your hotel room on that first day in Scotland? That it was you who, when you arrived at the room, began kissing her?"

He shook his head, reddening now. "It was a long time ago, so I don't remember the exact order of events. But it definitely wasn't me who started it."

"You don't remember *exactly*, but you can say *definitely* that you didn't suggest she come to your room instead of drinking in the bar? You can say *definitely* that you didn't kiss her first?"

"Yes."

"I'd suggest, Mr. Milton, that it's a little more convenient for you to remember it that way, given you were engaged to be married at the time, isn't it?"

He sniffed. "It's the truth."

"On the subject of that engagement—what happened to that relationship?"

"We broke up."

"Because Katherine Cole told your fiancée that you were a cheat."

He gritted his teeth. "Yes."

"I can't imagine you felt kindly toward Miss Cole after that."

He let out a snort. "What kind of question is that?"

Judge McQuilliam fixed me with a beady look. "I'm inclined to agree, Mr. Rao—that wasn't a question."

"My apologies," I said, though inside I must confess I felt a soaring kind of pleasure. I felt like myself again. "My question, I suppose, is why, when Katherine Cole not only ruined your engagement and, according to you, acted so unreasonably that you began to feel 'terrified,' you'd resume a relationship with her several years later?"

He glared at me. "Like I said, I felt a bit sorry for her."

"Not because, having taken advantage of her age and inexperience once before, you thought you might as well do it again?"

"*No,*" he said hotly. "That wasn't what happened at all."

"Wasn't it?" I asked, and then changed tack, keen to widen the crack that was beginning to show in his cool demeanor. "Mr. Milton, you've told us that Katherine was offered a job by Lucian Wrightman after she interrupted your drinks with him."

"That's correct."

"You implied that this was the result she wanted from the conversation."

He raised an eyebrow, knowing, as I did, that he'd done more than imply it. "I'm certain that was her intention, yes."

"And why do you think she did that?"

"She did it to stay close to me," he said, just as I hoped he would. "It was like she was stalking me."

"So not because she believed some kind of wild conspiracy theory about the club, then?"

Verity bristled, leaning over to whisper something to her junior.

Milton shrugged. "Can't it be both?"

"It would certainly be very convenient, wouldn't it?" I kept my voice arch, hoping to convey to the jury how unlikely I found this. Sarcasm is a high-wire act in the courtroom, and it can very easily go wrong. I moved on swiftly, not allowing Milton to respond. "You never heard Miss Cole talking about such a conspiracy theory, did you?"

"I didn't," he said, quiet now.

"In fact, she never talked to you about *any* conspiracy theories, did she?"

"No." He shot you a look. "She probably knew I'd think they were all bollocks."

"And she never spoke to you about any other grievance with any of the victims either, did she?"

"No," he said, through gritted teeth.

I cocked my head, put on an expression of faint confusion. "So no conspiracy obsession, no bad blood between them—despite your intimate relationship, Katherine never gave you any indication of any motive for these murders, did she?"

He stared at me for a long moment, his jaw clenched. "No," he said eventually, but I had the uncomfortable sensation that that was not what he truly wished to say.

89

Conrad

"Wildcat"

I COULD SLOW-FADE YOU ALL I wanted; ignoring your messages was no good when I'd show up to the club and you were there, giving me the kicked-puppy eyes from across the room.

The first time: a quiet lunch with Lucian, our monthly meeting made more regular as I got ready to move over from Kindred to the new business. And there you were, appearing at the table before we'd even sat down, your white shirt open one button too far, the lace of your bra visible through it.

"What can I do for you?" you asked, all eager, your eyes burning a hole in my head as I fiddled with my phone.

"Our newest star waitress," Lucian said. "I'd love an Earl Grey."

"Coming up," you said, though your eyes were still on me.

I couldn't be rude in front of Lucian. I looked up at you and smiled, gave my order.

You were all butter-wouldn't-melt when I overheard your conversations with other people. All *yes sir, no sir, of course sir,* long lashes batted down as if you were too timid to meet their eyes half the time.

It was a different act to the girl who'd clawed at my clothes in the middle of a field, in the back of taxis, and grudgingly, I admired it.

And wanted no part of it.

A week later, I turned up for a drink after work on my own, and you were there, serving a table by the window. The hem on your skirt coming down at the back, your hair messy.

I asked Camilla to seat me at the bar, assuming it would mean you couldn't come over, but you appeared barely five minutes later.

"You didn't reply to my messages," you said, pouting.

"I've been busy," I told you. The bartender put my pint in front of me, and I thanked him, hoping you'd be too embarrassed to continue.

But you don't embarrass easily, do you, wildcat?

"Well, you're not busy now," you said. "Why are you doing this to me again?"

There were a lot of people in the lounge, the club never quiet on a Thursday night. You weren't keeping your voice down. "I'm sorry," I said. "It's just been mad lately. Honestly."

You frowned. "Have you met someone else?"

"No!" I said, though it probably would've been easier to say *yes*, invent someone. "It's not that. When things are quieter, I'll let you know, yeah?"

Thinking: surely even you could read between those lines.

Apparently not.

Sometimes you'd message when I was in the middle of a conversation. Sitting there listening to Lucian and Harris discussing potential properties and the Article 4 restrictions currently in place across the City of London and Kensington and Chelsea, while my phone buzzed incessantly in my pocket: *you look so hot. i want you. shall i come over tonight?*

Every time I looked up, there you'd be, staring at me as you set down someone's drink from a tray.

Then you showed up on my doorstep again, this time with a bottle of wine that you must have stolen from the club.

"I know it's your favorite," you said. "Are you going to let me in?"

It was three in the morning. You'd probably just finished work.

"No," I said.

"No?" You blinked, like you'd never heard the word.

"It's the middle of the fucking night."

"That's never bothered you before."

I rubbed a hand over my face. I was still in boxers and a T-shirt I'd pulled over my head, dragged from sleep and deeply regretting answering the door. "You were invited before."

"What, and now I'm not?" You were getting louder.

"No. You're not. I don't know what you're doing here, but you're not coming in."

Now you became practically shrill. "Why are you being like this? I was your girlf—"

"You were *not* my girlfriend," I said. "This is insane."

I started to close the door, which seemed to make you angrier. You hurled the bottle of wine at me and it shattered in a spectacular mess of red against the white door. Glass falling like rain round your feet.

We both stood there for a second, you breathing hard.

"Don't ever come back here," I said. "This is insane. You're insane."

I closed the door on you. Found my phone in the bedroom and blocked your number. Only noticing as I did that my hands were shaking.

90

Max

"Killer Kate"

ON SATURDAY MORNING, I DEBATED sending another message to Gabriel. I just had this feeling that he might be my key to Mr. E, or at least
might be the perfect interviewee for my book—if he was as much of a
Manson girl as you were, it would be an unrivaled insight into the Rabbit Hole and the damage it had done. But repeat messaging might make
me look desperate, I thought; I found Bart's profile and sent him one
instead, chancing my luck: *Hey, never heard from your friend Gabe. Any
way you could give me an email address?*

While I waited for him to reply, I scrolled back through the notes
from my interview with Hunter Wrightman, hoping I'd be able to find a
decent quote to make an article out of. Keep up the momentum over the
weekend, until the trial resumed on Monday. There wasn't really a lot
to choose from. That he'd been miserable as a child, or that he'd been a
problem Lucian wanted to solve? Interesting, sure, but not really something I could use. I was annoyed with myself because I could see how he
had diverted me from the most important question—what he thought
of you—by asking me what *I* thought. It was a smooth move, one right
out of my playbook.

Frustrated that neither lead was offering me much material, I searched
through the other twenty open tabs on my browser, wondering which
thread to follow next. I settled on the searches I'd made trying to track
down Peter Walters, the local man you'd accused of being a pedophile.
I'd got the gym's name, Olympia, from the Facebook post, but when I

found its website, all I'd got was a 404. This time, tinkering around with date filters on the Wayback Machine, I found an archived version.

It was pretty basic—a yellow home page with the club's logo in green across the top and a few tabs for Fees, Programs, and Testimonials. I clicked around a bit, looking at the photos, wondering how long I had before Anya and Albie came back from Ukulele Club. Sometimes I thought she invented this stuff to wind me up.

I quickly got bored of the pictures of various bendy kids doing various unnatural things on the wooden horses, balance beams, and vaults I had dim and unpleasant memories of from school. I was about to click away when one caught my eye: a teenage boy chalking his hands, a determined look on his face, the parallel bars waiting in the background.

I leaned closer, studying the picture. I was pretty sure that it was your brother Bobby, and that the woman watching from the sidelines was your mum. I downloaded it, opened it in my picture viewer, enlarging it. Yep—definitely Bobby, and now my pulse was ticking up with the satisfaction of finding a new lead.

Not just a local man you'd made up a lie about, but your brother's coach. That was very interesting indeed, Kate.

I heard Anya's key in the door, Albie's excited chatter, and the rustle of plastic bags. "I've got the shopping," she yelled up. "Are you in?"

"Coming," I called, and I got up, though not before checking the photo again.

91

Tarun

"Katherine"

THE WEEKEND ARRIVED WITH UNWELCOME timing. I had found my footing, begun to feel at home in the courtroom again, and the interruption made me anxious. Being alone left me too much time to think, and I lay awake long before dawn, eventually wandering out into the living room, where I could stand in front of your case, rereading witness statements I'd long ago committed to memory. Studying the photos I had taken at March House, the guest list from that night—the notes pinned around it that I had made on each of the handful of other patrons who had come in and out of the club that day.

Trying to stop my mind turning to thoughts of you in the courtroom, replaying those moments when I might have seen a change in your face, a slyness slipping through. Trying to stop Marla's features replacing yours.

I turned away from the wall and opened my laptop, a self-destructive urge driving me to news sites, to all the coverage of your trial. The headlines did not make for pretty reading. Conrad Milton's testimony had been fertile ground—"Kate Cole's March House Lover Was 'Terrified'" read one headline by Max Todd, who'd been particularly vocal during Marla's trial; "Desperate Housewife" had been one memorable front page of his. I scrolled through some of the others he'd written about you, and the articles on other news sites, all of them similarly damning.

It wasn't unexpected for this point in proceedings and shouldn't have unduly concerned me; the papers had only the prosecution's case to report on, could only record what had happened each day in court. We would have our time to make our case, to turn the tide of public opinion.

But your story seemed to be creeping outward, your name appearing in articles that weren't to do with your trial. "One Third of Population Believe Cost of Living Crisis Is a Government Plot to Control Public" read one broadsheet headline, alongside a photo of you leaving court. "Protestors Gather at 5G Mast" read another, a different photo of you accompanying the article.

You were becoming the poster child for conspiracy theorists, and I didn't know how easy it would be for you—for us—to shake that off.

I didn't venture onto social media. I'd learned that much at least.

I went for a walk on Sunday morning and found myself pining for Elliot, something else I no longer allowed myself to do. I remembered the way he had pried the laptop from my hands during the weekends of other trials, forcing me out on expeditions into corners of the city we hadn't yet explored. The pop-up restaurants he always managed to hear about, the tiny galleries and food festivals, the obscure international films.

I remembered the way he'd come to the flat after Ursula had told him about my breakdown. The carrier bags of food, carefully chosen from the organic shop around the corner, the memory stick he'd loaded with films he thought I'd like. The way I'd watched him through the peephole as he stood on the doorstep, and waited for him to leave.

I walked down Marylebone High Street and wandered into Daunt's, picking up and replacing books from the shelves. It was the place in London I found most peaceful, but that day, the quiet felt stifling, the dark wood and vaulted ceiling too reminiscent of the courtroom.

I went out and carried on walking, realizing that I was—and had always been—heading for March House.

As I cut away from the high street, my brain began its comforting habit of worrying at the knots in your case, retreading much-worn tracks in hope of finding a new way to untangle them. I returned to the guest list, the ten other patrons who had been in the club lounge of March House over the course of the evening. The possibility that one of them had prior knowledge that Lucian's party were dining that evening, and had slipped in at just the right moment to have avoided detection. Camilla Johnson and Sebastian Dwyer both had more opportunity in this respect, and either of them could have been dishonest in their witness statements. But despite my interrogation of Camilla on the stand, I wasn't convinced she was a plausible suspect.

I chose the street that backed onto the club, where the courtyard gate stood inconspicuously in the middle of the long stone wall. A sleek black keypad was the mode of entry, the code given to staff and, of course, to the resident of the apartment above the club, Hunter Wrightman. Though I'd found no flaws in his alibi, it was entirely possible that he had given that code to someone else, a theory that I intended to present to the court.

This, though, also required knowledge of the party's booking, along with precise timing and execution. There was no forensic evidence, no fingerprints or DNA, that supported an unknown party entering the Voltaire Room that night, and though I could competently dismiss that in court—gloves could be worn, after all; it was not always true that every contact leaves a trace—it was an insubstantial, nebulous alternative to your guilt to sell to a jury.

The other possibility, the one that I kept returning to, was that the brandy had come in with one of the men themselves. But if so, who had given it to them—someone known to them, someone trusted? And could I convince a jury of it, when the simpler solution, the most obvious one, was standing in the dock in front of them?

I walked back up the street and round into Dexter Square, doubling back toward the now-familiar mews. There, standing a little way down the street and staring up at the club, was your father. He looked up as I approached, his brow furrowing.

"I wasn't sure what to do with myself," he said. "I've been going mad, sitting at the flat on my own." He looked up at the club. "Though maybe it's madder, being here."

"Let's get a coffee," I said.

I found us a café nearby and went to order, leaving your father to take a seat. As I waited at the counter, I noticed how thin he looked. He was in his late fifties, I thought, only a decade or so ahead of me, but he seemed far older.

"Thank you," he said as I put his drink in front of him, though his hands stayed clasped in his lap.

I drank a little of my espresso—something I'd ordered on autopilot, a habit from a long-ago time, and was now regretting.

After a while, he picked up a sachet of sugar from the pot, laid it beside his saucer. "So much of what they've been saying . . . it feels surreal. Like they're talking about someone else. Not Kit."

"I understand," I said. "Are you getting any support?"

I noticed he was still wearing a wedding ring, and wondered again where your mother might be.

He waved the suggestion away. "I'm fine. I just need to be there for Kit."

"I can tell it's bringing her a great deal of comfort, seeing you in the gallery."

He smiled tightly, picked up the sugar sachet again. "My wife always thought I spoilt her," he said. "My ex-wife," he corrected himself.

I hesitated, unsure how to respond. "I suppose we're all guilty of that, when it comes to the people we care about."

"I can't help looking back," he said, his gaze still locked on mine. There was a faint sense of desperation in his voice. "I keep questioning the way I remember things, wondering if she was right. If I was blind to it all along."

"Blind to what?" I put down my espresso, my chest beginning to feel tight.

"Maybe I've always wanted her to be someone she isn't," he said. He rubbed at the corner of one eye. "I'm sorry. Ignore me. Like I said, I've been going a bit mad on my own."

I felt as though the room had started to shrink, the tight, sharp pain of a headache beginning at my temples.

"Are you worried about something that's been said in court?"

"No, no." He put up a hand to stop me, but I thought there was still that trace of desperation as he said, "Really, ignore me. It's been a difficult time."

"Of course," I said, though I was now afraid that, whether he was able to admit it to himself or not, your father was losing faith in you.

As I walked home afterward, the headache swelled and intensified.

92

Conrad

"Wildcat"

YOU WENT SILENT AFTER THAT. Just long enough to lull me into a false sense of security. No texts, no late-night calls, no staring at me from across the room like you were starving and I was edible. You acted as if I weren't there at all.

Fuck me, the relief.

Molly had started posting more on Instagram. Her and the new boyfriend, dressed up for the races, in first-class seats on a flight to Dubai. I lay awake at night and stared at them, half the time imagining myself by her side, half the time hating her for falling for someone so predictable, some boring toff with a trust fund and zero personality.

All of the time hating you for wrecking it for me.

Then the emails began. The sender's name just a string of numbers and letters.

You deserve to suffer, one read.

You'll wish you were dead.

A chain that began at three a.m. one morning, one insult after another. The mouth on you, wildcat. It might have impressed me before.

Instead I lay awake wondering how it was going to end.

Lucian threw one of his dinners: me, him, Harris Lowe, and some of the other directors from the Wrightman Group. His favorite private room, the Voltaire, down on the ground floor of the club. I felt like I'd made it to the next level, one big step closer to his inner circle. His new favorite, smiling modestly as he talked me up to everyone.

"Big plans for this one," he said, and the guy next to me, Lucian's finance director, who had maybe twenty years and ten times the salary on me, nudged my shoulder.

"He said that about me once. Now look."

I laughed along with all their jokes, tried not to drink too much of the wine. That was difficult, though—Lucian was a determined host, didn't take no for an answer. Kept calling you over, getting you to refill everyone's glasses.

I wasn't going to let you ruin it for me. I acted as if it didn't bother me at all, you being there. As if we barely knew each other.

You deserve to suffer, you whispered in my head.

At the end of the night, you served the brandy Lucian ordered. "Victoire," he said to me. "Haut-Armagnac, very rare. You'll like it."

You modeled the bottle for me, with its flat, circular body and stubby neck, and I ignored you.

You'll wish you were dead.

"The best of the best," Lucian said. "Thanks, Katie, sweetheart."

When no one was looking, I took a photo of my glass. Making sure none of the other men were in shot, so it looked like I could have been dining with anyone. *The best way to end a night,* I captioned it, then tagged the brand: *#victoire.* Hoping Molly would be curious, google it, and see how expensive it was.

I went out to the toilet after that, passing Camilla at the wait station. She was frowning down at a notebook, adding figures to the laptop in front of her.

"Lucian works you too hard," I said.

She glanced up. "I could say the same to you," she said.

"We should start a support group," I said. "Or at least compare notes."

As she laughed, I glanced up and saw you.

An hour later, you stopped me on my way out. Your hand gripping my arm. "Why are you doing this?" you asked, your face reddening.

"I'm not doing anything," I told you.

"Ignoring me, flirting with people right in front of me. Don't you care about my feelings at all?" You were practically shouting now, your voice watery, embarrassing.

"Grow up," I said. "And let go of me."

"Grow up?" you repeated, even louder now.

"It was just sex, for fuck's sake," I told you, shaking you off. "Stop harassing me—you're humiliating yourself."

You started crying properly at that. Pushed past me and ran off.

I turned to leave and saw Lucian standing in the doorway to the Voltaire Room, a knowing look on his face.

I gave him a shrug—a *what can you do?*—and headed for the exit. Wondering why an uncomfortable feeling of shame had crept over me, and hating you for it.

93

Max

"Killer Kate"

I WENT TO PADDINGTON THAT afternoon, stood on the platform where you'd been arrested, replaying the bodycam footage in my head as everyday people went about their lives, carting suitcases past me and talking on their phones. I retraced your steps back from that point and visited the military cemetery where your brother was buried. It was a big place, row after row of stark white headstones, a Union Jack flapping solemnly in the breeze, and it took me a while to find Stephen. The day was moody, with a drizzly rain—nicely atmospheric, I supposed, taking a few photos with my phone in case they ended up featuring in the book.

Stephen was near the center of a well-maintained row, the soil around each grave planted neatly. Your parents had chosen rosemary and a white flowering shrub for his plot, but there was nothing else personal there, no framed photos or trinkets that might have made it more interesting.

I stood there, looking at his name, and imagined you standing in the exact same place in the middle of the night. Nice of you to have stopped by for a final visit, I thought. It was an interesting detail about you, and I wondered what the public would think of it. Whether they might have some empathy for you, for being drawn into the Rabbit Hole's stories about the bad men who were to blame for the death of your beloved big brother, a core trauma at the heart of you that had made you ripe for Mr. E's radicalization.

I was glad I'd come. I put up my umbrella and headed for the Tube.

By the time I got to Wilbur's, it was winding down, half an hour left until closing, and there was only one barista working, with one of the young girls I recognized from the first time clearing and wiping tables. I ordered a green tea from the guy behind the counter, playing for time by hovering indecisively around the display of cakes. When there was still no sign of your brother, I went to pay and asked casually, "Is Bobby around?"

"He's away," the barista said, barely looking at me as he clicked the takeaway lid on my cup.

I wondered if he'd actually gone away or if he was just hiding in the flat upstairs, waiting for your trial to be over. I'd been paying careful attention, and he hadn't shown up to a single day of court proceedings, your dad there on his own time and time again. And now I had a feeling I knew why.

"Oh." I faked a confused look. "That's so weird. He told me to drop by. Do you think you could ask him to call me? I'm Max. I'm a friend of Peter's, you can tell him." I scribbled down my number on a napkin, passed it over with a grateful smile.

Half an hour later, my phone rang. Withheld number.

Bingo.

"Who is this?" he asked. He sounded like he was outside somewhere, and he did not seem in a good mood.

"Max Todd. I gave you my card a while back."

The shutters went down immediately. "I'm not interested."

"Just talk to me for a couple of minutes," I said, rushing in case he hung up. "Off the record. If you're still not interested, I'll leave you alone, okay?"

He said nothing. But the call stayed connected.

"When I first came to see you, it was interesting to hear you say you weren't shocked when you heard about the murders," I said.

"I said nothing Kit does would shock me," he said. "But I shouldn't have. Of course what happened to those men is shocking."

"But what did you mean by that? What else had Kate done that made you feel that way?"

There was a pause and then, with what sounded like reluctance, he said, "No comment."

"Okay," I said. "Let me tell you what I know. I know that she accused your gymnastics mentor of being a pedophile and had him hounded out of town, and I know that when he came back, she burned his house down."

He drew in a sharp breath. "Who said that?"

"Several reliable sources. Was she right about your coach?"

"No," he said hotly. "It wasn't true. Christ."

"That's a pretty serious thing to lie about."

He was breathing harder, like he was walking somewhere fast. "She was a troubled kid," he said. "She was just jealous of the attention I was getting."

"From an outsider's perspective, it seems like your 'troubled' kid sister made up a lie that wrecked a man's life and maybe even derailed your gymnastics career."

He was silent, and I decided to take that as an encouraging sign.

"And now, years later, you've set yourself up nicely with Wilbur's, and she's blown everything up again. Because I bet people are asking you about it a lot in the coffee shop, aren't they? You guys look alike, you have the same surname. Maybe word's got round—no one wants to worry about their latte being poisoned—and I'm guessing business is suffering."

I could hear the wind whistling at his end of the line. Wherever he was, it sounded bleak.

"No one would blame you," I pressed. "Anyone would understand the need to distance yourself from it. To make sure the truth was out there."

He scoffed at that. "To sell you my story, you mean."

"We could discuss that. If it felt like the right thing to do. For yourself, after everything that's happened."

There was the longest silence of all after that, and I crossed my fingers, waiting. *Come on.*

"No comment," he said. "Don't call again."

94

Gabriel

"K. C."

I COULDN'T SLEEP FOR DAYS after you left. I sat up all night rereading the March House threads on the Rabbit Hole on the laptop you'd left behind, trying to imagine you there, working for those men. Laughing and talking and drinking with them, like you didn't know anything at all.

It was his fault, I realized. He was the one who had changed you, messed with your head and made you someone else. He'd turned you into just another sheep, the kind of person the Rabbit Hole was always warning me about.

I looked at his Instagram profile one night, with all its stupid pictures of fancy meals and show-offy places, sometimes his own stupid handsome chiseled face with his manly stubble and perfect teeth. I scrolled further down and saw photos of a pretty girl with dark hair. There was one of them cuddled up together, and they looked stupidly happy, like they belonged in a catalog. I stared at it for ages, wondering why he couldn't have stayed with her and left you alone.

Feeling worse, I scrolled back to the top, to the most recent photo, a glass of some kind of booze. The location was tagged as March House, and the caption read *The best way to end a night #victoire*. For a second I got excited, thinking that maybe it was a girl's name, maybe he was on a date, but then, feeling like I'd been punched in the stomach, I saw that you'd liked it. I googled the word, saw that it was French but also a brandy company. Because he was a grown-up man who drank grown-up drinks like brandy, probably in front of an open fire while he stroked his manly stubble and smiled at you. Touched you. Poisoned you against me and all the things we'd believed in.

I hated him I hated him I hated him.

I'd finally fallen asleep the first time the police came. I woke up to the sounds of their radios echoing up the stairwell, the heavy thump of boots on the concrete. I peered out from behind my curtain as they came through the door, a man and a woman. He was tall with a gingery beard; she had her hair scraped back into a tiny ponytail that didn't really seem worth the effort.

"All right," he said. "Let's not drag this out. You know why we're here."

Rudy stood up, folding his arms. "Actually, we don't."

"The owners of this building have notified us that you're squatting. And they're not very happy about that, as you might expect."

Rudy smirked. I could see Polly scowling from her place beside him, while Leah shrank back in her seat, looking scared. "My heart bleeds for them," Rudy said. "But squatting in a commercial property is *not a crime*." He gave a little singsong emphasis to the last three words, fixing them with a stare that felt like a challenge.

"Using utilities without permission is, though," the female officer said, tucking her thumbs into the armholes of her vest. "You want to brush up on your law a bit more, mate."

"The owners have applied for an interim possession order," the man said. He sounded tired. "Once the court approves it, you'll have twenty-four hours to get out. I'd suggest you leave before that and make this easier on all of us."

"How long will it take, this order?" Anneka asked. "We'd like to get legal advice too."

"Don't waste your time and ours." The man's radio crackled, and he reached down and silenced it. "Trust me. Get on your way and find somewhere you can legally live, before this gets nasty."

"I really hope that's not a threat," Polly said.

"Just a friendly suggestion," the woman said, and as she turned to leave, she looked round at the place we'd made home. "Nice luxury flats, it's gonna be," she said. "Very fancy. They aren't going to mess around when there's that kind of money involved."

After they left, Rudy picked up a chair and threw it at the window, cracking another of the panes.

"Fuck this," he said. "Fuck this and fuck them."

"Can they really do it?" Leah asked, looking scared.

"They can do whatever they want," Rudy said. "They don't play by the fucking rules, these people, so why should we?"

95

Conrad

"Wildcat"

I WAS SUMMONED TO THE club for a chat with Lucian one lunchtime and found him sitting at a window table with his berk of a son in tow. He was a good-looking kid, if a bit pretty that whole Chalamet thing going on with the pale, pointy little face and the messy hair that needed a wash and a cut. A chain round his neck that probably cost a bomb, wrinkled T-shirt definitely designer.

"This is Hunter," Lucian said, and the kid grunted at me.

"Hey," I said. So this was the teenage waster, the one with the written-off car.

"You go and pick up coffees," Lucian said to him. "And I'll see you back at the office."

The kid nodded, looking miserable, and loped off without saying goodbye to either of us.

"I'm trying to get him involved in the business," Lucian said. "Keep him on the straight and narrow, you know."

"Sure," I said. Thinking: What is this, community service?

"I'm glad we've got a moment to ourselves," he added, laying his hands flat on the table. "There's something I wanted to raise with you. It's a little delicate."

"Okay," I said. Thinking: this doesn't sound fucking good.

"The other night," he said. Eyeing me with that cool blue stare. "Katie."

"About that—"

He put up a hand to stop me.

"I don't need the details. I'm sure you know what you're doing. But I've got a daughter not far off that age. And I'd hope that when Hunter gets to yours . . ."

He gave this little shrug.

"Well," he said. "It's none of my business."

Except we both knew that it was. That I was part of his business now. And you were fucking ruining it for me.

"Anyway," he said. "I needed to update you on some conversations I've been having. A little awkward, I'm afraid."

"Sure," I said. As if it weren't already arse-clenchingly awkward for me.

"Harris has someone in mind to head up the new company. If it was up to me, it'd be yours, but . . ."

I thought: You're Lucian Wrightman. It's up to you.

But I smiled. Said, "Sure. I get it. No problem."

"He's the expert."

"No, of course."

"And you're doing great things with Kindred. Don't think I don't have big plans for you there."

"I'm sure," I said.

Thinking: take your big plans and your shitty fancy booze and fucking choke on them.

96

John

"Kit-Kat"

I VISITED STEPHEN ON SUNDAY afternoon, unable to get permission to come and see you at HMP Peterborough. The shrubs we'd planted at his headstone—rosemary, for remembrance, and white forget-me-nots, the flower you'd chosen, aged eleven—had grown wilder since my last visit. Before your arrest, I'd always suspected that you were the one keeping it tidy, often noticed that the headstone looked cleaner than the ones around it when I came up to the city to visit.

Now I imagined you there on the night of the murders. You'd left the club and come here, a place where I imagined you felt safe. Why? What had happened that night that made you need that comfort, that reassurance?

I remembered the smile on your face in the bus CCTV footage, an expression I hadn't recognized. A smile that had frightened me. I pushed the thought away.

I broke off some of the wilted stems and leaves and tamped down the soil, then used my handkerchief to wipe the grime from the letters of Stephen's name. I crouched with my hand against the cool marble for a while, thinking of him and the man he would have been.

Afterward, I walked across the east quadrant of the graveyard and found your great-grandfather to pay my respects. Godfrey, the farm's namesake, and a man the three of you had often asked to hear stories about. You and Stephen had played soldiers on our holidays at the farm after looking at old photographs of Godfrey in his uniform, disappearing into the barns and the woods for hours at a time. Your uncle rigged up lookouts for you, showed you how to paint camouflage across your faces.

I sat down on one of the benches nearby and called your mum. When she answered, she sounded groggy.

"Is everything okay?" I asked. "Did I wake you?"

"I just lay down for a second," she said, immediately defensive. "Headache. I'm fine."

"You're probably exhausted. Try and rest."

"I can't. The whole place is a mess, the fields are jungles or they're dead." She sighed. "Bobby and I hacked down a hedge that must have been seven feet deep today—we filled the van twice before he left. That's what it's been like every day, and it still looks like no one's been here for twenty years. I just can't believe he let it get like this."

"You don't need to do all that. Hire someone. Or just sell the place as it is."

She made a frustrated noise. "I *can't*. I should've helped more. I should've been here. This is the least I can do."

"You're making yourself ill."

"I'll survive," she snapped. "And it's none of your business anymore, is it?"

That stung, and I supposed I deserved it. But as the seconds wore on and neither of us spoke, I felt my own anger rising.

"Are you even going to ask how she is?"

There was a long silence, and when she spoke, she sounded tearful. "I don't need this right now, John," she said. "I really don't."

And she hung up.

97

Max

"Killer Kate"

I HAD A MESSAGE ON Instagram that afternoon and got my hopes up, thinking it might be your mate Gabe. But when I opened my inbox, it was a belated response from Tiffany Lowe, Harris's daughter.

I'd never talk to a rag like yours, but thanks.

Charming. I sent her a passive-aggressive thumbs-up back.

Mood punctured, I went back to my laptop. Since your brother wouldn't talk to me, I'd gone back to my search on Peter Walters himself. The first life you'd ruined. An interview with *him* would be gold.

But my first few attempts got me nowhere, and a couple of hours wasted on a hundred social media profiles also proved futile.

I searched through Companies House and eventually, an hour later, wondered if I'd found him. A Walter G. Peters was listed as company director for a gym in Portsmouth in 2002, the company showing as dissolved two years later. If it *was* the same guy, he'd at some point reversed his first and surnames.

Now even more interested, I stuck the new name into Google and got nothing in the first page or two.

But I had the bit between my teeth. I kept looking, trawling through fruitless result after result. Halfway down the sixth page, there it was. A subreddit dedicated to weeding out sex offenders in communities, a group of vigilantes with a lot of time on their hands and little respect for due process.

Walter Peters—Manchester, one of them had posted, almost eight years after he'd left Combe Little. *Served twenty-six weeks for distribution of indecent images of children (Category C). Sometimes goes by "Peter."*

I sat back and stared at the screen.

He'd gotten away with it in Devon, but apparently not the next time he'd tried.

You hadn't been lying.

My phone bleeped—an Instagram message. I opened it and saw that it was just Hasan, sending me a stupid football meme. I sent him a laughing emoji out of charity and sat there, staring into space for a second.

You'd been telling the truth about your brother's coach. What did that mean for you?

How did it fit with the version of you I'd built in my head?

When I went back to my message list, I saw the thread with Hunter Wrightman. Idly, I clicked on his profile. It was about as wanky as I expected—photos of pretty boys and beautiful girls in bars and at parties, all with a filter on to make them look like they'd been taken with an old camera.

I paused over a close-up of a girl, wondering why she looked familiar—pale face and pale blond hair, big sad eyes like some kind of oil-painted orphan. Then it clicked: she was the girl who'd made a show of trying to escape the public gallery earlier in the week. Hunter's caption read *Sister assisting*, and she'd been tagged for good measure: @vwright. So this was Lucian's daughter—no wonder she'd looked like she was going to puke listening to the toxicologist.

There were only two of Hunter himself: a photo taken in March House, of him drinking a glass of whiskey or brandy and talking to someone out of shot, and the other a mirror selfie in what looked like a dive bar toilet with his phone mostly covering his face. Both of them were a couple of years old, and his arms were notably less tattooed—the biggest, the staff with two snakes wrapped around it and wings at the top, was alone on his forearm in the mirror selfie, stark against his pale skin, while in the second one at March House six months later, he had two newer ones, a quote I couldn't read and some kind of plant or flower.

I looked at the first picture again, zooming in on the tattoo, and then I turned back to my laptop and opened YouTube.

98

Gabriel

"K. C."

YOU'D BEEN GONE ALMOST THREE weeks by the time the interim possession order the police had warned us about was served. It was serious, scary enough that Leah and Grace and some of the others packed up and left immediately. Rudy read it aloud. "Claimant: Lowe Estates. Fucking Harris Lowe again. The wealthiest property company in London, and they're kicking us out of our *home*."

"Fuck them," Polly said. "Let's trash the place. Let's set fire to it."

"Direct action," Rudy said. "Are you in, Angel Gabriel?"

I wasn't well. When I look back at that time, everything is stretched and yawning and weird, like a nightmare. I hadn't slept in days, hadn't done anything except scroll the Rabbit Hole, reading about the things Mr. E said were happening at March House. Reading the comments over and over and over, until my head was a jumble of voices and thoughts and fears. So when I tell you I don't remember everything clearly, I hope you believe me.

I remember that I put your laptop and some of your things into a backpack and slipped out of the Cally. I'd spent a while studying the route to March House online, but I still felt underprepared. Shaky. I kept checking the sky, the buildings, the cars driving endlessly past. Feeling like there was a target on my back, on everyone's.

Mayfair looked different, like another country. I felt like an alien, looking at the people sitting outside under striped awnings drinking cocktails and wine, my face all white and puffy in the windows of the expensive shops.

I remember everyone staring at me from their sleek cars and black cabs, from crowded tables in fancy restaurants, the doormen in their suits staring at me too. I kept my head down, felt like crying. I couldn't stop wondering who they all were, what they had done. The Group would have spies everywhere—Mr. E had said that so many times. We had to keep our eyes open.

I couldn't breathe. Even when I left the busier streets for the quiet square behind March House, I felt them watching me. A thousand security cameras turning in my direction, the dark windows of the townhouses hiding faces behind their curtains, the railings like weapons.

Then there it was. The club, towering over the little cobbled street like a haunted house, with a thousand voices inside my head whispering what went on in there.

I didn't dare get any closer. I waited for over an hour at the end of the mews, wishing I could curl up in a ball and hide, until finally you came round the corner, a can of cream soda in your hand. You jumped when you saw me.

"Hi," you said, and I couldn't help noticing that you looked worried, that your eyes flicked around to see who might be watching us.

"I brought some of your stuff," I said, holding out the bag. "We have to leave the Cally."

"Oh." You took it from me. "Thanks."

"Don't go in there, please. Come with me now, we can get away from here. It's not too late."

You looked sad, like you didn't understand. "I'm going to work now. And I think maybe you need to go home, get some sleep."

"Please, you have to listen to Mr. E—"

"Stop," you said, but you sounded angry now. "I don't want to talk about Mr. E, Gabe. None of that is real."

I laughed. This big, harsh sound that burst out of me like puke. "You're wrong."

You turned away. "I can't talk about this right now. If I'm late again—"

"You know one of Lucian Wrightman's companies is a defense

contractor?" My hands were shaking as I grabbed my phone, tried to find the right website for you. "Night vision and targeting systems."

"Stop," you said again, not looking at the page I was trying to show you. "I don't want—"

"Do you know how much money they made, the year your brother died?" I shouted, my voice trembling. I felt like I was looking down on both of us, like I wasn't in my own body anymore. "He's *dead* because of the Group and you don't even care!"

You took a big, shaky breath, and I wished I could reach out and cram the words back into my mouth.

"Wrightman made money out of that war," I said. Feeling sick and giddy as the words kept spilling out. "Just like Mr. E said."

"Stop," you whispered.

"And people in there made money out of Covid," I said. "With bad PPE and tests that didn't work. You can check the records. It's just like Mr. E told us."

You clenched your fists.

"They're lying to us," I said. "It's all lies, all of it."

When you spoke again, your voice was small and didn't sound like you anymore.

"I think you should go."

I stood there and watched as you walked into work and my whole world fell down. I stood and looked at March House, and knew that I'd lost you. That I was losing everything that really mattered.

That they had taken it from me.

99

John

"Kit-Kat"

I WENT BACK TO THE flat after I left the cemetery. Washed the cup and plate I'd used that morning, put my shirts and socks in the washing machine, and tried to translate the symbols on each of the space-age dials. Wiped down the counters and then the cupboard doors, even though Bobby kept the place spotless. Finally I sat down on the leather sofa and started flicking through TV channels, watching strangers judging each other's dinner parties and strangers going on first dates and finally finding an old film you'd all liked as kids, *Back to the Future*. I made pasta, ate it with little appetite as the film finished and its sequel came on.

Bobby came in at a little after ten. He dumped his bag at the front door and peered through to the living space. "Hi, Dad." He looked exhausted.

"Hi." I went over to hug him. He responded stiffly. "Have you eaten? There's pasta."

He shook his head. "I'll just have some toast or something."

He opened a drawer and found a blister pack of paracetamol. As he filled a pint glass with water, he nodded at the TV, where Doc and Marty were clambering into the DeLorean. "A classic." He punched the last two tablets out of the pack, tossing them into his mouth.

"You're not ill as well?"

He shook his head. "I'm fine. Just a headache. It's been a long few days."

I turned and filled the kettle. "Do you want tea?"

"Thanks." He leaned against the counter, sipping his water, as I got down mugs and tea bags.

"How was your mum?"

He pulled a face. "Stoic. You know how she is."

"I'm glad you were with her."

He put down his glass. "The state of it, Dad," he said, shaking his head. "All the outbuildings have just been left to rot. And the farmhouse was . . . There's this terrible feeling there now. Worse than it ever was."

I sighed. "I wish she'd sell it. I know we all have happy memories there, we all loved Neil, but after this . . ."

The kettle began rumbling on its stand. I put tea bags into the mugs, put the box back in the cupboard. When I glanced up, Bobby was looking thoughtful.

"Is that really how you remember it?" he asked.

"What do you mean?"

"Never mind." He shook his head, went to the fridge for milk.

I took it from him, put it down on the side. "No, tell me. Is that really how I remember what?"

"Going to Godfrey's." He looked bemused. "That we were all happy there."

The kettle boiled and clicked off. I ignored it. "Weren't we?"

"I was fucking terrified of Neil," he said. "So was Stevie."

I stopped, taken aback by the matter-of-fact way he'd said it. "Terrified?"

"He used to threaten us. Talk about feeding us to the pigs or sending us to the abattoir if we were naughty. When you took me there when I was eighteen, he marched me out to the loch and said he'd drown me if I didn't buck my ideas up. That he'd get me out of yours and Mum's hair once and for all."

"He had a dark sense of humor, I know, but—"

"He wasn't kidding, Dad." He went over to his bag, took out a battered old notebook. "Look at this," he said, flicking through the pages. I saw Neil's scrawled writing, lots of lines scribbled out. Bobby found what he was looking for and held it out to me. At the center of the page, a list of names.

I studied them. There were several I didn't recognize; a couple that I did. Conrad Milton. You. Me.

"What is this?" I asked.

He shrugged, flicked through the pages again. He showed me another, the words inked over several times so that they'd bled into the page. *They can all suffer now.* "The whole thing is like that," he said, putting the notebook down on the side. "It's poisonous. Horrible. I didn't want Mum to see."

I picked it up but didn't open it.

"He was always like that," Bobby said. "It just got worse after the business failed. But he always had that streak."

"Why didn't you ever say anything?"

He raised an eyebrow. "You two had enough problems, don't you think?"

A wave of guilt hit me. "I'm sorry," I said, reaching out to touch his arm. "I really am, Bobby."

"I know." He turned away, started making the tea I'd abandoned.

"Look, about tomorrow—"

"Don't," he said, without looking up. "We shouldn't talk about it."

100

Tarun

"Katherine"

I SPENT SUNDAY STANDING IN front of the wall, my thoughts racing anxiously from one document to the next. The prospect of the prosecution ending their case loomed; it would soon be time to begin presenting our defense. Your testimony was crucial, the single most important thing I could offer the jury—and yet I still had no idea how you would perform on the stand. I'd begun to pace, running through the possibilities, when I looked down at my phone and saw a text from Elliot: *Are you home?*

I looked around at the disorderly flat, and then down at the jogging bottoms I'd put on.

I am. Why? I wrote back with one hand, as I headed for the wall and started pulling down all the pages I'd taped there.

Be there in ten, he replied, and I crashed around the place, scooping clothes into the wardrobe and plates into the dishwasher.

The bell rang promptly nine minutes later, and I buzzed him in and met him at the front door of the flat, wondering belatedly if I'd remembered to apply deodorant that morning.

Elliot was wearing shorts and a baseball cap and carrying a bottle of wine.

"Thought I'd better check up on you," he said cheerfully. "Make sure you're remembering to eat and sleep this time."

"Kind of you." I took the bottle from him. "Come in."

"It's nonalcoholic," he said, as he closed the door and kicked off his shoes. "I wasn't sure if you were still . . ."

"It's great." I went to the kitchen and got out a corkscrew and two glasses.

"Looks good in here," he said. "You finally swapped those chairs round."

"Yes. You were right, it does look better."

I flushed, wondering if he had any idea how often I had imagined him reading in the one now positioned by the bay window. How many times I'd taken out my phone to send a photo but been too afraid of being met by silence.

I poured the wine, and he pulled out one of the stools at the breakfast bar.

"Look, there was something else." He fiddled with the stem of his wineglass, and I felt a little leap of anticipation. "A colleague of mine heard I was interested in Lucian and March House and came to chat to me—Florence, do you remember her?"

"Of course." I scrambled through my memory, trying to place the name. A vague image of a woman with a severe bob and elaborate glasses surfaced.

"She was at Lucian's sixtieth birthday party a few years back, doing a profile on him, and she mentioned something that struck me as interesting."

"Go on." I pulled out the stool next to him, took a sip of my wine.

"There was a bit of drama at the end of the night, she said. Someone had collapsed after drinking from a display of champagne. Lucian's daughter, Violet."

I put my glass back down.

"Florence was told Violet had just been enjoying the bar a bit too much for someone underage, all very normal, what can you do, these kids today kind of thing. But it sounds like Lucian was *very* keen to keep it under wraps."

"Because perhaps it was something more sinister than that," I mused.

"Exactly."

"When was this?"

"Twenty nineteen, she said. Pre-pandemic."

"So it predates Katherine Cole starting work and even Mr. E starting his posts on the Rabbit Hole," I said.

"Precisely. Someone might have had it in for Lucian all this time?"

"Maybe." Instinctively, I looked toward the wall, forgetting I'd removed all my papers. "The question is, who?"

101

Max

"Killer Kate"

I ARRIVED AT MARCH HOUSE that evening just in time to see Hunter leaving. He was coming down the steps in baggy jogging bottoms and another battered-looking sweatshirt, the sleeves pushed up. Black YSL sunglasses on even though it was dark, his hair greasy.

"I know it was you," I said, and he stiffened.

"What was?"

I smiled and nodded to his arm. "The tattoo. A staff entwined with snakes. The caduceus. Symbol of Hermes, right?"

He watched me without speaking.

"Hermes was the son of Zeus," I said casually, like I hadn't memorized it off Wikipedia after replaying DeeDee's Mr. E video a hundred times to make sure the tattoo definitely matched. "One of the youngest Olympians."

"I don't know what you're talking about," Hunter said, but he tugged his sleeve down to his wrist.

"He was the messenger of the gods," I said.

"If you say so."

"Able to move freely between the mortal and divine realms," I said, as if we were just two guys shooting the breeze. "They called him 'the divine trickster.'"

"I'll look him up," he said, trying to move past me. I stepped into his path.

"The thing about Mr. E," I said, "is that, for all his made-up bullshit about pandemics and wars and bunkers, he was pretty accurate about which high-profile members were visiting 'Olympus' at any given time and what they were eating and drinking."

Hunter was silent.

"Was it a game?" I asked. "Something to do during lockdown? Wind up all the crazies on the internet, see how far you could take it?"

He grimaced, turned away from me.

"I bet you sat there laughing, didn't you?" I asked. "Wondering what else you could dream up to see if they believed you?"

"No comment," he said, but he looked scared now. A scared little boy.

"Except it wasn't a game," I said. "It had consequences. *Real-world* consequences. A woman is on trial right now because of what you wrote. Your own father is—"

"No *comment*," he said, and pushed past me.

102

John

"Kit-Kat"

THE DAY I'D BEEN DREADING arrived, and when I first woke up, I had a horrible urge to pull the covers over my head, to stay there all day.

Instead I got up, showered and shaved, then dressed and walked to the bus stop. As I rode the bus, I stared out at the city and wished, more than ever, that you had never set foot in it.

I bought a muffin from the coffee shop nearest the court, so dry when I tried to eat it that my throat felt clogged, the crumbs like sand as I brushed off my shirt. I bought a bottle of water, drank some with a shaking hand. I forgot I couldn't bring it into the court with me and tried to drink the rest quickly as the security guard watched, spilling some down myself.

Inside the court, my legs shook as I climbed the steps, and I was relieved to take my seat, turning my body away from the rest of the gallery.

I met your eye as Bobby took the stand, smiling to reassure you. When I looked across at your brother, he turned away.

Naylor opened with some questions about the two of you growing up, about our life. Warming him up, the way I'd noticed her do with each of her witnesses. He answered calmly and clearly but I could see he was trying hard not to look at you.

"What were things like at home, after Stephen's death?" she asked, her voice gentle.

"Tense. My parents' marriage was on the rocks. Neither of them ever got over losing him, and life was very different after that."

My stomach dropped.

"How do you think your sister coped?"

"Badly. I would say she struggled the most."

I saw Tarun frown, scribbling a note to his junior.

"What was she like as a child?"

"A bit of a nerd. She loved reading about nature and history and the world, because those were things that Stephen liked. But she was creative too, into drawing, that kind of thing."

"And as you got older, what was your relationship like with your sister?"

"Poor. She—" He hesitated and I thought, *Please don't. Please don't say it.* "We argued a lot," he continued. "We were very different and I guess we were both hotheaded as teenagers."

"And as adults?"

"My contact with her was very limited. She cut all of us off for a while, and moved to London on her own."

"Why was that?"

I swallowed, my mouth dry.

Now Bobby glanced at you. "There was an argument with my uncle. Kit felt that my parents should've taken her side."

I let out a shaky breath. I didn't know when he'd decided to omit Peter, the fire. The farm closing down. I thought that he must've known it wasn't you, that you couldn't have killed them. And he was trying to help you.

"When did your sister get back in touch?"

"Last year, she didn't have anywhere to live. She called my dad and he asked me to let her move in with me."

I thought about the night you'd called me in tears, told me you had nowhere to go. You'd fallen out with friends, you said. You didn't know what to do. The relief I'd felt at finally hearing from you, at finally being able to offer help.

"Can you remember specifically when in 2022 that was?"

"Last summer. August."

"So Katherine was living with you while she was working at March House?"

"Yes."

There was a new tension in the room, everyone realizing why he'd been called as the last witness. I could feel the back of my collar getting damp with sweat.

"Did you discuss her job there?"

"Not really. We avoided each other as best we could. It was awkward, really. We were like strangers by then."

"How did your sister seem, when your paths did cross?"

"Quiet," Bobby said. "Like she was stewing over something, the way she did when we were kids sometimes."

You looked up at that, hurt. Bobby avoided your gaze.

"Do you recall the evening of August tenth, 2022?"

"Yes. I'd been on a date that night, so I'd gone to bed late. Then Kit came into my room around two a.m., and woke me up just as I was drifting off."

"Why did she do that?"

"She was upset. She said she needed to talk to someone."

My heart started thumping.

"She was upset?" Naylor prompted him.

"Yes. She was crying."

"What was she upset about?"

He looked at the floor. "'I don't know. She wasn't making much sense. I thought she was drunk. She used to do that as a teenager, get drunk and start crying, making a drama out of nothing."

"What did she say?"

"She said . . ." He frowned, like he was trying to picture you. "She said she'd made a mistake. She kept saying that she wanted to go home."

I closed my eyes.

"How did you respond?"

"I was angry with her for waking me up. I'd just taken a sleeping pill, I was confused . . . I told her to go to bed. And in the morning, when I woke up, she was gone. I thought I'd dreamt it, to be honest."

As Naylor confirmed she had no further questions, I tried to tell myself not to imagine it. Not to wonder what you'd have said to Bobby if he'd listened, if he'd been kind to you. If he'd sat up in bed and asked you what had happened. What you'd done.

103

Conrad

"Wildcat"

THE GIFT ARRIVED THE DAY after Lucian had shot me down for the new job. I came back from a meeting with one of our gin distilleries, and it was there waiting on my desk: a plain brown box with parcel tape stuck messily across the flaps.

I opened it, wondering if I'd drunk-ordered something the night before, and found a black gift box, the kind you get champagne or whatever in.

I thought of you immediately. Your sycophantic baby voice. *You deserve nice things.*

I lifted it out and opened it, my headache getting worse.

There it was. A bottle of Victoire, a special vintage.

A peace offering, probably, in your twisted little mind. I pushed it away from me, listened to the rain hammering against my window.

Then, thinking better of it, I stood up. Closed the box again and picked it up.

It was the end of the day, the office mostly empty. When I went up, Lucian was alone: a first. Almost like it was meant to be. He was on his way out, a Selfridges bag in hand, and it felt like luck was on my side.

"Conrad." Maybe I was imagining it, but his tone wasn't friendly.

"I just wanted to say no hard feelings," I said. "About the new role. And I wanted to say thank you for involving me so far."

I held the brandy out, box open. Like a fucking engagement ring.

"No, really, that's not necessary," Lucian said, embarrassed. But he stepped closer to look. "Is that the 1972?"

"It is," I said, as if that meant anything to me.

Lucian took the bottle from the box, turned it over in his hands. Admiring it. "Now, this is a special drink."

I stepped back, open box still in my hands. Like now he couldn't give it back. "Just a token of my appreciation," I said. "Really. And I hope we'll continue to work together."

And I left the office before he had a chance to reply.

Max

"Killer Kate"

WATCHING YOUR BROTHER IN COURT, I felt torn.

On the one hand: not my monkeys, not my circus. Who was I, some random journalist, to roll up and tell him that, actually, he'd been wrong about his beloved coach? It felt like something way beyond the realms of my duty to follow up, especially when he'd made it pretty clear he didn't want to talk to me again. It also hadn't escaped my notice that he hadn't mentioned it in court, that it wasn't part of the case against you.

On the other: you'd been telling the truth. And that felt important too. It felt like something he should know.

I kept looking at you, the whole time he was talking. Because you had told the truth one time, sure—but did that make you innocent?

I didn't think so. Not with that little story about you waking him up crying, panicking about what you'd done.

And yet something was bugging me, Kate. The whole thing was bugging me, in a way I couldn't put my finger on.

When I checked my phone during the break, I saw I had a new message from Hunter Wrightman.

Can we meet?

Gabriel

"K. C."

A COUPLE OF DAYS AFTER I moved back home, my mum came into my room and pulled open the curtains with a big dramatic flourish like a magician.

"Rise and shine, precious firstborn," she singsonged.

I pulled the covers over my head. She tugged them back down.

"We're out of tea bags. Any chance you could pop to the shop while I make lunch?"

I mumbled something about needing more sleep, and she pulled the duvet down further.

"Tea," she said, in her firmest head teacher slash drill sergeant voice.

I knew she'd just invented an errand to make me leave the house, but I was too tired to argue with her, so I dragged myself off the bed, pulled a hoodie on, and went out.

It was hot out, too hot for the sweatshirt, but I felt like hiding in it, and I kept the hood up. Even with the sky blue and the sun out, the familiar sound of the waves washing against the beach didn't calm me down the way it used to. I still felt like I was in a dream, like everything was wrong, like I wanted to run and never stop.

I thought about us sitting together on the dunes, all the things we'd shared and planned and laughed about, and it felt like remembering another lifetime, another universe. As I skidded down the last one, heading up off the beach toward the high street, I walked faster, trying to shut the memories out.

I'd picked the wrong route and realized too late that now I had to walk past Peter Walters's old place. For years afterward, I'd dreamt about that house, about being trapped in it, about it swallowing me whole, but in the bright blue summer daylight, it wasn't how I expected. They'd fixed it up really well, like you'd never even have known the way it looked before, with the black charred marks licking up the white walls like tongues reaching out from the windows, the roof all fallen in.

But as I stopped on the corner and looked up at the place, it all came flooding back. I remembered the fury on your face as you talked about him, the way I'd caught that feeling too, as easy as a virus beating right through my veins. *He's a monster,* you'd said, and I'd known what to do.

I remembered how easy it had been to pick up the rock, the way the window glass had sounded like music as it shattered and fell.

Remembered the way you took the lighter from your pocket, how loud the flint sounded against your thumb. The flicker of the flame in the dark as you leaned through the broken window and held it to the curtain.

It went up so fast, and it felt so right, at least at first. It was like the anger had jumped right out of us, like it was a living thing, something beautiful and powerful and amazing.

We ran away so fast I thought my heart was going to explode. And when we stopped and you reached out and squeezed my hand, it nearly did.

I bought the tea and walked back home feeling more miserable than ever.

"In here," my mum called as I took off my shoes, and I went into the living room, where she was watching the TV.

"Have you seen this?" she said, glancing up at me. "They're saying that girl is from here."

I looked at the screen and saw you.

"Waitress Arrested After Four Men Poisoned at London Members' Club," the headline along the bottom of the screen read as the picture changed to footage from outside March House, crime scene tape across the street, but my ears were ringing too much to hear what the newsreader was saying.

"Do you recognize her?" Mum asked.

"Yeah." My voice sounded far away and like it belonged to someone who wasn't me. "Yeah, she was in my year at school."

Mum pressed a hand to her face as your name appeared in the next line of text: "Katherine Cole, Aged 22, Was Charged This Morning in London." "God. Did you know her?"

I couldn't tell her that you were the K.C. I'd talked about, the name she'd probably always heard the way it sounded: Casey. It felt like there was something hard in my throat, something it was almost impossible to squeeze even the smallest word round. "No," I heard myself say. "No, I didn't really know her at all."

106

Tarun

"Katherine"

YOU LOOKED TEARFUL AS MY cross-examination of your brother began, and I could see several jurors studying you. I felt deflated myself, the weight of Bobby's testimony about that night as significant as I'd feared. The information that Elliot had brought me about another possible incident at March House seemed suddenly less hopeful, a tall order for me to spin in the face of the case Verity had presented against you.

The thought frustrated me as I rose to speak.

"Mr. Cole, you resented the fact your father had forced you to let Katherine stay with you, didn't you?"

He blinked. "I wouldn't say . . . It was awkward, yes. Of course."

"The little sister you'd never got on with, who, by your own admission, you argued with a lot, had always sucked up all the attention in the family with her drama and now was living rent free in your home. You were angry about that, weren't you?"

He drew back. "I mean, I wasn't thrilled about it, but I wouldn't say angry . . ."

"Well, you were hardly feeling well-disposed toward her when she came to you for advice that night, were you?"

"It was the middle of the night," he said sullenly. "I was asleep."

"Yes, that's right," I said, consulting my notes. "You'd taken a sleeping pill, hadn't you?"

"Yes."

"You said yourself, 'I was confused.'"

He stared at me. "Yes."

"You didn't listen to her properly, did you? You didn't want to listen."

"Like I said, it was the middle of the night."

"She'd just walked out of a job she hated and had her heart broken by a man she'd been seeing, and the only person she had to turn to at that moment was you. And you rejected her, didn't you?"

His face hardened. "I didn't know any of that at the time."

"In fact, had you shown your sister some kindness, she might not have felt so alone that she left your flat and headed to Paddington to catch a train home. Your coldness toward her was the only reason she was 'fleeing' the city, as the prosecution would have us believe, wasn't it?"

Now he looked at you. "I don't know."

You looked back at him, your lips pressed together so tightly they'd turned pale, and for a moment, I couldn't tell if it was anger or sadness I saw on your face.

107

John

"Kit-Kat"

WHEN THE JUDGE SENT US for a coffee break, I walked up Holborn Viaduct to a phone box and called your mum.

"How did it go?" she asked.

I studied a crack in one of the glass panes, wondering how to answer that.

"As well as it probably could," I said. "And it's done now."

"I've just been sitting here, thinking about it. Thinking about them both. I should be there. I know I should. Everything is just . . . I can't . . ."

"It's okay," I said, unnerved by the way she seemed to be unraveling.

"It all feels like a nightmare. Like I'm not really here."

"Have you been sleeping?"

"Last night I slept like the dead. And I . . . John, I drove into the village earlier to get some paracetamol for my head, and I saw Stacey."

I dimly recalled the local vet who'd once come to dinner with us at the farm, a woman who'd drunk two bottles of wine and tried to teach us all the Haymaker's Jig.

"She said she'd seen me out in the field with the van, with all the cuttings, and that I ought to be careful. Cut cherry laurel branches are toxic, they release a form of—"

I felt a rush of ice down my spine. "Cyanide," I said.

"Yes. Stacey remembered because she said the pigs got sick once, eating it. Neil had to move them out of that field."

I turned and looked back in the direction of the court, my brain running back and forth over this information like it was a loose tooth.

"John? Are you there?"

"It's just that cyanide is . . ."

"I know," she said. "That's what I mean. It feels like a nightmare. None of it feels real."

I thought about the notebook that Bobby had shown me, the list of names etched in dark scratched letters. The pigs had been sick, and Conrad Milton's name had been on that list.

"I need you to check something for me," I said slowly, the idea coming into focus. "Do you have access to Neil's emails?"

When she answered, she sounded scared. "Why?"

"Please trust me," I said. Something I hadn't asked of her in a long time.

"There's the computer in the study. I don't even know if it still works."

"Can you find out?"

"Why?" she asked again, more forceful now. "I don't understand. What's going on?"

I explained, and told her that I'd call back.

I caught Ursula walking back toward the courtroom, her heels clicking briskly across the marble floor.

"John." She put a comforting hand on my arm. "How are you holding up?"

I swallowed. "I'm okay. I . . ." I didn't know how to voice the thoughts that were muddling together in my head. "I just spoke to my wife, my ex-wife, and she mentioned something that might be relevant . . ."

She stopped walking, her expression patient.

"My brother-in-law, Neil, recently died."

"I'm very sorry," she said, brow furrowing.

"It's come to my attention that he may have been the one sending Conrad Milton hate mail."

"I see." Her frown deepened.

"But, the thing is . . . there was cherry laurel growing on the farm grounds, and I remembered the toxicologist the other day . . ." As I said it out loud, I realized how ridiculous it sounded. "It's just . . . For him to do that, with a shotgun, the day before Kit's trial—and now this." I looked at her helplessly. "I can't stop feeling that somehow it's connected."

I waited for Ursula to dismiss me. To kindly tell me that I needed to rest, or to go home. But instead, still frowning, she reached out and squeezed my arm again.

"Leave it with me," she said.

108

Gabriel

"K. C."

I VISITED YOU A MONTH after you were arrested. I was scared, so, so scared, going through the security, imagining that when I turned to go home, none of the gates and doors would open, that I'd be locked in there forever, that all of this was a trap.

But I knew I had to do it. I had to see you. I sat down at the table they sent me to, and you came out in jeans and a jumper I recognized, and you looked at me and your eyes went kind of big and watery like you were going to cry.

"You came," you said, and I thought about how happy you'd been to see me when I arrived in London for the first time, and that made me feel like I was going to cry too.

I stood up and hugged you and you felt small and like you weren't strong anymore, not how I remembered you.

"What happened?" I asked, and a guard yelled at us to sit down.

"I don't know." You had your hands clasped together in front of you, and your fingers looked red and sore where you kept clenching them, picking at them. "I think I'm in really big trouble, Gabe."

"What they're saying . . ." I asked. "Is it true?"

You looked shocked, your hands suddenly still on the table. "Of course it isn't. How could you ask me that?"

Because I didn't know what to believe anymore, about anything at all, and because I'd been worried, night after night, that the things I'd told you about Mr. E and the men inside that club had made you as angry as me. As angry as you'd been about Peter Walters.

"I'm sorry," I said. "I didn't know . . ."

You sighed. "I was worried it was you. How crazy is that?"

I felt a giant wave of sadness, like if I didn't hold on to the table, I could be swept away by it. "That *is* crazy."

"I know." You reached out and covered my hand with yours. "I do know that. It just messes with your head, in here. Turning over everything." You bit your lip. "I've been worrying about Rudy and Polly. The things they said about Aleksandr and Lucian and Harris. You don't think . . . ?"

I shook my head. "They left, the day I came to see you at the club. They went to stay with her family in Sandbanks. She's been messaging me since she saw the news—I don't think they'd do something like that."

You nodded, like you'd never really expected me to say anything else.

"I'm too scared to tell anyone about any of it," you said. "I'm scared it all just makes me look more guilty."

"What are you going to do?"

You swallowed, looking tearful again. "I have this lawyer. My dad says he's really good and I should trust him. That he'll be able to help."

"Okay," I said, even though my head kept going to the Rabbit Hole and everything I'd ever read about the police and the courts.

"Promise me something," you said. "Can you stay away from the Rabbit Hole?"

I hesitated.

"Gabriel, please believe me. Mr. E isn't real. After everything, after all of this . . . I just need to know you're going to be okay."

And I told you that I would be. I promised it to you, even though I didn't know if it was a promise I could keep, even though the Rabbit Hole was the only place I felt safe still.

I promised it to you even though you were wrong about Mr. E. I knew you had to be.

109

Max

"Killer Kate"

HUNTER WAS WAITING FOR ME in a pub close to the Old Bailey, a dusty old boozer with a red-painted ceiling and beer-soaked floorboards, a place a million miles from the grandeur of March House. He was sitting at a table near the saloon doors in a hoodie and jeans, his eyes tracking me warily as I bought a pint and sat down.

I could tell right away that he was drunk. That he'd probably been up all night, his eyes hollow and bloodshot, his breath pure meths.

"You have no proof," he said when I sat down.

"Who says?"

He scowled and picked up his gin and tonic, sloshing it in the glass. "So what are you going to do? Are you going to run a story on me, with this supposed proof?" The words slurring together into a sludgy whine.

"I'm not sure," I said. "I'd prefer to run one *with* you."

He balked at that, didn't dignify it with a response. We sat in a stalemate for a couple of minutes, listening to the conversation of a group of suits behind us.

I took a careful sip of my pint. "Have you actually read any of the threats that people on that site write to journalists like me?"

He chewed at the inside of his mouth. "No," he admitted eventually.

"Maybe if you had, you'd have realized how dangerous it was to start messing around on there."

He gave me the death stare at that, but at the end of the day, he was the one who'd invited me.

"Look, I understand that it probably started out as a joke. Maybe you were drunk or high or whatever, maybe it was someone else's idea. Then, before you know it, there's all these people replying, and I don't know, maybe you kind of enjoy it. Hundreds of them, hanging on your every word, joining in with this fantasy you're creating. I can see how that could maybe start to get addictive."

He raised an eyebrow. "There are a lot of maybes there."

"*Maybe* you're finally getting the attention you want," I said. "Maybe you're finally the most important person in the room, even if that room is an anonymous forum where half the users believe Joe Biden is a robot and the Earth is flat."

"Don't psychoanalyze me," he said. "It's beneath you." He hiccupped.

"Probably best left to a professional."

"That's a work in progress." He ran his tongue across his teeth, looked around the room.

"Hunter, it doesn't have to be like this. I can help you."

He cocked his head, a mock expression of interest—but he was too drunk to pull off the bravado, and he just looked scared. He looked broken.

"Okay, let me tell you what's bothering me." I took another sip of my pint, put it carefully down. "Most of Mr. E's posts were rooted in fact," I said. "Especially at the beginning."

He looked away.

"That first post. 'Sacrifices are made at Olympus,'" I continued. "'Lives taken to further the Group's dark deeds.'"

Even though I could tell he didn't want to, he met my gaze again.

"Who were you talking about, Hunter?"

110

John

"Kit-Kat"

I WAITED OUTSIDE THE COURT for Bobby, my stomach churning. I kept thinking of the list of names, your mother in the van full of cut laurel. It had to be a coincidence. It had to be. And yet everything in me was telling me that it wasn't. That this was how we'd save you.

Bobby appeared at the end of the hallway, his mouth set in a grim line.

"Do you hate me?" he asked, when he reached me.

"*No.* God, Bobby, how could you think that?"

He grimaced. "I just gave evidence against my own sister."

I put a hand on his shoulder. "You were in a difficult position."

"What he said, her barrister. That I resented her, that I was angry with her . . . It made me feel awful. Because it was true, wasn't it?"

I released him. "Those were normal things to feel. It was my fault for forcing the two of you together."

"But what did she want to tell me, Dad?"

A question I had asked myself, over and over. "I don't know."

"Maybe I always should've been kinder to her. When she was a little kid, I just . . ." He trailed off, looking miserable.

"I think it was always complicated," I said carefully, as I guided him out onto the street. "And after Peter . . ."

Neither of us had said that name in a long time.

He swallowed. "A journalist has been pestering me about that. Max Todd. Has he contacted you?"

I grimaced. "I lost track of all the people who've called."

"Well, this one's persistent. And someone's been speaking to him."

"Who?"

"Someone from home, I don't know. He knows about the fire. About Peter, about all of it. Where are we going?"

I tugged open the phone box door. "I just need to call your mum."

She answered on the second ring.

"You were right," she said, her voice shaking. "In the sent items, messages to Conrad Milton." She let out a shuddery breath. "Horrible things. Awful." She started to cry.

"Sarah, it's okay—"

"I've found a receipt," she said, talking over me. "In the inbox, from last year. I found a receipt for a bottle of brandy."

111

Max

"Killer Kate"

I'D THOUGHT MAYBE HE'D BITE right away, but Hunter just looked back at me, jaw clenched so tight that his mouth was trembling.

"You were trying to say something with those posts. It wasn't just a game, was it?"

He looked pointedly at his empty gin glass, but I ignored him. I could justify the muddy moral waters of letting him talk while he was clearly wasted—up to a point—but I wasn't about to start plying him with more booze.

"Hunter, if something happened at March House that you wanted the world to know about, I can help."

He snorted. "Yeah, you're very interested in justice, aren't you? I've read your stuff."

"I am," I said.

"A big believer in the system."

"I wouldn't go that far. And I'm not the system."

He tugged at his hair, slumped back in his seat.

"I can help," I said. And then, chancing it, "What happened to you in that club?"

He shook his head, no longer meeting my eye. His voice quiet as he said, "Not me. My sister."

I remembered her up there in the public gallery, watery looking and emotional, a vague likeness of Lucian in her features. "I've seen her in court. Violet, right?"

He made a bitter face. "I don't know why she keeps going."

"What happened to Violet?" He looked up at me and I could see him right there, on the brink. I put my hands up, a gesture of surrender. "Off the record." And then, gentler: "Let me help."

His gaze dropped away again. "It was a few years ago. Dad's birthday party, his sixtieth. Vi was seventeen, I was fourteen. He wheels us out, makes us play nice with Leandro by bribing us all with cash. Playing the big family man for all his guests. He even tried to get my mother to come, as if she and Mimi could just stand there drinking cocktails and sharing notes on alimony, while he swanned around with Ilse and his new kids."

"Families are complicated," I said. "The party was at March House?"

Hunter nodded. "He didn't pay any attention to us once the photographer he'd hired had clocked off for the night. Leandro and I got high in the courtyard, and Vi spent the night drinking with Ollie Lowe."

"Harris's son?"

He pointed at me with both index fingers: *bingo.* "You know what they called him at Harrow?"

I waited.

He leaned in, like he was delivering a punch line. Whispered it in a fug of booze. "Benzo Lowe."

"He liked prescription drugs."

Hunter eyed me. "That's one way to put it."

"Did he give Violet drugs?"

His lip curled, and he looked away. "That's one way to put it," he said again.

"He spiked her?"

"Yeah. Vi would never have touched anything like that willingly. And when she started complaining about feeling weird, when she fell over in front of everyone, he shepherded her off to one of the private rooms." His face puckered. "She wakes up there at four in the morning, still completely out of it, but she knew . . ."

"He'd assaulted her," I said grimly.

He nodded. Rubbed at his eyes like a little boy. "If you could see . . ."

He scrunched up his face, shook his head like he was trying to clear it. "If you'd seen what it did to her afterward, how she changed . . ."

"Did she tell anyone?"

"She told Dad." His bloodshot eyes met mine. "She was the favorite. They were close."

I already knew what was coming. "And nothing happened," I said, feeling sickened.

"Harris is too important a contact to Dad," Hunter said, then caught himself. "Was." He moistened his lips, started picking at a scab on his hand. "He told Violet she was making it up. That she'd just got too drunk and Ollie had helped her."

I took a bleak swig of my beer, wanting to wash the acid taste out of my mouth. "She believed him."

Another set of double finger guns. "She did. Or at least she tried to. She started uni, she dropped out of uni. He got her therapy, sent her off to all these retreats for 'her nerves,' for the fact she got so agoraphobic she didn't leave the house for months sometimes. And when she finally told me what had happened, why she was feeling like that . . ."

"You were angry."

"I was angry. For a long time." He began drumming his fingers against the edge of the table, foot tapping restlessly. "Now do you get it?" he asked, and he seemed to actually care about my answer. "Now do you understand why? Why I hated him?"

"Sure, but—"

"It wasn't like you said. I didn't want the attention. I'm not a bad person." He looked down at the table, and I couldn't work out if he was bleary-eyed or genuinely tearful. "I'm not," he said. "It was, like, a way to get it out. All the stuff I used to hear around the club, the way those men talked to each other. The way they acted." He shook his head. "Half the stuff I wrote never felt like fiction."

I didn't respond. He nodded as if I had anyway.

"It got out of hand. It did. The crazy stuff all the Mr. E fans started posting, it . . . I guess it made me feel better. Creating monsters out of them. It did turn into a game."

"It wasn't."

He scowled. "I didn't know it would end up with someone doing . . . something like *this*."

Because he hadn't expected someone like you to be reading.

He reached out and picked up the remaining half of my pint, taking a long gulp. "So there it is. That's the story behind big bad Mr. E. What are you going to do with it?"

112

Tarun

"Katherine"

"THERE WAS CHERRY LAUREL ON the farm," Ursula finished. "It seems a stretch, but it's an interesting connection."

"Yes," I said, musing on this. Unnerved to find that my first thought was that you had also been on that farm, many times. That you had even been there, perhaps, when the pigs had fallen sick.

"Neil Flack's grudge seems to have been against Milton, though," Ruth mused.

"But Milton was working for a Wrightman company," I said. "It's worth looking into, as quickly as possible."

Then your father came to see me.

As was customary to close their case, the prosecution were adducing their final piece of evidence, your record of interview, in court that afternoon. This was the interview you had given in custody once Ursula had arrived to advocate for you, and as was conventional, it would be read out, rather than a recording played.

You looked bemused as the officer who had interviewed you on that day, DC Hasan Darwish, took the witness stand. He and Verity began reading out the transcript that both sides had agreed could be admitted into evidence.

I felt restless, listening to their careful, monotonous inflection. My brain turning endlessly over this new information, wondering what was unfolding, right at that moment, outside the courtroom.

"'What happened to the men in that room?'" DC Darwish read aloud, as I scribbled notes to myself.

"'I don't know,'" Verity said. "'When I left, they were alive. They were fine. I don't know anything. I just wanted to go home.'"

When I glanced across at you, you were watching me curiously, as if you could read my mind. You frowned, a silent question, and I smiled at you, returned my attention to Verity.

113

John

"Kit-Kat"

I DROVE AS FAST AS I could to the farm, eight hours of motorway and countryside passing by in a dark blur. Bobby in the passenger seat beside me, the two of us silent and tense. I thought of the notebook he'd brought back from the farm with him. The key to the flat I'd given to Tarun's junior, Ruth, so that she could collect it.

"I did believe it," Bobby said quietly, as the sky turned dark around us. "There were times—a lot of times—when I thought Kit could've killed them."

I switched lanes, pressed the accelerator all the way to the floor.

Your mum was waiting for me in the open doorway as I pulled up the rutted old driveway, light flooding out behind her. She was wearing an old woollen jumper of mine, moth-eaten and stretched, her arms wrapped round herself as she watched me climbing out of the car, walking up the path.

"This can't be happening," she said, and she let me fold her into a hug.

In the farmhouse behind her, two police officers continued their search.

Bobby eventually fell asleep on the sofa, but your mum and I were still awake at dawn. I made tea and sat down beside her at the kitchen table, watching as more officers arrived to search the old outbuildings.

"He was a good person," she said, not for the first time that night.

I drank some of my tea, the liquid still scalding.

"I know he was angry," she said. "I know he'd gone to a dark place. But not this."

We watched as a police van drove across the paddock, as the officers who got out began donning white suits, blue plastic gloves.

"You couldn't have known this." I put my hand over hers.

She closed her eyes. "Maybe I should've. Maybe I should've listened properly. Done something. But he was my big brother. The person who hid me away when I was little and it all got bad, and who looked after me when my mum left and Dad went to pieces. The person who picked me up after Stephen . . ." She pressed her lips together.

"It's okay." I squeezed her hand tighter. She'd so rarely spoken about the violent temper of her mother or the chaos she'd left behind when she'd abandoned them all for another man. Had always avoided talking to you about her childhood, which she had been so determined yours would be nothing like.

"I keep thinking about her. My mum."

I looked at her, nodded at her to go on..

"All this time, I suppose that, deep down, I thought that it was proof, Kit going off the way she did. History repeating itself. But I've realized that isn't right, is it? It was me. I pushed her away. I was frightened and I pushed her away and I believed . . . God, John, a part of me really believed she could have killed those men, when all along . . ."

I put my arm around her and, finding no resistance, pulled her toward me. She leaned against me, her head finding its old spot on my shoulder. We watched in silence as the police trudged back across the field toward us.

114

Tarun

"Katherine"

I TOOK A CAB TO court that morning, repeatedly refreshing my inbox. Ruth, Ursula, and I had only parted ways at chambers at three a.m. after a long evening and night of sending emails and making calls, and as my driver swore at yet another red light, a new message from Ruth appeared.

From the post office, read the subject line.

Attached was a video file. It was twelve hours long, the file name 07-08-22, a date three days before the murders. My pulse tripped up a gear. In the body of Ruth's email, she had included a simple instruction: *Skip to 5:22.*

It seemed to take an age to load, and when it did, I dragged the playhead to the five-hour-and-twenty mark.

It was grainy footage, a dated CCTV system, but I could make out the shelves in the background, the back of the worker's head as she stood behind the counter with its Perspex screen. She moved across the screen jerkily, the video buffering badly, and I used my thumb to edge the playhead along a little further, waiting.

Then your uncle entered the frame. His head held down, a box under his arm.

I paused the video and called Ruth.

"Yes, I am amazing," she said, by way of greeting.

"Do they remember him?"

"When I finally got through to the woman who served him, yes. She said he was memorably rude to her, keen to get out of there. Chose not to send it recorded delivery."

"Unsurprising."

"That's not even the best part."

"Tell me."

"He didn't want to leave his details, but they still have a record of it being sent. Including the addressee. It's Milton. Milton received the bottle and, at some point, passed it to one of them."

"To Lucian," I said. "They worked in the same office."

"I've forwarded it on to the police."

"Great. There have been some further developments overnight—the police in Tayside have found the equipment used to distill the laurel water in one of the outbuildings at Godfrey's Farm."

"Wow." I heard the sound of traffic at the other end of the line, Ruth already heading back to chambers. "What will happen now?"

115

Conrad

"Wildcat"

I'D BEEN WAITING FOR IT, I guess.

Or maybe I hadn't. Maybe I'd stopped losing sleep, stopped shitting myself every time the door went, stopped seeing Lucian's face, Alek's, Harris's, whenever I closed my eyes. Maybe I'd finally relaxed, started to even forgive myself, now that you were on trial.

Big mistake.

The Met banged on my door at the crack of dawn, watching me as I threw clothes on and went meekly down to the car with them, hoping this was all a bad dream.

A feeling I'd had a lot since I met you, Kate.

They'd figured out that I'd given the brandy to Lucian, and yeah, that was bad. I didn't need to be told that.

But as far as I was concerned, you'd poisoned it. You'd intended it for me, but you were still the person responsible for their murders. I wasn't sorry you were in the dock for it.

I hadn't thought about your uncle in years. When they told me at the station that it'd been him who'd sent the brandy, that he'd been harboring that hatred for all that time, I actually almost felt sorry for him. Until I realized the guy had tried to kill me.

For a confused, sleep-deprived minute, I thought maybe the police really did just want my help with working out what had happened. Then they started throwing around phrases like perverting the course of justice and involuntary manslaughter, and I started to understand how deep the shit I was in really was.

116

Tarun

"Katherine"

MY HANDS WERE SHAKING AS I explained to Judge McQuilliam why I felt the trial could not continue. I'd stopped for a double espresso on the way into court, an old cure after all-nighters, and propranolol seemed no match for the combination of caffeine and adrenaline.

"Your Honor, new evidence has been discovered, compelling new evidence. The CPS have been made aware of this."

Judge McQuilliam glanced at Verity, who nodded bleakly.

"In light of this new evidence, Your Honor," I continued, my palms beginning to sweat, "I believe that my client can no longer receive a fair trial. I'd like to make an application that the jury is dismissed on this basis."

McQuilliam flinched. "*That* is a drastic suggestion, Mr. Rao, at this stage in proceedings. Mrs. Naylor, what's your opinion on this?"

Verity pursed her lips. "I'm afraid I have to agree, Your Honor. The new evidence is significant, and the Crown will need to review it."

Judge McQuilliam sighed. "I really rather hoped we were rattling through this one." She shook her head. "Very well. Mrs. Naylor, I will set a hearing date of two weeks from today, at which the CPS must inform the court if it wishes to pursue a new trial. Mr. Rao, your client will remain on remand in the meantime."

We both nodded, my shoulders sinking in relief. The first hurdle behind us.

Judge McQuilliam nodded at the usher. "You can bring the jury in. Let's tell them their weekend will be starting early."

I came down to the cells to speak with you. You stood up immediately, seeing something new in my expression.

"What's happened?" you asked, and I suggested we sit back down as finally I told you everything.

Your eyes widened and filled immediately with tears. "Sorry," you said. "I just . . . I can't . . . Neil dead . . ."

"I understand it's a lot to take in."

"But . . . why? Why would he do that, with the brandy?"

"The intended recipient was Conrad Milton."

You looked horrified. "Because of the farm?"

"It seems that way."

"Oh my god," you said. You looked away, repeated it again, quieter now. "Oh my god."

I waited, giving you some space.

Your eyes narrowed. "I don't understand—if he meant it for Conrad, how . . . ?"

"That I'm not entirely clear on," I admitted. "But Mr. Milton is currently assisting police with their inquiries."

You sank back in your seat, emotions I couldn't read passing over your face.

"But what does this mean? What's going to happen to me now?"

I explained the timeline the judge had set out.

You nodded, blew out a slow breath.

"Two weeks," you echoed. "And then . . ."

"Let's get there first," I suggested.

"Two weeks," you said again. "Okay."

117

Max

"Killer Kate"

I LEFT THE COURT, STUNNED. Jury dismissed, a retrial hanging in the balance.

Something big was happening. An unsettled feeling started growing in my gut, and I sent Hasan a text: *What's going on with Kate Cole trial? Jury dismissed?!*

On the Tube on the way home, I filed a quick article explaining what had happened for the handful of ghouls who showed up religiously in the comments every day. No response from Hasan.

I let myself in, the house quiet, and sat for a while in front of my laptop, wondering what to do with myself. Trying to shove down that niggle of doubt, to ignore the question marks now hovering over everything.

I still had one thing on my to-do list, and after a cup of tea and a few walks around the living room, psyching myself up, I called your brother.

When he answered, he sounded dazed—but not so caught off guard that he was friendly. "I told you I don't want to talk to you."

"Actually, it's not about that," I said. Wondering why I'd tried to be sensitive, hadn't just sent a message instead. "I just wanted to let you know about something I discovered while researching Peter Walters."

I kept it brief, gave him the facts in a neutral tone. "Just thought you might want to know," I finished lamely. "I can send you the conviction information, if you want to verify it. There's a court record."

He was so quiet I took the phone away from my ear to check whether he'd hung up. "No," he said eventually. "That's not necessary."

And then he did hang up.

I sat looking into space for a minute, and then I went through to the kitchen. I set about finally making that Bolognese for when Anya and Albie got home, keeping myself busy while I tried not to wonder what the hell was going on with you.

118

Tarun

"Katherine"

THE HOURS SEEMED IMPOSSIBLY LONG before I received a call from an unknown number.

"Tarun? It's Verity."

I slowed, the bustle of the South Bank continuing around me. "Verity, hi." I made an apologetic face at Elliot, stepping closer to the railing and the water, pressing a finger to my other ear.

"Milton has confessed to passing the bottle to Wrightman. He's claiming he thought it was a gift from Katherine."

"Perverting the course of justice?"

"At the very least." She tutted, and I heard a car horn, the sound of an indicator clicking. "Anyway. Just wanted to keep you in the loop."

"I appreciate it."

As I hung up, Elliot approached. "Good news?"

"I think so."

"Great." He checked his watch. "The film's about to start. Ready?"

"I am." We walked through the crowds, a polite distance between us. "Thanks for coming out," I said.

"Happy to be a distraction." He grinned at me. "How many other friends do you have who can abandon work in the middle of the day?"

"None with decent taste in cinema, sadly."

"You always have known how to make me feel special."

I willed myself to reach out and take his hand. To tell him that I could be different this time.

Willed myself to stop thinking about you.

Ten days later, I watched you enter the dock. You were wearing a black dress and blazer, your hair tied back. You looked elegant, older. For a moment, you looked calm, and then you caught my eye, and I saw how tightly your jaw was clenched, how your hands were gripped into fists.

The judge began proceedings, eyeing both Verity and me with a wary look.

"Mrs. Naylor, has the Crown made a decision on whether it would like to pursue a retrial against Katherine Cole?"

Verity cleared her throat. "Your Honor, we will be offering no evidence on the indictment."

Ursula and I looked at each other. I exhaled, long and slow, as the words sank in.

"In that case," Judge McQuilliam said, her attention now on you, "the defendant is found not guilty. And this will conclude proceedings."

You would be released from custody immediately.

You seemed stunned as the usher came to direct you, as Ursula and I strode over to meet you.

"Is this real?" you asked, your hands pressed to your cheeks.

"Yes!" Ursula laughed. "It's really happening. You're going home."

"I can't believe it." You stifled a sob.

"But it's true," Ursula said firmly. "It's over. You're going home."

"I can't believe it," you said again. Breathless. "Thank you. Thank you so much."

And then you turned to me and hugged me. "Thank you," you repeated.

Startled by the unexpected physical contact, I found myself hugging you back.

Over your shoulder, I saw your father. Moving quickly, as if he were afraid to believe it too. I stepped back from you, watching your face crumple as you turned and saw him. When he reached you, he folded you into his arms as you started to cry in earnest. Your mother hovered two steps behind him.

"You did it," Ursula said beside me.

"We did," I said.

Picturing, out of nowhere, the snarl on your face as you'd turned in the bodycam footage, the way you'd said, *They deserved it.*

119

John

"Kit-Kat"

WE WALKED OUT OF COURT together on that cold autumn morning, your breath fogging on the air. Your mother carrying the small plastic bag of your things. Your arm looped through mine.

You stood for a second and closed your eyes. Breathed in and smiled.

"It's over," I told you.

"At my hearing," you said, "I tried to tell you. I wanted you to know." I thought about the words you had said. *I love you. I'm sorry.*

"You have nothing to be sorry for," I told you.

At the car, you climbed into the back and pulled the old blanket over your lap, clicked your seat belt on.

You leaned your head against the window and were quiet as we drove. Your mother put the radio on, and every now and again, I'd hear the faint sound of you humming along to a song you liked, as you watched the unfamiliar roads turning into ones you recognized.

When we first came in sight of the sea, I caught your eye in the rearview mirror and you grinned.

120

Max

"Kate"

AFTER YOU WERE RELEASED, I spent days trying to get rid of the guilty feeling I had. I told myself I'd just been doing my job, had reported all the facts on you that were available to me. I was an experienced court reporter and journalist, and the case against you, in the beginning, had appeared to everyone to be ironclad.

But I couldn't shake it. Couldn't help feeling floored by the way my assumptions had been proven wrong, one by one.

I told myself to snap out of it.

Because there was another story that needed to be told now.

The post appeared on the Rabbit Hole two days later. It was short, honest, and clearly remorseful:

My name is Hunter Wrightman, and in early 2020, I began posting anonymously on this website, mostly because I was bored and angry with my father. I used the username Mr. E, and before long, the joke had got out of hand. The Group do not exist. I am deeply sorry for the trouble this has caused, and for the pain I have caused my family.

It felt like it had been written by an advisor of some kind, but it did the job. The comments beneath it, which multiplied exponentially as the minutes passed, ranged from the furious to the heartbroken to the disbelieving: *This can't be true. The Group have got to E. We need to save him.*

Sometimes you can't get the conspiracy cat back into the bag. But he'd done the right thing. Now it was my turn.

Violet Wrightman was waiting for me on the corner of Northumberland Avenue, just as we'd arranged. She was dressed in jeans and a long coat, the collar turned up around her face, and she looked like she was having second thoughts.

"Violet." I shook her hand. "It's good to meet you."

She smiled weakly. "Thank you for coming."

"Shall we?"

I led her down the pavement, noticing the way she wrapped her coat more closely around her, the way her steps slowed as we approached our destination. I shoved my hands in my pockets, found a plastic spider Albie had snuck in there, one of his favorite tricks. I turned it over in my fingers, surprised by how nervous I was.

"I know this might be difficult to talk about," I said. "But I want to make it as easy as possible for you."

She took a deep breath, looking up at the glass building in front of us. "Okay," she said.

I held the door open for her, and we stepped into the lobby, where Hasan and a female officer were waiting for us.

121

Gabriel

"K. C."

WHEN I READ THAT POST, I had to walk away from my computer. Had to walk out of the house and down the street and keep walking, until the thud of my steps drowned out all of my thoughts.

It couldn't be true. It just couldn't. Somebody had hacked Mr. E's account, made it up as a joke.

But I could feel the knowledge already worming its way inside my head, bits of my brain lighting up like traitorous little Christmas lights as all the things I thought I knew changed shape or crumbled away, and I started to feel shaky and weird.

I walked to the dunes and sat down in the grass. I tried not to think about all of the time I'd spent talking about Mr. E, hiding from the things he told me I should hide from, being angry about all of the things he told me I should be angry about.

You'd tried to warn me, and I hadn't listened to you.

He wasn't real. None of it was real.

I pressed my hands into my eyes, trying to stop myself from crying, because who cries about some kid making up stories on the internet?

I heard the swish of marram grass, footsteps sinking through the sand behind me.

"I thought you might be here," you said. "I saw the news."

You sat down next to me.

"When did you get back?" I asked.

"Yesterday." You leaned back on your hands, breathed in the sea air the way you always used to.

"How does it feel?"

You gave me a sideways look, half a smile starting. "I can't tell yet. But better than prison for sure."

"I'm so happy you're out." The breaking news alert on my phone had made me bounce around the room like a kid on a space hopper.

"I'm sorry," you said, a serious look on your face. "About Mr. E. I know it was . . . I know it must be a shock."

"It doesn't matter." I looked out at the sea. Taking a long, deep breath, all cold salt sting, and knowing that eventually I'd be okay.

Hoping that you would be too.

122

Tarun

"Katherine"

I WAS READING A NEW brief when Ruth knocked on my door.

"Sorry to disturb you," she said, peering round, her glasses perched on the top of her head. "But I was just passing reception, and there's a visitor for you."

I looked up, surprised. I wasn't expecting anyone.

"It's Katherine Cole," she said.

I gave her a questioning look, and she shrugged. "Good luck," she said.

I came down to find you sitting on the wall outside, a backpack at your feet.

"Katherine," I said. "This is a nice surprise."

"Really?" you asked. "I bet you thought you'd seen the last of me."

I shoved my hands in my pockets, leaning against the wall beside you. "What can I do for you?"

"I just came to thank you," you said. "I was in town."

"There was really no need."

You shrugged. "Actually, I think there was. I don't think you realized how much it mattered to me that you believed me."

It had mattered to me too, more than it should have.

"I just did my job," I said.

"And with such warmth and affection too."

I shot you a look.

"I'll miss you side-eyeing me," you said. You slid down from the wall. "I'd say I'll see you around, but I think we should both hope that isn't the case."

You hitched your bag onto your back.

"Heading anywhere nice?" I asked.

You smiled as you turned. "Let's see."

There it was again. That memory of you on the platform at Paddington, the defiant, unapologetic way you'd said it. *They deserved it.*

I watched you walk away and then, trying to shrug off my disquiet, I went back inside to work.

123

Katie

I GO TO VISIT STEPHEN. Feel something lift from me as soon as I step through the gates. A calm settling over me as I find his row, kneel down by his grave. And maybe it's only now, only in this moment, that I get it: It's really over. I'm really here.

It feels good, this old routine of mine. I tug up tiny weeds, trim back the rosemary, the forget-me-nots. Scrub at the stone till it shines, every letter of his name kept clean and clear.

When it's done, I sit back against his headstone, stretch out my legs. "I'm sorry it's been so long," I say.

I tell him everything. About prison and how, when I was afraid, I thought about Pancake and Howard and the WotsitPotsit Bird, tried to remember all of the stories he'd told me. All of the places we wanted to see. I tell him how I thought of all the times I was scared or sad and he was there for me. How, even now, I always feel he is.

I tell him about Neil. About him losing the farm and the barn where he brewed poison and how I took the blame for both of those things. About Mum and the quiet space between us now, the way it's closing, slowly, so slowly. Two people moving over a frozen lake together, wondering if they'll ever reach solid ground.

"I miss you," I tell him.

When the sun goes down and the cemetery is empty, I get up. Place a hand on the headstone, tell Stephen I'll be back soon.

I couldn't keep that promise last time. That night last August, when I ran from here so fast, the fear setting in. Because I knew then that they'd be coming after me. Was already regretting what I'd done.

Wondering where to hide. I shudder, remembering the terror of it. The thrill.

I'd turned to Bobby, and that was a mistake. The panic sending me to Paddington; the police there too fast for me to make the train.

A lot has changed since then. But I can hope. Luck, lately, has been on my side.

So: I sneak past the gates, past the groundskeeper's hut. Trace the fence on the east side, away from the main road, away from the last of the sunset, to an old potting shed. I thought the groundskeeper might have realized the lock was loose by now, replaced it. But no: I slide it free, open the door just wide enough to slip in.

I stand in the dim light for a second, wondering if it's possible that it could still be here.

More money than we got when Stephen died. More than his life was supposed to be worth. Left in the yellow Selfridges bag, discarded by the coat stand in the Voltaire Room that night. Those neat stacks of fifties, Ainsworth's fee, tucked up beneath a four-thousand-pound dress.

And now I lift the old tarpaulin, send spiders scuttling. Dust thick in the air.

It's still here. All of it.

I put it in the backpack as quickly as I can. Worried this is all another dream, that I'll wake up in my cell again.

I try to move fast. Try not to think about Peru, the Inca Trail. The Great Barrier Reef, the Great Wall of China. All of those things Stephen should have seen. All of the things I'll go and see now, for him.

I put the last stack into my bag, zip it closed. I know it was wrong, stealing it.

But it was so easy to dip in when their backs were turned. Moving quickly, quietly. Be unimposing, invisible: the first rule of being a good waitress. I was better at it than you might think.

And I thought they deserved it.

Acknowledgments

It took me a while to work out what this book would be, and I want to thank my agent, Cathryn Summerhayes, for waiting while I did, and for being the perfect champion for Katie. Thank you to Lily Dolin and Gráinne Fox for making my dreams come true in the States; to Georgie Mellor for working international wonders; and to Jess Molloy, Annabel White, Jason Richman, Anna Weguelin, Gemma Craig, and everyone at Curtis Brown/UTA.

Katie Ellis-Brown and Danielle Dieterich formed a transatlantic editorial superteam—you've both been so brilliant to work with, and I feel incredibly lucky that the book found the perfect homes in Harvill Secker and William Morrow. I'm also really grateful to Anouska Levy, Sam Stocker, Graeme Hall, Shona Abhyankar, Ellie Pilcher, Sam Rees-Williams, and the whole Harvill Secker team; and to Grace Vainisi, Michelle Meredith, Marie Rossi, Yeon Kim, Bonni Leon-Berman, Liz Psaltis, Tess Day, Eliza Rosenberry, Kelsey Manning, and everyone at William Morrow. An extra big thank you to Hayley Shepherd and Ana Deboo for copyedits on both sides of the Atlantic.

Jeanette Ashmole provided not one but two incredibly helpful manuscript reads to advise on the legal side and Tarun's chapters in particular—thank you for explaining why the original ending was wrong! And for all of your guidance and suggestions.

A huge and heartfelt thank you to my writer friends, especially the St. Tropez writers and the Ladykillers, who are the most inspiring, generous, talented group of women and the best (and funniest) company to have on this publishing journey.

Thanks to Claire Lewzey for getting me in trouble with our GCSE English teacher and for being a bad influence and a perfect friend ever since.

And to Hayley Richardson for being the best beta. Always. And Sian Richardson for making me tea (not your way) and making me laugh, and always getting it.

Thank you to Margaret and Richard Cloke for . . . so much, really. For being the most supportive, understanding parents. For reading first drafts and celebrating all the wins and listening to all my worries. For Luton games and shopping trips and lockdown wine. For always having the answer to my "How do I . . . ?" calls. I'm so lucky I have you, and I'll be forever grateful.

Thank you to Dan Cloke for being the best brother and friend. For answering my police questions and never laughing at my life ones. For showing me what hard work, determination, and a bit of self-belief can do (whether it's in front of a heavy bag or a first draft). And for always finding the right dog meme exactly when it's needed.

And thank you, Chris Whitaker, for having faith that I'd find this story and for making me believe it too. For bagels and sweet pots and endless songs. Road trips and a million air miles and midweek homecoming roasts. Character chats and plot problem-solving in a blue chair (or on the long dark walk to find a Guinness). For dreaming big and small. You'll say this isn't true, but you inspire me every day. I love you (is it nice, thank you?).